CHASING HONOR

THE NEXT GENERATION
BOOK 2

RILEY EDWARDS

Chasing Honor
The Next Generation

Cover design: Jena Brignola

Written by: Riley Edwards

Published by: Rebels Romance

Edited by: Eve Arroyo

Proofreader: Kendall Barnett

Chasing Honor

SPECIAL EDITION

Paperback ISBN: 978-1-951567-34-7

First edition – December 26, 2022

CONTENTS

CHASING HONOR AUDIO

Performed By: Troy Duran & Devon Grace

PROLOGUE

"I'm pregnant."

"What?" I rolled to my side to get a better look at Chrissy. The full moon providing enough light I could make out her pretty features. I brushed her after-sex, messy hair from her face and noticed she was crying. "But we always use protection."

She shivered, and I pulled the sleeping bag over her chilled skin.

"I don't know, Ethan. It had to have broken, or you didn't put it on right. I've missed three periods; I took a test a few days ago."

A thousand thoughts sprinted through my mind. This couldn't be happening. I was sixteen. We couldn't have a baby. Fuck. My parents were going to kill me, but I had to make this right.

"Marry me," I blurted.

"Why?" Her eyes widened in shock.

"We'll get married, and I'll take care of you and the baby. Everything will be okay, Chrissy. I promise."

"I've already talked to my parents. I'll finish out the last month of school then move to Arizona with my aunt before I'm showing. They talked to an adoption agency out there. All you need to do is sign the paperwork."

I rolled to my back and looked up at the tiny, sparkling lights in the midnight sky. I should've been happy, Chrissy and her parents had everything planned. She'd move, have the baby, and the problem would be taken care of.

Baby. My baby—not a fucking problem.

I should've felt relief but I didn't. I was pissed at the universe for stealing my youth and dreams and angry at her that she'd give my baby away.

Fuck.

MAYBE MY COUSIN Nick's backyard barbeque wasn't the best place to have this conversation with my parents, but I couldn't keep my secret any longer. Every morning for the past week my mom had been waiting, like always, in the kitchen with breakfast ready—she'd kissed both my brother, Carter, and me on the cheek before she sent us off to school with a smile. She wouldn't have been smiling if she'd known what I'd done.

Sometime after dinner and before he and my mom went to bed, my dad would come into my room to ask how my day had been, how baseball practice was going, my grades, my friends, how Chrissy was. I'd been living a lie and I couldn't do it anymore. I couldn't listen to my dad tell me how proud he was of me one more time.

Fuck. My mom was going to cry. I hated seeing her sad, thankfully it didn't happen often. Dad had taught Carter and me from as far back as I could remember we needed to take care of Mom. All the women in our lives, in fact. That included our aunts and cousins. It was those lessons that had led me to my decision.

"Mom. Dad. Can I talk to you a minute?"

My mom looked up and frowned.

"What's wrong?" she asked.

That was another thing about my mom, she always knew when one of her boys was in trouble. Goddamn, how could I have been so stupid? She was going to be crushed. I could take my father's anger—I deserved it, but I didn't think I'd survive my mom's disappointment.

I almost said never mind and chickened out until my dad spoke.

"Fuck," he muttered.

I'd always been unable to hide my discomfort from my father. It wasn't often I screwed up; I was a straight-A student and excelled at sports. My parents had instilled in me to always be respectful; my coaches and teachers loved me. So did the cheerleaders, and that was how my current problem started. "As long as no one's knocked up, we can fix anything."

"Lenox." My mother slapped his shoulder.

I tried to keep my face blank and stop the flinch, but it was too late. My father saw it.

"Shit," he mumbled and leveled me with one of his famous "you've fucked up now" stares. "Chrissy?"

I nodded, and my mom looked between my dad and me.

"Wait. What? Are you serious?" my mom asked.

I still couldn't speak, so once again I nodded.

"Goddamn it, Ethan," Dad growled. "Follow me." The three of us walked inside, and my dad pointed to the couch. "Sit."

For the first time in my life I defied my father's wishes. "I think I'd rather stand if you don't mind."

"How did this happen?" Mom asked.

Dad looked at her with his eyebrow raised. "Seriously, Lily?"

"You know what I mean. We've taught you to be safe."

"We were. The condom broke." Shit it was embarrassing talking about my sex life with my parents. They knew I was sexually active. They'd always been open and honest with both Carter and me. Mom always stocked the bathroom with condoms, and Dad had talked to us a million times about how to treat girls. But talking about it in the abstract was far different than talking about Chrissy and me doing it.

"What are you going to do?" Dad asked.

I sucked in a breath and stood tall, trying to convey to them something I wasn't—confident.

"I'm keeping the baby."

"*You* are?" Confusion laced my mom's question. "What about Chrissy?"

"She and her parents talked it over and they've decided to put the baby up for adoption. I've thought about it and I won't sign the paperwork. She can give it up, and I'll take the baby. I'll raise my child without her."

"Son," Dad started. "You're sixteen. I think we need to sit down and weigh the options before you make a life changing decision based on emotion rather than logic."

"Would you have given away either of your children?"

"Fuck no," he answered.

"Then how could you ask me to give away mine?"

"We weren't sixteen, Ethan. We were adults when your mom got pregnant with Carter."

"But if it'd happened when she was sixteen, would you have then?"

My dad's face turned red, and I knew I had him. He didn't need to answer, I knew he would've never entertained the idea of his child being given up for adoption.

"Ethan," Mom whispered, the tears I'd dreaded brimming in her eyes. "Your dad and I want what's best for you. Taking care of a baby is hard work. Being a parent is forever. I don't think you understand how hard it will be to do it alone."

I looked at the two people I loved most in the world, shock, disappointment, and anger shone in their eyes. My stomach twisted knowing I'd done that to them.

"I know you're both worried for me. I know you're disappointed and pissed. I hope one day you'll both forgive me, because I know I can't do this alone—I'll need both of you. I may only be sixteen, but dad has shown me every day what it is to be a good dad, a good man. This is my child. Mine. I will not give up on it before he or she is even born. You've both taught me better than that. I'm taking responsibility. Chrissy and her parents have made their choice, and I've made mine. This baby is a Lenox and will be raised as one."

"You're finishing school," my mom instructed. "When Carter leaves in a few months for the Naval Academy, we'll move you into his room in the basement. There's enough space down there for you and the baby. I'll get together with your aunts and we'll get it baby proofed and ready."

"Thank you," I choked out.

"Lily, give me a minute alone with Ethan."

My mom closed the short distance between us and pulled me into a hug, rolling up on her toes she kissed my cheek.

"I love you, Ethan."

"I love you, Mama."

My dad waited for my mom to leave the room, and I braced for his ire. He'd kept himself in check in front of my mom, but I saw the blast coming.

"Fucking hell, Ethan."

"I'm sorry, Dad."

"A little late for sorry, don't you think?" I didn't answer, not that he was expecting me to. "You have no idea what it means to be a parent. The sacrifice, the sleepless nights, the fucking worry your kid is gonna pull some stupid shit." He stopped and shook his head. "Think long and hard about this. Once you do it, there's no going back, *ever*."

"I have thought about it."

"No, son, I don't think you have. I think you were

so wrapped up in working your way through all the available cheerleaders you never stopped to think about shit."

"You're right, Dad. I hadn't thought about it then. But I've thought of nothing else since Chrissy told me. It's all I can think about. I've thought about how I'd feel knowing my kid was out there somewhere being raised by strangers. I can't do it, you might as well rip my fucking heart from my chest, Dad. I can't breathe thinking I'll have a child I'll never know or hold or watch grow up. Adoption is not an option for me. Then, I thought about how you and Mom and Carter would look at me knowing I didn't have the balls to stand up and be a man."

"Christ, you don't make this easy." My dad's face twisted, and he offered me his hand. I cautiously took it, and he tugged my arm, making me stumble forward. "Welcome to fatherhood, son. I'm still pissed the fuck off, but I couldn't be prouder of you."

"YOU'RE DOING GREAT, CHRISSY," I told her.

"I'm too tired," she whined.

"Almost there. The doctor said one more push and you'd be done."

It hadn't taken one more push, it had been closer to

ten more. Mr. and Mrs. Krier, Chrissy's parents, were in the waiting room along with my family, making it hard to concentrate on Chrissy. Things were tense between our families, although both sides had tried to keep interactions as respectful as they could. The Krier's had sold their house in Georgia and were moving to Arizona for a fresh start. I was still in shock Chrissy was really going through with signing over her parental rights to me. I'd been holding onto some sort of stupid hope she'd want to be a part of our baby's life. But she'd refused. She was completely disconnected from the baby. Even at the ultrasound she wouldn't look at the monitor. I didn't understand how she could do this. It took everything inside of me to stop myself from yelling at her and telling her how hurt and angry I was.

"It's a girl," the doctor announced. "Ethan, would you like to cut the cord?"

I pried my hand from Chrissy's hulk-like grip and took the surgical scissors from the nurse. I barely remembered cutting the cord, my daughter's tiny body holding my attention.

I had a daughter.

I was a dad.

She was so small and screaming her slime-covered head off.

"Should she be crying like that?" I asked.

"She's exercising her lungs," the nurse smiled and took my daughter from the doctor, walking over to the scale where she weighed her and measured her length before placing her in the prepared bassinet. "Would you like to put on your first diaper?"

"Yes." I stepped forward and waited for the nurse to clean her off with a washcloth. When she was finished she moved to the side, allowing me to touch her for the first time.

I had no clue what I was doing, and the nurse took pity on me.

"You won't hurt her, just be careful not to cover the cord clamp with the diaper. You're doing great. Roll down the top of the diaper and fasten it." I did as instructed, and next the nurse taught me how to properly swaddle her, explaining that babies like to be "snug as a bug in a rug." "You can pick her up now."

I must've looked as stupid as I felt, and then she laughed. "Go on, Ethan. Just pick her up, support her neck and hold her close to you so she can feel you. You can talk to her too you know."

"Hey, baby," I whispered after I had her situated in my arms. "I'm your daddy." I kissed the top of my daughter's head and, for the first time in a long time, I felt tears rolling down my cheeks.

If someone would've told me an hour before I could love something so much, so thoroughly and completely in the matter of seconds I would've laughed. But holding my baby girl for the first time, I knew I'd never loved someone so much.

I walked back to Chrissy's side, the doctor had taken her legs down, and she was covered with a blanket, her face turned away from me.

"Chrissy? Would you like to hold her?"

"No." Her voice was flat, and she refused to look at us.

"You sure?" I tried again.

"No, Ethan. She's yours, just take her away. Please." She sounded dead inside, and, for the first time since it all started, I realized how hard this was on her. She wasn't ready to be a mom, but she'd quelled her own feelings to give our child life. Whether she wanted to admit it or not, that was what being a mom was, loving and sacrificing for your child.

Careful to balance the baby in my arms I leaned down and kissed the side of Chrissy's head.

"Thank you," I whispered. "Thank you so much for her. Take care of yourself."

The nurse was waiting by the door with a wheelchair. Hospital rules said I couldn't walk out of the room with the baby. The staff knew our situation and had arranged for the baby and me to leave the room as soon as possible, moving us down the hall to a private room as far away from the Kriers as they could.

"Does she have a name?" the nurse asked.

"She does."

"You're not gonna tell me?" She laughed teasingly.

"I want to tell my mom first."

The nurse patted my shoulder and wheeled us into the room. A few minutes later my family piled in, eager to meet the new addition.

My mom and dad stepped forward, and the tears I'd been trying to keep in check once again leaked from my eyes.

"Mom. Dad. I want you to meet my daughter, Carson Rose."

1

Eight years later

"Yo, Ethan you headed to the bar with us tonight?" Officer Oscar Lorenz, my partner, asked.

"Nope. Got a date."

"A date?" His eyes widened in shock. "You finally getting over your ten-year dry spell?"

"It hasn't been ten years, fucker. And no. I'm taking Carson out for a movie and dinner."

"You know, Maria and I would love to watch her if you'd like to go out. You know, on a date with a woman your own age."

He'd been offering for the last three years. I appreciated the gesture, but I always turned them down. I'd much rather spend time with my daughter than going on a pointless date. Carson and I were regulars at the Lorenz's dinner table. They had kids around Carson's age, but I never left her there, even when Maria begged for her to stay. They had boys, and Maria said she liked having a girl in the house.

"'Preciate it, man. But I'm good."

"Ethan, dude, one of these days you're gonna need to put yourself out there again."

"I haven't been a monk," I reminded him.

When Carson was about two, it was my mom who finally insisted I started giving her "alone time" with her granddaughter, telling me I needed to spend time away from her and with people my own age. After months of being pestered I relented. It didn't take but a few times going out with my old friends to be reminded I wasn't one of them anymore. I may've been eighteen but I had responsibilities and a daughter. They were all carefree and were still worried about their cars and chasing ass. I didn't have that luxury.

Much to my mother's dismay I'd quit public school, opting to finish my junior and senior years home schooled, and taking online classes. I hadn't wanted Carson in daycare. The guilt I'd felt was overwhelming. She'd lost her mother, and I never wanted her to feel like she didn't have me. Everyone said I was crazy, that she was too young to understand, but I did. I understood.

I finished two years of high school in under eighteen months and immediately enrolled in online college classes. I didn't have time to fuck around, I needed to provide for Carson and myself. My parents had supported us while I was in school. My dad had laid down the law and told me my education and future were what was most important.

I still made time to go out occasionally, mostly when the stress of single fatherhood weighed heavy. From time to time, those nights I'd gone out had led me back to a woman's bed. However, I made no promises. There would be no tomorrows, only sex with no strings. I had nothing more to offer; all my time belonged to my daughter.

"Biannual pussy doesn't count," he chuckled. "You're a twenty-something virgin."

"Crude much?" I shook my head. "And to think you kiss your pretty wife with that mouth."

"Don't you worry about Maria. She loves my crude mouth." He wagged his brows and continued to gather his belongings.

I was almost to the door when he called out. "Get some rest. Tomorrow's gonna suck," he reminded me.

"Congressional detail always does. See you tomorrow."

I checked my watch and saw I still had plenty of time to pick up Carson from my parents' house and grab dinner before the movie.

I climbed into my Yukon bone tired and prayed I

could make it through tomorrow. Congressman Harris was a pretentious prick. We'd have to follow him around the city tomorrow while he put on his dog and pony show for his supporters. Too bad none of them saw or heard how he behaved in private. His wife had died a few years ago giving him the leg up he'd needed to win that year's election. He had the grieving widower act down to a "T" and he'd gotten the sympathy vote easily. His son was a politician-in-training and an even bigger douche. Thankfully, they didn't come into town very often.

I pulled up to the house I'd grown up in and found Carson in the front yard with my mom, working in the flower garden. She had on a pair of bright yellow rain boots with god-awful red ladybugs all over them. Carson turned to watch me pull into the driveway, her pretty, chestnut curls bouncing with her movement, and my rough day melted away.

"Daddy! You're finally here. I thought you'd never get here. Gran said I was acting like I had ants in my pants. That's gross. I don't have ants in my undies," Carson said before my feet could hit the concrete.

"Hi, sweetheart. I told you I'd be here at five. It's only four thirty," I reminded her.

"I know. But I really, really, really want to see *Incredibles* 2. Everyone else has seen it already."

A familiar guilt hit my gut at Carson's declaration.

Most of her friends had two parents. Even if they were divorced there was always one available. She only had me. And even though my captain tried his best to keep me on days, knowing I was a single dad, there were months I had night and weekend shifts. With only three years on the job, I didn't have much seniority.

"That's a lot of reallys. We better get going if you want to stop at The Freeze to get burgers and milkshakes first." I picked Carson up, bringing her face level with mine and kissed her forehead before I set her back on her feet. "Go say bye to Gran and change your shoes please."

She hurried off, disappearing into the house, and I walked over to my mom.

"Hey, Mom. How was she?"

"Perfect. As always." She smiled.

"The flowers look great," I told her, noting the addition of pink daisies this year.

"Thank you, Ethan. Listen, I was thinking about the roommate situation—"

"Mom. I know what you're going to say. I'm a cop. I'll do a background check before I let anyone move in. I don't want anyone around Carson I can't trust."

"But—"

"I got this. I have a huge house for just Carson and me. If I rent a room out it brings in a little money.

Carson's been asking about cheer camp on top of dance classes. I can't afford both."

"My God, you're just like your father." My mom scowled, making me smile. It wasn't the first time she'd complained that my brother and I were like my dad. "Would you stop interrupting me and listen for a second? You don't need to rent the room. Your dad and I want to pay for Carson's classes."

"No way!"

"Ethan."

"No!"

"But we're her grandparents. We're allowed to spoil her. It's our right," she tried.

"No way, Mom. Thank you, but no. You spoil her enough. That was the excuse you gave when you put the pool in the backyard for her. And the last three times you took us to Disneyworld on vacation. And all the other countless things you do for her—and me. I appreciate everything you and dad have done and still do. But I'm not taking money from my parents to raise my kid."

"Told you, he'd never go for it," my dad said, joining the conversation.

"I had to try." My mom looked thoroughly dejected. "I just want to help."

"Mama, you help me all the time. You watch Carson after school until I get off work. You keep her overnight if I have a shift. And if I get called out in the middle of the night, you never complain when you wake up and she's at the house. There's nothing more I could possibly ask for."

"I hate the thought of a stranger being in your house."

"I do too. But I have two more years until I can take the detective exam. Until then, we're gonna have to scrape by." We'd had this talk a hundred times.

"We have the money, Ethan. We want to spend it on you, Carson, and Carter."

"Mom!"

"Leave it, Lily." My mom cut her eyes to my dad and his face softened. "You rolling your pretty eyes at me, woman?"

Oh, hell. I knew where this was headed. Over the years my parents had never hidden their attraction for each other.

"Yes." Her hand went to her hip, and my dad smirked. He always told us he loved when mom caught an attitude with him. I thought he was crazy. When my mom was in a tizzy, there was nothing cute about it.

"It's a good thing Ethan's here to pick up our granddaughter then."

"Please don't start," I begged.

My dad chuckled and tagged my mom around the waist, pulling her tightly against his chest. He whispered something that turned her face red and that was my cue to leave.

"Carson," I bellowed.

"Right here, Daddy. Keep your pants on." Carson trotted up next to me and, blissfully unaware her grandparents were randy, she announced, "We're going to the movies. Thank you, Gran, for making me cookies." My mom tried to hide her smile as Carson inadvertently threw her under the bus. It didn't matter how many times I'd asked my mom to stop giving her cookies every day, especially when she knew I was taking Carson for milkshakes and junk food, she never listened. Her reply was always the same—it was her right as a grandmother.

"Have fun with Daddy."

"Pop?"

"Right here, Princess," my dad answered.

"Are we still going fishing this weekend?"

"We sure are. Uncle Jasper is coming, too."

"Awesome." She fist-bumped the air. "He doesn't make me touch the worms like you do."

"Come on, Squirt, we're gonna be late."

We said our goodbyes, and I helped Carson buckle up before I headed in the direction of The Freeze.

Carson prattled on about her day with my mom and dad. I had my best girl next to me, smiling and happy, and all was right in my world.

2

Two hundred and fifty miles wasn't far but returning to the place that held happy memories gave me hope.

It was a start.

Two hundred and fifty miles smelled a lot like freedom.

I stepped out of the motel room I'd been living in for the past week and inhaled. Yes, indeed, freedom. I'd picked this motel because it wasn't terribly expensive and still in a nicer part of town, and I didn't feel like I was going to be mugged every time I left the safety of the locked door.

It was a beautiful, sunny afternoon, and, with nothing to do for the next few hours, I decided on a walk. Hitching my camera strap over my shoulder, I double-checked I had my new pay-as-you-go phone and room key. Getting a new cellphone plan was on my long list of to-dos, but first things first—a place to live that wasn't pay by the night. Hopefully, that would be taken care of later this afternoon.

There was a cute, little park down the block with the most beautiful magnolia trees. I'd already taken at least a hundred images of the blooms, but I couldn't get enough. The small pond attracted both mallards and sunbathing snapping turtles, there was always something to photograph. My mom used to joke about me never leaving the house without my camera. She complained I was experiencing life through the narrow viewfinder instead of with all my senses. Maybe she'd been right. However, now that she was gone all I had left of her were the pictures I'd taken, and I was grateful to have them. Each time I looked at the images I could draw up a memory to go with what I'd captured. All of them wonderful until she'd met and married Franklin. And with Frank came Samuel, his equally dreadful son.

The pavement gave way to plush, green grass, and I smiled thinking about how angry Franklin must've been at my defection. The man had a perverted sense of family and had to know I'd never go along with his plans. It didn't matter how many times he'd threatened to kick me out of his sprawling mansion or take away my allowance, I never followed his orders. In a way, I was grateful for his ultimatum, I should've moved out of his house long ago. My mom had been gone for four years, and I'd stayed in that house of horrors four years too long. I'd been too devastated at the time to make a change. If I'd had my wits about me, I would've flipped Frank and Sam the bird and been on my merry way.

A little girl squealed in delight, pulling my attention away from the cream-colored flower. Beautiful, brown curls flew behind the girl as her dad pushed her on the swing, her legs stretching out on the way up and curling back on the way down. With each push she was gaining altitude. She threw her head back and laughed.

The sight was too good to pass up. I lifted my camera and pressed the shutter release, capturing the girl in midflight. I lowered my camera and saw her dad staring at me. Even with a scowl on his face he was hot. Maybe he wasn't the dad, he looked too young to have a child as old as the girl on the swing. He stopped the swing, said something to the girl, and started toward me in a fast and angry clip.

Shit.

"Hey," he called out. "What do you think you're doing?"

"Um . . ."

I was frozen in place. Not only had I not expected him to yell at me, but the closer he got, the clearer I could see his face. I'd been wrong. He wasn't hot. He was smokin' hot. Light-sandy-brown hair, greenish eyes, a perfect nose, and a square, chiseled jaw line. What I wouldn't have given to have him in front of my lens. Maybe with his shirt off, showcasing those bulging muscles under the T-shirt pulled tight across his broad chest.

"Well?" he barked.

"Well what?"

"Why are you taking pictures of my daughter?"

"Huh?"

I studied his face and thought about how unfair it was that men aged so much better than women. There wasn't a line on his face. After looking at him for a moment or two, I realized he had to be close to my age, I glanced over his shoulder at the little girl, now standing by the swings, she had to be nine or ten—there was no way.

"Serious as shit. Right now, lady, tell me why you took my kid's picture."

"I'm a photographer."

"And?" He motioned for me to keep going as if my explanation wasn't good enough.

"I didn't mean to offend you. I'll delete the picture. I heard her laughing and when I glanced over, she looked so happy and carefree I could help it."

"Delete it," he demanded.

What an asshole.

"Okay."

"Now."

"You're kinda a jerk," I told him. I said I was sorry. "Don't you think you're being a tad over-the-top?"

"A jerk?" He recoiled. "You haven't seen over-the-top yet. It's fucking rude to take pictures of other people's children. You could be some sicko for all I know."

"Never mind, you're not a jerk, you're an asshole." I pulled my camera body up and scrolled to the image, flashing the LCD screen in his direction so he could see me deleting the picture. Before I could pull my camera back, his large hand covered mine and stilled my movements. Goose bumps raced down my arms at his touch.

"That's good," he said narrowing his eyes.

"That's because I'm good," I told him, yanking my camera free.

I glanced at the screen, saddened to delete such a perfect moment in time. I hit the trash button on the back of my camera and the image disappeared. I hated deleting pictures, even the bad ones. They were moments in time you'd never get back.

"I hope you take a lot of pictures with her." I don't know why I said that, and when the man looked at me in bewilderment, I hurried to finish. "I lost my dad when I was about her age. I have one picture of the two of us together. Only one. I wish with all my heart I had more. When memories start to fade, it's important to have a reminder. Sorry for troubling you."

I turned to leave when the man stopped me.

"Listen, you were right. I was being a dick. I'm sorry. I'm a little crazy when it comes to my daughter. I'm a cop and, unfortunately, I see danger everywhere. It was a really great picture."

"Thanks. Enjoy your day."

I glanced at the little girl again, wishing I could remember if my dad had ever pushed me on the swings. And, if he had, did I laugh and smile like the cute little girl with wind-tangled curls? I like to think I did. My mom had told me stories about how much my dad loved me, but I had no way of knowing if those tales were made up to make a broken-hearted ten year old feel better.

Now I was a twenty-something orphan. No parents, no family. It was me, myself, and I against the world. I started back to the motel, needing to change before I went to meet a man about a room for rent. It was the second step on the road to independence. A place to live that was not a motel.

When I'd left Frank's house I took only what was mine. Either what I'd bought with my own money or what I'd had before my mom had married the prick. It wasn't a lot, but, truthfully, I didn't need much. I'd preferred it when it was just my mom and me in a small condo. Frank's mansion was cold and lonely. Thankfully, I had my car. I was happy that even when he'd complained the old Honda was a piece of shit, I'd never given into his desire to buy me a fancy, new car. My car was mine. Bought by me before Frank came into the picture. I wanted nothing from him.

I was so lost in my thoughts the short walk to the motel was a blur. I rushed a shower, dressed, and was in my car before long.

I grabbed the directions I'd written down and pulled out of the parking lot. The drive was short, and when I pulled into a nice neighborhood, I prayed the landlord wasn't a creep. I needed to find a place to live and get back to work before I blew through my savings.

I parked at the curb and got out, straightening my T-shirt the best I could.

Please. Please. Please. Be normal.

I lifted my hand and knocked. A few seconds later the door opened.

Well, fuck my life.

This sucked.

3

Shortly after the woman with the camera had interrupted us, Carson and I headed home. My head was pounding, and I was tired. I'd had a week from hell. Lorenz had been wrong, the congressman's detail hadn't sucked, it fucking blew. He'd had his son with him on the campaign trail, and with the congressman up for reelection he was stressed and took it out on everyone around him. His twit son thought he was Mr. Billy Badass and barked orders at the officers. Luckily, it only lasted two days and they'd headed back to the fiery pits of wherever they'd come from.

"Daddy? Can we go over to Gran's? I want to go swimming." Carson asked as I walked us in the front door.

I hated having to tell her no, but the last thing I wanted to do was go to my parents'. My mom would complain I looked tired, and, truthfully, I knew she meant well, but I didn't want to hear it. She'd be happy if Carson and I moved back into their basement where she could continue to take care of us both.

"No, Squirt. Someone is coming over to look at the room we're renting out. But you're going over tomorrow, remember?"

"I hope this one's not creepy like the other ones."

I looked down at Carson and smiled at her scrunched-up face.

"Me, too."

Shit, maybe my mom was right. Renting one of my extra rooms out seemed like it was a good answer. But after the last two guys that'd come over, I wasn't so sure. And the only women that had answered my ad wasn't much better. She'd been polite and nice to Carson but when she'd swung her eyes in my direction, she hadn't tried to hide that she liked what she saw. That was never going to happen; she had trouble written all over her.

"Why were you mad at the lady at the park?"

My gut twisted remembering what a dick I'd been. A bad week coupled with the always present fear Chrissy would try and pop back into our lives had me overreacting. It wasn't an excuse for my behavior, but when I saw the woman taking Carson's picture my imagination went into overdrive. I hadn't seen or heard from Chrissy since the day I'd been wheeled out of the hospital room with Carson tucked close. She'd done what she'd said she was going to do and had completely disappeared. But the what ifs plagued me.

"I wasn't mad. I was concerned because a stranger was taking your picture."

"Why, because it's not safe?"

"Yes, because it's not safe," I repeated.

There was a knock on the door, and I checked my watch. Right on time.

"Run upstairs and play in your room."

She was half way up the stairs when she yelled down, "Can I watch TV in your room?"

"Yes," I answered.

I opened the door and had to blink a few times before I understood what I was seeing. What the fuck? The photographer from the park was standing on my door step. Her smile faded, and she glanced from side to side before she looked back to me and cocked her head to side. Confusion marred her pretty face. My eyes narrowed as I wondered if she'd followed us home.

"You following me?"

"I must have the wrong address."

We both spoke at the same time.

Talking over each other again we both asked, "What?"

I gestured for her to go first.

"I said, I must have the wrong address. Sorry to have bothered you."

"What address are you looking for?" She rattled off my address, making me even more concerned she knew where I lived. "A friend's house?"

"No."

"Then why are you looking for that address?"

She placed her hand on her hip, much like my mom did when she was annoyed with my dad, and looked me over from top to toe.

"I'm sorry, but that's none of your business," she said.

"Come again?"

"You heard me. I'm not telling a stranger why I'm doing anything. For all I know you're a crazy person. Sorry to have bothered you—again. I'll go check the address."

I wondered if she was the woman coming to look at the room. The timing was right.

"What's your name?"

"Hello. Did you miss the part about you being a stranger and me not telling you anything?"

Something strange ticked inside of me. My dad would call it instinct, my mom would call it an aha moment. Whichever you called it, I suddenly understood what my father had been saying all these years. There was something sexy as fuck about this woman throwing me attitude. The cop in me was kind of proud she wasn't divulging any personal information. But the impulsive man in me wanted to yank her close and kiss the sass right off her tongue.

"Honor?" I asked.

She rocked back on her feet, and her green eyes sparked to life.

"How do you know my name?"

"A wild guess," I teased.

"Right. Because Honor is the first thing that pops into most people's head when they try and guess a name. Now if you'd said Mary or Donna or something as equally common, I might believe it was a wild guess."

"I bet you're looking for a room to rent."

It was fascinating what her face gave away. She wore her emotions boldly.

"Ethan?"

"That's me," I confirmed. "Would you like to come in and look around?"

I held the door open and stepped aside. She stood there, worrying her bottom lip between her teeth, then suddenly nodded as if she were having some sort of internal discussion.

"I'd like that," she mumbled and crossed the threshold, taking in the large, open downstairs.

The house was too much for Carson and me, but it

had been a foreclosure, and my dad and uncles had helped me fix it up.

"This is nice."

"Thanks. Around here is the kitchen." I led her farther into the room and around the corner into the breakfast nook.

"Now, this is amazing."

The kitchen was a housewarming present from my family; all of them, my aunts and uncles had pitched in too. My Aunt Emily had insisted the kitchen was the soul of a home and it should be the best room in the house. They'd gone all out with top-of-the-line appliances. Too bad I was a shitty cook.

"Through there is the laundry room and garage."

I turned and walked to the other side of the house and opened the door to the downstairs bed room.

"This is the room. It is a modified mother-in-law-suite. It has a private entrance going to the side yard and a private bathroom. You'll have to share the kitchen and laundry."

"May I?" She asked motioning to the door.

"Yeah. Take your time. I'll be out here."

She walked into the room, and I went back to the kitchen. For some reason I hoped she liked it and wanted to move in. I kept telling myself it was because I was too tired to keep showing the room and if I wanted Carson to have both cheer camp and dance, I needed the money. But that wasn't the entire truth. I could scrape by and give my daughter what she wanted without renting the room, and as lazy as I was, I'd wait until I found the right renter. There was just something about Honor that made me want *her* to move in. Which was crazy because the first time we'd exchanged words I was a dick to her, and this time she'd been in my house just a little over ten minutes.

"Um. The ad said four hundred a month, utilities included. Is that right?" she asked once again looking around the house.

"Yep."

"What's the catch?"

"The catch?" I questioned, not understanding where she was going.

"Four hundred a month for this house is a steal. Do you have other roommates? Throw wild sex parties. Drink too much?"

"No, no, and no. It's just Carson and me."

"Carson?"

"My daughter." I could see she had questions and before she could ask I continued. "There are a few rules. No boyfriends spend the night without me meeting and approving of them first. Always set the alarm when you leave. And clean up the kitchen after you use it."

"Boyfriends?" she huffed.

"Or girlfriends. Whatever floats your boat. My daughter lives here. All I ask is that you respect that and understand her safety is all that's important to me."

That was true, but I'd made up the boyfriend part on the fly. Partly to see if she had a boyfriend and because the thought of seeing Honor with a man made my fists clench.

"I work from home. Is that going to be a problem for you?"

"You're a photographer, right?"

"Yeah. I sell fine art still images. But I'm also a graphic artist."

"Daddy?" Carson called from the top of the stairs.

"Yeah, Squirt?"

"Can I come down and get a drink?"

"Sure."

Carson came bouncing down the stairs but stopped short when she saw Honor standing in the living room. She looked between the two of us then her gaze settled on me.

"It's okay. Come meet Honor."

Carson's nose scrunched. "That's a funny name."

"Carson Rose. That's not polite." I scolded.

"Sorry," she mumbled.

"It is funny, isn't it? My momma named me Honor because my dad was in the Army. He was actually on deployment when I was born and didn't get to meet me until I was six months old," Honor explained.

"My pop was in the Army," Carson beamed.

"That's cool."

"Yeah. He's retired. Now he just takes me fishing and plays football with me and helps me with my back-walk-overs."

"He sounds like a great pop. You're pretty lucky."

"I am. My pop says I'm the luckiest girl in the world because I have so many people who love me. But who couldn't help but love me?" Carson cocked her head to the side and batted her eyelashes. "Did it work? Gran says I need to work on it some more. But soon I'll be good enough Daddy won't be able to tell me no."

"Is that so?" I chuckled. "Gran's teaching you bad habits."

"She's allowed. She says it's her right."

Honor laughed at Carson's antics, then a sadness settled over her features.

"Thought you wanted something to drink?" I reminded Carson, wanting to change the subject.

"Oh, right." She skipped to the kitchen before turning to Honor. "Are you going to rent the room?"

"I'm talking to your dad about it. Would that be all right with you?"

I may've swayed on my feet with the effort of

picking my jaw off the floor. I couldn't believe Honor would think to ask Carson her opinion.

"You seem nice. But Daddy says—"

"Carson!" I stopped her before she could say something that offended Honor.

"Will you teach me how to take pictures?"

"Of course I will." Honor beamed. "I mean if your dad and I talk, and I rent the room."

"Cool."

"I take it you like the room?" I asked.

"I do. It's perfect. So much better than the motel I'm staying in."

Honor was laughing. I, however, was not. Different scenarios ran through my head about what could happen to a single woman living in a motel—all of them bad.

"Why are you living in a motel?"

She tugged at the hem of her shirt and diverted her eyes, the hair on the back of my neck prickled, and I knew she was getting ready to lie to me. Was she in some sort of trouble? And if she was, did I want to help?

"I moved here from Atlanta and didn't have a place lined up. I'm staying at the motel while I look around."

Hmm. A partial truth, but she'd omitted why she'd left Atlanta. My instincts were screaming at me that she was hiding something.

"What motel?"

She was quiet for a moment while she contemplated my question. Surely, she wasn't going to tell me I was a stranger again and not tell me.

"West End."

"The fuck?"

"What?" She looked around the room unaware it was her answer that had garnered the curse.

"That place is dangerous, Honor. I get called there at least once a week for a domestic disturbance."

"Yeah. It can get loud. But I don't leave my room after dark, so I don't mind."

Hell. To. The. No. Honor was not staying at the motel one more night. Fuck the background check, her ass would be in this house by nightfall. I checked my watch, seeing it was mid afternoon. Depending on how many trips we needed to make, we could get her moved in before dark.

"Squirt?"

"Yeah, Daddy?"

"Call Gran and ask her if you can go over and play for a few hours."

"She says, yes."

"You didn't call.".

"I don't need to. I know her answer. Gran says I'm welcome anytime, day or night and all the time between."

"Go get your bathing suit and towel. I'll call Gran."

Carson ran upstairs, and Honor stood staring at me confused by the abrupt change of subject.

I pulled my phone out and dialed my parents' number.

"Hello?" my dad answered.

"Busy?"

"Just got unbusy, whatcha got?"

I made a gagging sound, understanding full well what my father was implying.

"Something's come up. Would you mind, since you're *unbusy* now, if I dropped Carson off for a few hours?"

"You never have to ask," he replied.

"Yes, I do. You and mom are *busy* more than any two people I know. I'm still trying to recover from the time when I was thirteen and walked into the house and saw something no child ever wants to see. I'm avoiding the years of therapy for my daughter by calling first."

"You have a point, son. If you had a woman as—"

"Dad!" I cut him off.

He chuckled before he asked, "Everything okay?"

"Yeah. I need to help the woman who rented the room move her shit from the motel she's staying in."

"Which motel? You need backup?"

And just like that, with no questions asked, my dad

had my back. Just like when I was sixteen, and every day before and after that. He was there, pushing me forward, carrying the load when I thought I couldn't, and walking beside me as my best friend.

If I turned out to be half the man, half the father, he is, I'll have walked this life a good man.

4

What was happening? Why was Ethan making plans for Carson to go to his parents' house and for him to move my stuff?

Ethan was smiling when he hung up and put his phone back in his pocket.

"You good with the rent?" he asked.

"Yeah." I drew out the word still unsure what was going on.

"Great. There's only a week left in this month. Call it a move in special, first month's rent due on the first."

"What's happening, Ethan?"

"We're going to grab your stuff," he told me as if we'd already agreed I'd move in.

"And why are we doing that? I can manage on my own. I only have a few suitcases."

"Great, then we only need to take the Tahoe and make one trip. Wait, what about a bed and furniture? Do you have a storage unit or something?"

My face burned with embarrassment. I didn't want to admit I'd left my stepfather's house with just my clothes, camera gear, laptop, and what I'd salvaged of my mother's before Frank had banished all memories of her from his house.

"I'm going to buy new stuff." That was the truth, but the fact I was neglecting to tell him the rest didn't sit well. It shouldn't have mattered, he was no one to me, however I was overcome by an unsettling feeling, reminding me I was returning his kindness with lies. But I'd rather die a thousand deaths than tell Ethan the real reason for abandoning my old life: the disgusting plan Frank had come up with. No, that was a secret I'd rather keep to myself.

"I have a bed in the garage you can have," he offered.

"That's nice, but, no, thank you." His suggestion felt a lot like charity, something I didn't want. I moved away from Atlanta to learn to be on my own. A new start, a new life. I didn't ever want to depend on anyone again. I had to stand on my own two feet.

"Really, my Aunt Regan gave it to me when they remodeled one of their rooms. It was a guest bed, I don't think anyone's ever slept on it, and it's sitting in the garage collecting dust."

"I said, no, thank you. I'll buy something."

His eyes narrowed, but he didn't argue.

"Ready, Daddy. Are we leaving now?" Carson came down the stairs, interrupting our conversation.

"We sure are." Ethan looked at me with a raised eyebrow, almost daring me to argue with him in front of Carson. The thought crossed my mind to put my foot down and tell him to butt out, but then Carson turned to me and flashed the cutest little girl smile I'd ever seen, and the irritation melted away. Her grandmother was right, she did have the sly, give-me-what-I-want look down pat. She was going to give Ethan a run for his money when she was a teenager. And on that glorious thought of cosmic payback I relented to let Ethan help me move my stuff.

On the short drive to Ethan's parents' house, Carson told me all about the "awesome pool" her grandparents had put in a few years ago. Now all her cousins, even though they are much older than her and are really Ethan's cousins, her second cousins, liked to come over and swim too. She gave me a very thorough run down of the family tree. There were so many of them, I couldn't remember all the names except Ethan's older brother, Carter. Carson declared he was the best uncle of the bunch. He was in the Navy and lived in Virginia. Whenever he came home, he told her all about the places he'd been and always brought back foreign currency for her—she had quite the collection.

Nowhere in the conversation had she mentioned her mother. Not even in the abstract or in the past tense. It was simply as if the woman who'd given birth to her never existed. I was sad for her, but the interesting part was, she didn't seem upset or bothered by it. There were so many people around her who loved her she wasn't missing anything. That was something I'd never had. After my dad died, it was just me and my mom for a long time. She had been all I'd needed, but listening to Carson tell me stories I realized there's a big difference between need and want. I'd always wanted aunts and uncles and cousins—a family.

Ethan pulled into his parents' driveway, and a tall, imposing, very good-looking man stood on the porch waiting for our arrival. It was easy to see he was Ethan's dad. Ethan was a carbon copy, minus the graying hair. Talk about good genes. Some woman was going to get very lucky when she scooped up Ethan and Carson. Unwarranted jealousy bloomed in my chest at the thought of Ethan with a woman.

Shit. Maybe he had a woman in his life. It wasn't out of the realm of possibility. He was out of this world hot. He had a nice house, a good job, the sweetest little *Squirt* I'd ever met. A woman would have to be a flat-out idiot to turn him down. First impressions notwithstanding, he seemed like a nice guy. A little bossy but—

"Wanna come in and see the pool?" Carson cut through my thoughts.

"Another time. We need to start moving Honor's stuff," Ethan, thankfully, made an excuse for me.

Shit on a shingle, Ethan's dad was making his way to the truck.

"Sorry about this," Ethan mumbled and exited the truck, rounding the hood and coming to my side. Carson had already unbuckled and was waiting for her dad to open the back door for her when, much to my dismay, he opened mine first.

Well, hells bells, it looked like I was meeting his dad.

I tried not to fidget as Ethan made the introduction at the same time he let Carson out of the truck. She yelled hello to her grandfather and ran into the house.

"Dad, this Honor Sullivan. Honor, this is my father, Carter Lenox."

"Pleased to meet you, Mr. Lenox."

"Just, Lenox."

"I'm sorry?"

"No Mister. Just Lenox," he explained.

He had a funny look on his face as he studied me.

His stare was intense, and I was afraid he could read my innermost thoughts.

"Are you Buck Sully's daughter?" Lenox asked.

My body jolted, and Ethan's hands came to my shoulders to steady me. "Whoa."

"I am," I recovered.

"Anyone ever tell you you look just like him? But you have your mom's pretty, green eyes."

"No one has ever told me that," I choked out. "You knew my dad?"

My mom had been so heartbroken after my dad died she'd rarely spoken about him. I'd heard her in her room at night, crying herself to sleep. In the morning I'd sneak in and find the old letters my dad had written to her spread out over her bed. It was her private time with my dad, and I never intruded or asked about the letters. After she died, I tried to find them, the last of my father, but they were gone.

"Not well. We had a few deployments together. He talked about you and your mom all the time, and there were pictures of the two of you above his cot. He was a good man, I was sorry to hear about his passing. Did you know he was stationed here?"

"Thank you," I whispered. "I did. I don't remember it well, but my mom loved the area."

I was grateful Ethan hadn't removed his hands, they were the only thing anchoring me in place.

"Your name is fitting. Honor. He served with great honor and sacrifice."

Ethan must've felt my body start to shake because he finally spoke up.

"We'll be back to pick up Carson in a bit. It shouldn't take long to move Honor's stuff."

"Take your time," Lenox said, our eyes still locked, and I prayed he wasn't as observant as he looked. I didn't want him to see the hurt and sadness I tried to hide. "It was nice meeting you, Honor. I hope Ethan will bring you back when you can stay and visit."

Lenox finally looked over my head to Ethan and smiled at his son. Damn. I missed my mom smiling at me like that. With a nod he turned and walked back into the house.

Ethan helped me back into the truck and, without needing directions, headed to the motel.

"I'm sorry if my dad upset you."

"He didn't. I was just shocked."

"What happened to your dad?"

I took a few cleansing breaths before I could speak. It had been a long time since I'd been allowed to talk about my father. His very name had been off-limits in Frank's house. He'd made sure all memories of my mother's first husband had been wiped clean.

"He died on deployment in Kosovo. RPG took out the convoy. I was ten."

"Fuck, Honor, I'm so sorry."

"It was a long time ago."

"Doesn't matter how long ago it was." We'd been silent for a while when he asked his next question. "Where's your mom?"

That question was a direct hit to my heart. Talking about a father I barely knew was one thing, but my mom was different.

"She's gone."

He pulled into the parking lot of the motel, and I muttered my room number. He found a spot and rolled to a stop. Cutting the engine, he turned in his seat, his gaze assessing and full of something I hoped wasn't pity.

"She died four years ago in a car accident," I told him.

It almost felt good to say it out loud. Frank hadn't talked about my mom after her death. He said it was because it was too painful, he'd lost the true love of his life. He didn't mean those words, they were just for show; the grieving widower act made for great headlines. He had whores sneaking in the staff entrance before my mother's body was cold.

"Jesus, Honor. I can't imagine."

There was nothing to say to that, so I didn't speak. I got out of the truck and made my way to the room, trying to remember if I'd cleaned up before I'd left this afternoon. I didn't want my new landlord to think I was a slob and change his mind. I opened the door and looked around the small space. My belongings were neatly stacked against the wall.

"Is that it?" Ethan questioned, scanning the area for more.

"That's it. I have to grab a few things from the shower." I told him and went to gather my toiletries, leaving him alone by the door.

When I came back out Ethan was gone as well as some of the boxes. I was sorry I'd missed him picking up the heavy load. I'd wanted to watch his biceps flex like they had when he'd picked up Carson to help her into the truck. It was probably a little inappropriate for me to have drooled over the sexy way his muscles bulged, but I couldn't help it. He was a far cry from Sam and his soft, country club friends he'd brought around the house. It was laughable how they used to parade shirtless around the pool, their skinny bodies doing nothing for me, even as a teenager. Sam used to watch my reaction when his friends were over, and if I looked a little too long at one of them, he accused me of being a slut and wanting to fuck his friends. It was done under the pretense of him being a caring big brother. But as I got older, I saw it for what it was—him being an obsessive, disgusting asshole.

"One more trip and we'll be done if you can grab your suit cases," Ethan said appearing in the doorway.

"You can't carry those three boxes in one trip. I'll help you."

The sexy smirk that crossed his face was panty-melting or panty-dropping or let-me-take-my-panties-off-myself-and-throw-them-at-you hot. Shit on a shingle he was dangerous.

"Watch me."

Oh, no, I didn't want to watch anything. I had a few minutes before, but now that he'd smiled at me, and my undies had dampened, I no longer wanted to look.

He was my landlord—off-limits.

"Honor?"

"Yeah?"

"You ready?"

"Oh, um . . . sure."

Ethan's body shook as he silently chuckled before giving way to a deep, rich laugh that sent chills racing over my body. Damn, he was even better looking when he laughed.

Off-limits.

5

"You finally found someone," Lorenz said, coughing.

"Man, are you sure you're ready to come back to work? You still sound like shit."

"Used up all my sick days last week. Besides, I feel fine." The lung he'd almost hacked up proved his statement a lie. He looked like shit, sounded like it too.

"Yeah. I found a roommate. Moved in last week."

Talking about my sexy roommate had my body thrumming with lust. There was something about her that drove me crazy. The week had been smooth, she was doing her own thing, and Carson and I had our own schedule. Our interactions had been pleasant and friendly. There was nothing she'd done specifically to put my body on edge, it was simply the way she moved, the way she smiled at Carson, and her great laugh, which she shared often. There was no doubt Honor was beautiful, but it was more than that, she was sugar-sweet to her core with a side helping of wit. As the days passed, I could tell she was getting more comfortable around me, then last night, there was a hint of flirtation in her tone. Nothing overt, but it was definitely there. My heart rate had ticked up, and my cock had stirred. I knew it was a bad idea to allow myself to fantasize about my roommate, however, it hadn't stopped me from taking care of business in the shower with memories of the sexy sway of her hips or her flirty comebacks.

Normally, I hated having to work weekends. It meant getting up early and taking Carson to Mom and Dad's, disrupting their day. Even if they said I wasn't, I still felt that way. But this morning I was fucking thrilled to be up early. I came out to get a cup of coffee before I got dressed and caught Honor in the kitchen in a pair of tight as all hell work out shorts and a sports bra, sweaty from a run. I nearly swallowed my tongue as I took in her curves and tight ass. I had never been so thankful for the thick material of my sweatpants. I had to tuck my hardening dick into the waistband to prevent a tent she'd never forget.

She'd apologized profusely about her scantily clad attire and explained she didn't know I'd be up so early on a Saturday. I didn't bother explaining why I was up so early, I was enjoying her stuttering and discomfort far too much. Try as she might, her eyes kept dropping to my bare chest. I should've apologized as well. I was less dressed than she was, but I didn't. And when I told her not to change her clothes on my account, her cheeks turned a delicious shade of pink, the color extending down to her very impressive cleavage. I was skirting the line of what was deemed socially acceptable, but I couldn't give the first fuck.

Honor was the first woman since Carson was born I'd let my guard down with. A woman had never stepped foot in my home. Granted, she was renting a room, but it felt like more. I couldn't explain it and I didn't want to. For once, I just wanted to feel, not analyze it to death.

"And he checks out? Good people, you're comfortable with him being around Carson?"

I loved that Lorenz cared about Carson. He and Maria were good friends, honorary aunt and uncle.

"She."

"She?"

"A woman rented the room. Honor Sullivan."

"Is she hot?"

I should've told him to shove off, that it didn't matter what she looked like, she was just renting a room, not entering a beauty contest. But I didn't.

"She's all right," I lied.

There was nothing all right about Honor. She was a fucking knockout.

"I guess all that matters is she pays her rent on time and she's nice to Carson. Maybe she'll even babysit so you can finally get laid."

Lorenz's off the cuff comment had vivid images of Honor sprawled on my bed popping into my mind. Jesus Christ, the woman was sensational, but I shouldn't have been thinking about what she'd look like naked, and the sounds she'd make as I moved above her, and I really shouldn't have been imagining what she'd look like taking my dick in her mouth. But I had, and I was.

"One-Palmer-One, this is dispatch." The radio in the patrol car came to life.

"One-Palmer-One," I responded.

"One-Palmer-One, Two-Delta-Five requesting backup at 307 Main Street. Burglary in progress."

"One-Palmer-One, copy. Any further code response?"

"ASAP. One-Palmer-One."

"Copy that. One-Palmer-One en route."

Lorenz flipped on the lights and sirens and headed in the direction of the burglary.

"Think it's another convenience store?" he asked taking a right corner so fast I had to grab the oh shit bar to keep myself upright. "This would be number five in the last seven days."

With the drug problem being what it was in the area, increased armed robberies were on the rise. The crime rate had spiked over the last few months, leaving our chief's ass on the line, as if he could control the criminal behavior in the area. The department was short-staffed, hence most of us were pulling doubles and weekend duty. My once monthly on-call schedule had recently changed to once weekly. I didn't mind the overtime, but the burnout rate in the department was increasing. I didn't want to be next.

"One-Palmer-One. Be warned, shots fired. Repeat, shots fired."

"One-Palmer-One, copy," I answered.

"Dispatch requesting additional units to the scene, 307 Main. Call in," Sammy the dispatch operator came back over the air.

"Fuck," Lorenz barked.

Red and blue flashing lights greeted us as we pulled up to the scene. Two cars—four officers, none of them in sight.

We exited the car, and before pulling my Smith & Wesson .45 acp from my holster I rapped my fist against my bulletproof vest, a habit pressed upon me by my dad and uncles—verify your equipment. I double checked every time, without fail. In a smooth draw I had my weapon in hand. Pulling the radio from my shoulder, I called in our location.

"Two-Delta-Five. Coming in west side—" My transmission was interrupted by two loud bangs.

"Christ," Lorenz cursed.

"One-Palmer-One, two shots fired. Entering west side."

I clipped my radio back and waited for Lorenz to open the door. It was an ass pucker factor one-hundred when entering a building with no visual of what's waiting inside. I nodded, and he pushed it open. I went right, he went left. We had breaching a room down to as much of a science as one could when there were thousands of variables you couldn't account for.

"Clear," we both called out and continued through the stockroom.

The door to the hall was open, guns at the ready, we made our move.

"He's hit," an officer yelled.

I fumbled with my radio to call dispatch. "Officer down. Need a bus. ASAP."

"Suspect fled on foot. Jenkins and Tebbetts followed," Patterson told us, leaning over his downed partner, applying pressure to a leg wound. "Stay with me, Mike. Don't close your eyes."

"Fucking burns," Mike complained. The growing pool around his thigh was not a good sign.

"Jesus fucking Christ," Patterson yelled. "Where's that ambulance?"

And as if he'd called it up with his outburst, a wailing siren sounded as the ambulance pulled up out front. Lorenz jogged to the front of the store and I stood guard over the two officers.

My head reeled at seeing a fellow officer injured. I knew my job was dangerous; every day when I strapped on my vest and sidearm I was reminded of just how much. But seeing one of the good guys lying on the ground, bleeding, was a sock to the face. A gut check, reminding me that at any time I could be the one injured or killed in the line of duty. And where would that leave Carson? I was the only parent she had.

The EMT pushed his way in and Patterson stood, his partner's blood dripping from his hands. I looked around and found an open box of cleaning rags beside the stockroom door. I grabbed a few and tossed them at Patterson.

No words were exchanged—none were needed, all his concentration still on his partner. Mike was quickly loaded onto a gurney, Patterson following out the front door, leaving me and Lorenz alone to stare at a puddle of thick, red gore on the floor.

"Let's get to work." He slapped my shoulder, pulling my eyes from the horror.

"Yeah."

We spent the next two hours processing the scene and three more at the station doing paperwork. By the time four o'clock rolled around, and my shift was over, I was fucking done. I wanted nothing more than to pick up Carson, grab a pizza, go home, and sit out on the deck in silence.

Talk about a clusterfuck of a Saturday.

On my way to my parents' house I called the captain to check on Mike. He was out of surgery. Luckily, the doctor was able to repair the damage before he'd bled to death, and he'd make a full recovery. Thank the good Lord.

"DADDY!" Carson came running toward me at full speed as soon as I walked into my parents' house.

"Hey, little Squirt." I picked her up and spun in a circle before hugging her close.

"Ouch, Daddy. Your stuff is poking me," she complained.

My *stuff* being my vest and utility belt I still hadn't taken off.

"Sorry, baby. You ready to head home? I'm tired today."

"All ready. Gran packed up some of the cookies we made so Honor can try them."

Fuck. Honor.

How could I have forgotten about her? A burglary, an officer shot, and after-action reports from hell was how I'd forgotten about my sexy, new roommate.

"That was nice of you and Gran. I'm sure she'll like them. Go grab them."

Carson ran to the kitchen where I knew my mom was because there was loud clanking coming from that direction.

"What's Mom doing?"

"Cleaning out the cabinets." My dad rolled his eyes. There was no need to clean anything in my mom's kitchen. It was spotless. "What's wrong?"

Leave it to my dad to pick up on my demeanor.

"Officer was shot today. Mike Collins. He's recovering."

"The suspect?"

"At large. Fled on foot. Two officers gave chase, but they lost him."

"Another liquor store?"

"Yep."

"What is that five or six?" he asked.

"Five," I confirmed.

"Fuck. When's your next shift?"

"Monday." I hated how worried my dad look and I was quick to add, "I'm always safe."

My father's green eyes, the same color as mine, pinned me in place. My reminder did nothing to ease the worry etched into his face. He had the same apprehensive look when my brother was home. He'd always told us from a young age he'd support any career choice we made, from being a garbage man to any branch of the military. What he never wanted was for either of us to feel obligated to join the Army like he had. He'd always said he'd answered the call enough for both of us, but it would be our choice.

Carter had set his sights on the Naval Academy and accomplished just that. After he was commissioned, he answered another challenge and left for San Diego to go to BUD/s. Six months later he'd graduated and was pinned with a shiny, gold Trident. My brother was one tough son of a bitch.

When I'd left school to raise Carson, I'd also left behind ROTC and my plans to join the Army. Even though the military was no longer an option, I still had the deep-seated need to serve my community, so I became a cop. Now I wondered if my desire to follow my dreams was selfish.

"What was that thought, boy?" My dad's tone caught me off guard. "You're my son. I'm allowed to worry about you. But don't you think for one second,

I'm not proud as fuck you became a cop. Do not question your decision."

"You got all that from one look?"

"No. From twenty-four years of looks. There are a few things in life I'm good at. One is knowing my sons and what they're thinking before they do. The other, and maybe more important, is I know my wife and how to—"

"La la la. Do not finish that sentence." I looked around not seeing my daughter. "Carson. Come on."

"In a hurry?

"Yeah. I have a headache from hell and I'm hungry."

"I bet you are," he muttered.

"What's that supposed to mean?" I made the mistake of asking. The thing about Carter Lenox was, he didn't pull punches. He was a straight-shooter, even with his sons.

"It means, after all these years, there's a pretty woman in your house."

"And?"

"Son, if I have to spell it out for you then it has been longer for you than I feared."

"She's renting a room. Period. And she's met Carson, so that's a double strike. She's a no-go."

"Since when did you start lying to your old man?

And did you miss the part about me knowing what you're thinking before you do?"

I sighed and resigned myself to an uncomfortable conversation with my dad. I don't think we'd discussed my sex life since I was sixteen and told them a condom had broken and Chrissy was pregnant. I was happy with that; not discussing sex with my dad was a good thing.

"Fine, she's pretty. And the thought has crossed my mind." My dad chuckled, and I added, "A lot. I've thought about it a lot, but it doesn't change anything. I have to keep my distance. Carson—"

"Carson is and always will be fine. Stop using her as a shield and an excuse to stop living."

I was floored at my dad's accusation. "I don't use my daughter."

"Sure you do. How many women have you dated since she was born?"

"None. I was busy being a teenage dad and then a single dad with a career," I spat out.

"Right. How many women have you slept with?"

"What does that have to do with anything?" He gestured for me to answer, pissing me off even more. "I don't know. I haven't kept track. A few."

"Any of those women interest you for more than a roll?"

"No."

"Why do you think that is?"

Christ. Where was he going with this? If I'd thought I had a headache when I'd arrived, I now had an elephant sitting on my skull.

"No clue. Maybe I just wanted to blow off some steam and get laid. Your point?"

"No point. An observation. Wake up, the years are passing you by. Do you want to continue having meaningless fucks twice a year or do you want to be happy?"

"I am happy." *What the fuck?*

"No, you're content. You love Carson beyond measure. You're an excellent dad. You have a good family. But you've never known bone-deep, soul-consuming love. I know that to be a fact. Because, son, when you find that, you don't let it go. You hold on to it, you fight for it, you nurture it, and you wrap yourself up in it until there's no beginning or end to it. Then you'll be happy."

"Not everyone has what you and Mom have," I reminded him.

"No. Not everyone does. But one day you will, if you stop hiding behind the shield of parenthood."

"You ready, Daddy?" Carson came into the room with a big Tupperware container.

"Are those all cookies?"

"Yep. Gran taught me how to make oatmeal raisin today." She stopped and looked around, lowering her voice she whispered, "They're gross, but don't tell Gran. I think they're adult cookies because no kid likes raisins for a treat."

"I heard that, Carson," My mom called out. "Hey, Ethan. Good shift?"

"Yeah, Mom. Thanks for—"

"Don't you say it. I'm knee deep rearranging the cupboards. Hugs." She blew me a kiss and went back to work.

"Come on, Squirt. Time to go home." I turned to my dad. "Thanks."

"Any time."

He knew why I was thanking him, I didn't need to explain anything to him. As he'd said, he knew what I was thinking before I did.

The drive home was spent thinking about Honor and if what my dad had said was possible. Maybe Honor would be nothing more than a friend, but was there someone out there for me? Could I have what my parents had? I seriously doubted it. My mom and dad had a rare connection. One always knew what the other needed or wanted. My dad was one lucky man, my mother was one in a million.

Carson and I walked into the house, and I was immediately assaulted by the smell of garlic. My stomach growled, reminding me I'd been so lost in my thoughts I hadn't stopped to pick up a pizza for dinner.

"Hey, you guys are home." Honor said walking out of the kitchen. Jean shorts showcased her tanned, toned legs, and the tank top she wore clung to her ample breasts. Damn, she looked like heaven. "How was your day?"

"Good," I answered, and she frowned, not believing me. When had I become so transparent?

"Right. So, I didn't know what time you guys would be home for dinner, but I'm cooking. You haven't eaten, right?"

I shook my head, and she continued.

"Awesome. I made spaghetti sauce. An old family recipe. It's been simmering all day, but I thought I'd wait and make the meatballs and see if Carson wanted to help."

"You made dinner?" I stupidly asked.

"Is that all right? I thought maybe I'd save you the trouble since you worked all day. But . . ."

I looked down at my daughter, who, for once in her life, was speechless.

"Would you like to help Honor make meatballs?" Carson nodded, still staring wide-eyed at Honor. "Go wash your hands."

Carson took off, and I stalked toward Honor, stopping shy of knocking her over. I tagged her around the waist and pulled her into me, hugging her tightly.

"Thank you," I whispered. "You have no idea how much I needed this today."

I kissed the top of her head, and she started to wiggle in my arms.

"Ethan your stuff is poking me." I found it amusing she'd said the same thing Carson had said when I hugged her. I loosened my embrace, and her arms finally wrapped around my middle.

"Sorry you had a shit day. You can talk to me about it, or not, I'm here either way."

"Ready!" Carson bounced into the kitchen. The thought momentarily crossed my mind that Carson had never seen me touch or hug a woman. My first instinct was to pull away, but Honor felt right in my arms. A very close second to the happiness that thudded in my chest when Carson hugged me.

"Awesome." Honor pulled back. "Ethan why don't you go do what it is you do and let Carson and me take over the kitchen?"

I let go of Honor and watched her take Carson's hand, explaining how they were going to mix the ingredients with their hands. I took off to my room to change out of my uniform and thought about what Honor had said, *go do what it is you do*, and it hit me, I didn't know what it was *I* did. I hadn't been Ethan in a long time. I was Carson's dad. I was Officer Lenox. But who was Ethan and what did he want?

The answer came quickly and with astounding clarity.

I wanted what I'd just had. Honor waiting for me when I got home from work. A pretty smile on her face. My two best girls in the kitchen mashing ingredients together with their hands.

Flat-out—I wanted Honor.

6

Shit on a shingle. Ethan and Carson had come through the door, my heart had raced, and my mouth had gone dry. This morning, when we'd met at the coffee maker, his eyes had roamed my body with an appreciation I swore I could physically feel. And if he'd thought I couldn't see his morning wood—he was mistaken. The thick outline was easy to see through the material of his sweats. Which begged the question, could he see my puckered nipples through the spandex of my sports bra? I was so embarrassed I'd holed up in my room until they'd left, reeling from our exchange in the kitchen. Which was a shame because it meant I'd missed seeing him in his uniform. Wowza. Ethan looked hot in the jean and a T-shirt or bare chested with a hard-on, but in his uniform, he was super-duper hot. I never knew I had a thing for men in uniforms but, apparently, I did. Or maybe it was just Ethan, who could wear a paper bag and still be sexy.

The past week had been great. I'd spent time getting to know the area and scoping out new places to take pictures, I filled a few orders for a gallery that was showing my work, and I was slowly getting to know Ethan and Carson. Ethan was easy to talk to, and funny. His banter with Carson melted my heart, it was plain to see how much he adored his daughter. There still had been no mention of her mom, nor were there any reminders of the woman in the house. I was curious, but I didn't dare ask. I knew Ethan had caught me more than a few times openly staring at him. He probably thought I was some sort of stalker, but last night after Carson had gone to bed our conversation had turned a little flirty. So maybe he didn't. And then there was that hug when he got home tonight.

"Honor?"

"Right, here, darlin'."

"Me and Gran made you cookies today."

"You did? That was nice of you."

"Yeah. Don't worry if you don't like the ones with raisins in them. They're gross."

"I love raisins."

"You do?" Her eyes widened and she stopped mixing the raw meat and egg concoction.

"I do. You keep mixing. I'll pour in the bread crumbs."

Her little hands got back to work, reminding me of the first time my mom taught me how to make meatballs. I missed her so much.

After we'd kneaded and squished everything together, we rolled out the balls and arranged them on the cookie sheet I'd prepared.

"You're good at this," Carson commented.

"I've done it a time or two."

"Gran tried to teach daddy how to cook, but she says he's hopeless. I think she called him call-in-airy . . ."

"Culinary?" I offered.

"Does that mean cooker?"

"Something like that." I laughed.

"Culinary challenged."

"I resent that."

Carson and I startled, not expecting him to be finished so soon.

"How do you know we were talking about you?" I teased.

"Wild guess."

He looked eatable standing in the kitchen, hair damp from a shower, another T-shirt pulled tight over what I knew to be a very hard, muscular chest and stomach.

He cleared his throat and smirked.

Ass.

"Want something to drink?" he asked.

And before I could warn him I'd been to the store he opened the fridge.

"Holy shit," he muttered.

"Daddy!"

"Sorry, Squirt." Then turned his attention to me. "You've been busy today."

"I hope you don't mind. Since you gave me such a great move-in special, I thought I'd stock up on some groceries. The fridge was a little bare."

"You didn't have to do all this."

"And you didn't have to help me move my stuff and give me a free week's rent, but you did."

"Seriously, Honor."

"Seriously, Ethan," I mocked him, mimicking his stance.

His gaze dipped from my eyes then back up before he shook his head.

"Damn, I hate when my dad's right," he mumbled under his breath.

"What ewas that?"

"Nothing. Thank you for this. But in the future, if you wouldn't mind picking up some stuff for me and Carson, I'll leave you money. But no special trips."

"We'll see."

"Honor . . ."

"Ethan . . ."

"I'm serious."

"And so am I. If you two need something, and I need to make an extra trip, I'll make it. I work from home. I set my own hours. Some days I work eighteen hours, some days I work one. My schedule is flexible. I'm getting a room in a nice house for a steal. Not to mention it comes with a pretty little girl I get to cook with. If I want to pitch in and help where I can, I will, and you're not gonna argue with me. Got it?"

Ethan stood stock-still, his back ram-rod straight, and I was worried I'd crossed a line with him.

"Doesn't she remind you of Gran when Pop tries to tell her what to do?" Carson broke out in a fit of giggles next to me.

"Funny, I was thinking the same thing." His face went from unreadable to soft.

"Okay, smalls. But I'm leaving money. And that's non-negotiable."

"Smalls? I'm not small."

"Sure you are. You're barely taller than Carson. And compared to me you're a small, sassy thing."

"Back up, darlin' let me put these in the oven. Make sure it's set at 350 degrees, and they go on the middle rack."

Carson checked the digital read out on the oven,

and I ignored Ethan's comment. I also avoided looking at him. The silly nickname had felt good, too good. There was nothing intimate about the word smalls, but, for some stupid reason, it felt like I'd just been inducted into this family of two. Ethan called Carson, Squirt, more than by her name; it was a term of endearment said with love and adoration for his daughter.

"Oven's ready," she confirmed.

I placed the tray on the rack and closed the door.

"Perfect. Set the timer for thirty minutes, check that the sauce is on simmer, and we're done."

"Check and check." Carson said.

"Wash your hands again," I instructed.

She jumped off the chair she was standing on, and I picked it up to move it back to the table when Ethan stepped in my way.

"What just happened?"

I looked behind me trying to figure out what he was talking about. Nothing seemed out of place.

"What do you mean?"

"You went from smiling to looking like I'd punched you in the gut."

"I did?" I tried to play it off.

"Yeah, Honor, you did."

I tried to hide my disappointment that he'd called me by my name.

"There it is again. Smalls, you can't hide a damn

thing. Your pretty face shows everything you're feeling."

Warmth spread over me, and I wanted to deny I was pretty just to hear him say it again. Thankfully there was a chair between us because I wanted him to pull me close for another hug.

"Will you do me a favor?" he asked, and I nodded. "No matter how embarrassing, inappropriate, or mean, tell me the last thought that ran through your head. The one you had just when you looked at me. Complete honesty." My face flamed, and he smiled. "Yes, that thought."

I took in Ethan's hopeful expression and found I couldn't deny him. Or maybe I didn't want to. Maybe this was part of being the new me, brave and taking what I wanted instead of being a meek bystander too afraid to rock the proverbial boat.

Fuck it. Here goes nothing.

"I was thinking I was grateful there was a chair between us because now that your vest is off I wish I could feel your hard chest pressed against me."

If it was possible, my cheeks burned hotter, but Ethan didn't give me time before he moved the chair, the legs scraping on the tile floor, and yanked my hand until I was flush against him, my breasts smashed between us. He lowered his head to whisper in my ear.

"Smalls, I've been doing nothing all day but

thinking about how good you'd feel pressed up against me." I shivered at his words. Ethan, taking that as encouragement, went on. "I'm pleased as fuck to hear you're on the same page. But I'm not taking whatever this is between us any further until we're both sure."

I nodded in appreciation and, tucked there under his arm, I felt every bit of the nickname he'd given me. He could wrap both his arms around me and engulf my entire body in his embrace. Something I'd never felt before had taken root, safety.

He let me go as Carson came barreling back into the kitchen.

"Are they done yet?"

"No, darlin' we have some time left. Let's set the table and get the salad out."

"Do I have to eat the salad?" Her lips pinched together.

"That's up to your daddy. His rules. But if you don't eat the salad, you'll miss out on my homemade cheese crisps and special salad dressing."

"What are cheese crisps?"

"Yummy, delicious, fried cheese. You crumble it on top of your salad and pour my super-secret-recipe dressing over them. But, if you don't want any, more for me."

"Okay. I'll try it." Ethan was back to watching us,

and I hoped I wasn't overstepping his boundaries. "I'll show you where the plates are," Carson offered.

"Perfect."

The two of us moved around the kitchen, gathering everything we needed to set the table. By the time we were done, dinner was ready to be served.

I WAS PLEASED when Carson declared she loved the salad and Ethan went back for seconds. Complimenting me and Carson on how good the meatballs were.

Carson talked and talked and talked. The girl could chatter to a brick wall and never tire. Through it all Ethan had hung on her every word. He never told her to be quiet or interrupted one of her many stories. He let her carry the dinner conversation in any direction she wanted. And, for her part, she was smart and funny. It was obvious she'd spent a lot of time around adults and had soaked up all the information she could.

"What grade are you in?" I asked Carson while we were doing the dinner dishes.

"Third."

"You're pretty smart," I told her.

"Thank you. Pop says it's important to study. My daddy got straight As in school. Then, when I was born, he took extra classes and got out of school early, so he could start college."

"Wow. That's impressive."

"What is?" Ethan asked, bringing in the rest of the dishes from the table.

"I was telling Honor how smart you are. You finished school way early and college too."

"Are you bragging on your old man, Squirt?" He ruffled her curls, and she pushed his hand away.

"You're not old. All the teachers talk about how young and cute you are. It's gross."

Ethan turned scarlet and shook his head. "That is gross. Your teacher is older than Gran."

They both laughed and started loading the dishwasher. It was sweet to watch them.

By the time Ethan had taken Carson up to bed, I was exhausted. I had to hand it to him, I wasn't sure if I'd be able to keep up with all the energy Carson had, but he did it all on his own and with grace. I grabbed a bottle of water and turned off the lights in the kitchen. While I was debating whether or not to shut off the rest of the lights Ethan came back downstairs.

"I wasn't sure if you'd gone to bed and if I should turn everything off," I told him.

He looked like he had a lot on his mind and when he didn't answer me right away, I took that as my cue to go to my room and leave him in peace.

"Where are you going?" His words stopping me.

"I was gonna let you have some time to yourself. You look like you've had a long day."

"Thank you for dinner. And for being so patient with Carson. I know she can be a handful."

"She's not a handful. Full of life, maybe, but she's a good girl. I enjoyed cooking with her tonight."

"Yeah, she liked that, too. It was all she talked about when I was tucking her in."

The pensive look was back, and I didn't understand why.

"Is that a problem? I didn't mean to trample on your rules or anything."

"Sit with me a minute?"

Dread washed over me. I'd lived here a week and I was afraid he was getting ready to give me the boot. I sat next to him on the couch, and my body slumped when he sighed. Oh, no. He didn't look happy.

"Other than my mom, aunts, and female cousins, Carson has never had a woman around. Certainly not in the house, cooking with her."

I waited for him to say something more, but he didn't.

"If you'd rather me not, I won't. I just thought she'd like it. I always loved cooking with my mom." Ethan's entire being changed and I rushed on. "That came out wrong. I didn't mean . . . I don't mean . . . I . . . fuck.

Ethan I wasn't saying I'm anything more than a room-mate. I enjoy cooking and thought it would be fun for her as well. I swear, I wasn't trying to push myself into your life."

His next words shocked and saddened me at the same time.

"I was sixteen when Carson's mother got pregnant. She wanted to give her up for adoption, but I wouldn't agree. I couldn't. Chrissy never wavered, not even after she'd given birth. She wouldn't even look at Carson, let alone hold her. Not even ten minutes after Carson was born I left the delivery room with her, and, as promised, we've never heard from her again. A few hours later, her parents' attorney dropped off the paperwork relinquishing Chrissy's parental rights, and I took over all responsibility for Carson.

"There are some days, like today, I question what kind of father I am. Between my job being as dangerous as it is, and raising Carson without a mom, I wonder if I'm a selfish prick. I wouldn't give up my daughter for anything, but I've never entertained the idea of dating or what it must be like for her not to have a woman in the house."

"Don't do that." He stopped brushing imaginary lint off the couch and looked up at me. "I had two parents. My dad was rarely home. I knew he loved me and my mom, but he loved the military more. He'd volunteer for deployment even when he'd only been home a few months. I've heard men like your father tell stories about the great Buck Sully, but the truth is, he may've been a great soldier, but he sucked as a dad. I had a mom, a good one when she wasn't lost in her grief over losing a husband who'd promised year after year things would be different. Looking back, I wonder if she was grieving the love of the man, or the loss of a future she knew he'd never provide. She loved me, but she never let me rattle on about my day and listen with her entire soul like you do for Carson.

"I've known Carson a week, and I can tell you with certainty that little girl wants for nothing. She is surrounded by love. There's no way she'd be as bold and talkative if she was unsure about the people around her. Your job *is* dangerous. But that doesn't make you selfish. I doubt you'd be happy working behind the counter in a hardware store. That's not how you're wired. And if you're not happy, how are you supposed to make her happy?"

"And the dating part? Now that you've properly put me in my place for feeling sorry for myself do you have anything to say about that?" He smiled.

I hadn't meant to come off sounding preachy, but he was selling himself short.

"You haven't dated since she was born?" I asked.

"Before that, actually. I'd been dating Chrissy for

six months when she got pregnant. The night she told me, everything between us changed. We were over. It was like a switch had been flipped, and she wanted nothing more to do with me. I've never told anyone this, not even my parents, I asked her to marry me that night. I told her we'd raise the baby together. She told me no." His laugh sounded hollow.

"I guess you haven't found the right woman to be Carson's mom." He averted his gaze from me. "You know any woman you find has to not only be right for you but Carson, too. It's easy to trust your heart, but I suppose it would be difficult to trust someone with hers."

"I'm going to kiss you, smalls. I know what I said earlier, and we'll go slow until we both know this is something we want to explore. But I have to taste you." He leaned in and cupped my face. "Tell me now, if you don't want this."

"I want this," I whispered.

He quickly closed the scant distance between us and, instead of going for it like I would've allowed, he slowly explored my mouth with his. When he finally licked the seam of my lips, I was panting with anticipation. The first swipe of his tongue tasted like paradise. It didn't take long for him to scoot closer and angle my face where he wanted it. The kiss became demanding, and I wanted nothing more than to submit. I met him stroke for stroke, completely lost on the most erotic voyage of my life, trusting Ethan would steer us where he wanted to go. It may've been five minutes or two hours when he slowed the kiss and sweetly brushed the corners of my mouth before pulling back, leaving me dazed.

With his hands still cupping my cheeks he spoke. "I thought I was sure before that kiss but now I'm absolutely positive I want to see where this goes. I'm scared as fuck because I've never let anyone close to us before. But, smalls, I've never been kissed like that. I've never felt a spark of excitement so deep I never wanted to breathe again. I swear we'll go as slowly as you need, as long as we're moving forward."

"And if I don't want slow?"

He closed the distance again and softly kissed me.

"I need slow. I've never done the whole dating thing as an adult and I'm sure I'm gonna fuck it up. Bear with me?"

"Is that what this is? Dating?"

"I don't know what you'd call what I'm feeling, but, whatever it is, I want more of it."

"Okay. But I need something from you, too."

"Anything."

"I need patience. The last time I had a boyfriend I was a senior in high school, and it didn't go so well."

He studied me for a second before asking. "Did he

hurt you?"

"Yeah. But not the way you're thinking. After I gave him my virginity, he told the whole school about it. Then he gave a blow by blow description of the night and offered to share me with his buddies on the lacrosse team."

"What a dick."

"He totally was. The rest of the year was spent trying to restore my reputation. But it never worked. Once you're deemed a slut in high school, there's no changing it."

"I'm sorry that happened to you."

He situated himself on the couch and pulled me back into his arms to cuddle. It felt nice sitting and sharing with Ethan.

"Eh. It was a long time ago. After I graduated, I started design school and was so caught up learning new stuff and getting my portfolio together, dating and sex were the last thing on my mind. Then my mom died. Nothing seemed important after that."

"Tell me about her?"

I shifted and curled up even closer to Ethan. With my head still spinning from the information he'd given me, my heart pounding from our closeness, and wet undies from our scorching hot kiss, I relaxed and told him stories about my mom—the good ones before Franklin came into our lives.

7

"Can Honor come?" Carson asked, sitting on my bed, waiting for me to finish getting ready.

"If she wants. But, Squirt, don't be disappointed if she says, no. She may have to work today."

"But it's a Saturday," she said, telling me something I already knew.

It had been almost a month since I'd first kissed Honor. And in the four-weeks since, there had been more stolen kisses after Carson had gone to bed. My hands had never moved from her face or back. I'd kept my promise and my dick in check. That didn't mean after our goodnight kisses I'd hadn't gone up to my room and jerked off thinking about all the things I wanted to do to her.

Honor, however, was getting braver; her hands roamed my chest as I devoured her mouth. Last night, as I had her pressed against her bedroom door, her touch had ventured south, and she rubbed my dick over the outside of my pants. Her tiny hand stroked over the material, and I was a moment away from coming when I pulled her hand away. She'd almost broken my will. I wanted her so badly I could barely stand to wait any longer. But I'd walked away, leaving her breathless, and both of us needing more. I had lain in my bed with my dick in my hand wondering why I was waiting. I could've walked back to Honor's room and made love to her until we were both satisfied.

The truth was, I was scared. What if the excitement and anticipation waned after we had sex? What if she wasn't as perfect as I thought she was? What if I fucked this up and hurt her? And what about Carson? Over the last few weeks, they'd cooked together, gone out back and Honor showed Carson how to use her camera, they'd painted together, they even went grocery shopping—just the two of them. I'd stayed home to set up Honor's new TV and Blu-ray player for her, and the girls had left. Bottom line, Carson was attached; she liked Honor. Case in point, she wanted to invite Honor to come along with us to Savannah. This was our time, Carson had never wanted anyone to come with us on our trips to the city—not even my parents.

Fuck.

I was at a loss. Did I pull back and pump the brakes, or did I give in to my desires and lift the temporary ban on sex and go for it? And why the fuck was I mixing sex with emotion? We were both adults. Surely we could get hot and sweaty between the sheets and still behave like rational people. But, as much as I didn't want to admit it, I knew why I was holding back. It had been a month, and I was already half in love with Honor. If I took her to my bed, I wouldn't be able to keep my emotions out of it. I wouldn't be fucking her, I'd be making love to her. She was so different from the other women I'd been with, they weren't even in the same universe. I could see Honor in our lives for the long haul.

Carson jumped off my bed and headed for the door.

"Carson, if she says no, don't bat your pretty eyes at her and try and convince her. She has deadlines, and her work is important."

"Fine," she huffed and went in search of Honor.

A few minutes later, as I was brushing my teeth, Honor appeared in the doorway of my bathroom,

"Hey there, handsome." She smiled.

I had a mouthful of toothpaste, so I opted for a chin lift in response.

"Carson invited me to tag along on your big day out. I wanted to check that was cool with you. Last night you were excited about some one-on-one time with her. I don't want to intrude."

I rinsed my mouth and thought about what she'd asked. Honor was always careful not to *intrude*. She always asked before she did anything with Carson, she didn't even take her into the backyard without permission. She respected my time with my daughter and would sneak away if she saw Carson and me cuddled on the couch, watching a show. I wasn't sure if that made her the world's most perfect woman, caring about my time with my kid, or if it made me an asshole because I'd made Honor think she was an interloper when I'd invited her into our circle.

Time to shit or get off the pot. With my mind made up, I dried my face and listened for Carson. The slamming of a cabinet door downstairs told me everything I needed to know. I was alone with Honor.

Two strides and I was face to face with the woman who'd plagued my dreams and turned my world upside down.

"I want you to come," I told her. "I'm sorry if I've made you feel otherwise."

"You haven't, but your time with Carson is important."

"You're important, too."

"Thank you, Ethan," she whispered.

"Are you sure about where we're headed? You want to try this with Carson and me?"

"I promise, I've thought a lot about it. It's not just you and me. I'd never do anything to hurt Carson. Never. I like you." She stopped and smiled. "A lot. I want to see where this goes. And for the record, I'm done with taking things slowly with you. But, I want my friendship with Carson to be separate from my relationship with you. Does that make sense?"

"It does."

"It's important she never feels like I'm taking her daddy's time away from her. And I want her and me to gradually get to know each other better. I only have one shot with her and I won't fuck it up by pushing; we move at her pace. It won't matter if what we have is perfect, if Carson isn't comfortable, that's a deal breaker for me."

Yep, world's most perfect woman. I was happy she'd said exactly what I was feeling. Eight years ago, I gave my life to my daughter, I never knew how or where a woman would fit into our world, but Honor had shown me. One step at a time.

"I'm gonna kiss you, smalls. And, tonight, after I get Carson to sleep we're taking our goodnight kiss behind closed doors."

"Is that right?"

"It is. And just so you're forewarned, you may need a nap. It's gonna be a long night," I informed her.

"You think so?"

"I know so."

"We'll see. Maybe you're the one who should take a nap."

The mischief that sparked in her eyes meant good things for me later.

"Smalls, every night for the past twenty-nine days I've come upstairs after I've kissed you senseless and stroked my dick, imagining all the ways I want to make you come. On my fingers, in my mouth, all over my cock until the bed is soaked. I've thought up a hundred filthy ways to make you beg for more. Trust me, you'll need the nap."

I pushed forward and pressed my dick against her stomach, letting her see how affected I was by the images.

"Kiss me, Ethan."

I lowered my mouth to hers and took my time enjoying the taste of her. Sunshine and promise. It should've worried me how she could bring me to my knees with just the brush of her tongue. But it didn't, instead it filled me with hope. Honor Sullivan was everything I never thought I'd find.

"Honor!" Carson called from the landing outside my bedroom and we both jumped apart.

"Oops." She wiped her mouth and answered Carson. "Coming."

"Not yet you're not. But you will tonight," I quietly added.

"Promises, promises." She threw her comeback over her shoulder and left me standing in my bathroom adjusting my throbbing hard-on.

Fuck yeah, it was a promise. A promise I fully intended to make good on. Multiple times in a multitude of ways.

***

"DADDY, can we take Honor to the candy store then to the ice cream shop next door?" Carson asked as we strolled down the river walk, passing the tourist shops that lined the path.

"We can after dinner."

"Do they have Swedish Fish at this candy store?" Honor asked.

"Yes. Every candy you can imagine. They even have fried crickets."

"Fried crickets? Gross."

"Totally gross. We bought some for Pop. He ate the whole bag and said they were pretty good. But Pop will eat anything, so I don't believe him."

"True story," I laughed. "My dad will eat just about anything."

We found a restaurant across from the Echo Square and walked the two flights of stairs to our table. It had a perfect view of the Savannah River, complete with the old-time riverboat replica docked nearby.

I watched as the girls sat close, heads together, scrolling through all the pictures Honor had taken.

"There are a lot of pictures of me and daddy."

"There are. The two of you are perfect subjects. Always smiling."

"What's a subject?" Carson asked.

I zoned out during Honor's explanation. I hadn't seen the pictures she'd taken but I had noticed her taking them. It seemed every time I turned around Honor's camera was in front of her face, and she was snapping pictures. It had dawned on me that Honor had documented our day, sans her. I pulled out my cellphone, opened the camera app and took a picture of the girls together.

I vowed right then and there, Honor would never be left out again. I remembered what she'd said the first time I'd met her in the park.

When memories start to fade it's important to have a reminder.

I wasn't planning on forgetting, but I saw the beauty in the reminder.

Our dinner came and Carson, as usual, dominated the conversation but this time it was different, she wasn't directing all her questions at me. Honor and Carson carried on like Honor had always been part of our lives. They poked fun of me and laughed together. Carson filled Honor in on the latest family news—including that my brother was coming home on leave for a few days. It was a good time. No . . . a great time.

We stopped at the candy store, loading up on enough treats for Carson to have a sugar rush for a month. Honor had insisted on getting the friend crickets. One package for her and Carson to try and a second for my dad.

With ice cream cones in hand we walked River Street, taking in more sights, until we got to the Waving Girl statue that Carson was dying to see, even though she'd seen it every time we'd come to Savannah. She climbed onto the bench and threw her hands out, mimicking the sculpture. Honor's camera came up and she started snapping pictures. I quickly pulled out my cell and, also caught the moment. Only I was focused on Honor focusing on Carson.

DESPITE THE ICE cream and handful of M&M's Carson had eaten, she'd passed out in the backseat thirty minutes into our forty-five-minute drive home. She barely stirred when I carried her inside and changed her into her jammies and tucked her into bed. I hovered over her, staring down at my daughter. It was hard to believe she was eight. It was both just yesterday and a lifetime ago she came into my life. My parents had been right about one thing, I'd been too young to understand all the ways my life would change when I'd decided to keep Carson. But there has never been a second I regretted it. I couldn't imagine what it would be like not having my daughter. She was the best part of me.

I turned off her light and shut her door and made my way down the stairs to where Honor was waiting for me. I prayed I had enough left to give her. She deserved a man who could and would love her with his whole being. The kind of love my dad gave my mom. If Carson held my heart, would there be room for Honor?

I found Honor in the kitchen rooting through the pantry moving boxes around in search of something.

"Whatcha' looking for?" I asked, and she jumped, banging her elbow on the open door.

"Shit on a shingle you scared me to death." She rubbed her elbow and went back to riffling through the fully stocked, thanks to her, pantry. "I thought Carson and I could make waffles tomorrow, but I don't know if we have baking powder."

We.

I liked that.

"There's a box of waffle mix right in front of you."

She glanced over her shoulder and scowled, completely affronted I would dare making such a ludicrous suggestion.

"You don't make homemade, Sunday-morning waffle goodness out of a box, Ethan. You spread out all the ingredients, measure, make a mess, whisk everything by hand, and watch the batter turn into fluffy golden delights."

I shouldn't have worried, there was more than enough room in my heart for this amazing woman and her Sunday-morning golden delights.

"I better up my gym time. With all the delicious food you make, I'm gonna get fat."

"Right. Because your six pack and arms of steel are going to disappear overnight."

"Arms of steel?" I laughed.

"Ethan Lenox, are you fishing for compliments?"

"From you? Always."

She abandoned her quest to find baking powder and stalked toward me. When she was within arm's reach, her palms went to my chest before they moved lower to my stomach.

"I thought you were taking me to bed?"

"In a hurry?" I joked.

"Yes."

No games. No playing coy. Honor was straight up honest about what she wanted.

I covered her hand with mine and laced our fingers together, pulling her toward the front door, I double checked the alarm was set before I stopped in front of her bedroom door.

"You're sure?"

"So sure."

"I don't want to stop tonight."

"You wanna go all the way with me, handsome?"

"Fuck, yeah."

"Good. Because if you stop, I might die."

"Can't have that, smalls."

I closed her door with a soft click and a turn of the lock, then we were alone in her room with the bed less than ten feet behind us.

"I want you naked."

My hands went to the hem of her T-shirt, and I yanked it over her head. Following my lead, her hand went to mine, and she pulled it off and tossed it on the floor with hers.

She found the button of my jeans before I could unsnap her shorts.

Both of us pushed the material down and soon they were pooled around our ankles. We kicked them to the side, and she smiled shyly.

"You are so beautiful," I told her and ran my knuckles over the swell of her breasts, down to her lace covered nipples. "So damn perfect."

Her hands weren't still, they roamed my chest and stomach, up and down over my skin until she stopped at the waistband of my boxers.

I was almost paralyzed with indecision. I wanted to go slowly, take my time and enjoy the gift she was giving me. But the sight of her standing in front of me in only her underwear had my dick aching and my hands shaking with need.

When had I ever wanted a woman so badly?

Never.

High school sex, didn't count for shit. It was fueled by hormones and was completely uncoordinated. I'd had no idea how to really please a woman then. Over the last few years sex had simply been a means to an end, a mutually beneficial release. This was something altogether different. Something more. I wanted to consume Honor, own her, and I needed her to fall as fast and hard for me as I was for her.

8

I was trembling and nervous as all get out.

This wasn't just sex, at least it didn't feel that way to me. Ethan's gaze traveled down my body until he brought his eyes back to mine. Heat, lust, and desire swirled together making me shiver once more. How could he make me ache with just a look?

Ethan's arms wrapped around my back and he found the clasp of my bra. With a flick of his fingers it was unfastened. He held my gaze while he pulled the straps down my arms. When the garment was freed and thrown to the side his eyes dropped to my chest.

"Jesus Christ," he said, and his hands cupped both my breasts.

His head lowered and licked both my nipples in turn, before sucking one into his mouth. Ethan's hand never stopped squeezing and massaging my overly large boobs.

I'd always hated how big they were, but now with Ethan obviously enjoying what I had to offer I no longer cared I had breasts the size of an augmented stripper. His mouth moved over and lavished attention to my other nipple, and my head fell back.

"I could spend all night playing with your tits."

"They're not too big?" Old insecurities die hard.

"They're big and soft, and this part . . ." He traced his finger around my areola. "Sexy as hell." He kissed both nipples and continued. "Your tits are the perfect size for me to put you on your back, straddle your chest, squeeze them together, then slide my cock between them while you suck me off."

We were moving toward the bed, and before I could recover from the sexy images he'd invoked, the back of my legs hit the mattress, and Ethan was easing me down. My back hit the cool fabric of my comforter, and his scorching-hot chest covered mine. His weight smooshed us together, and he finally kissed me. This kiss was not like the others where he'd always held himself back, if only by a fraction. This time he gave me everything. His hips ground down, the ridged shaft of his dick grinding the lace of my panties against my wet center. Our tongues mingled, and our bodies heated. As good as he felt on top of me, I wanted more.

My hands moved over his back, appreciating the smooth skin before I finally made it to the waistband of his boxer briefs. I tugged on them, and he lifted, helping me move the elastic over his hard-on.

"It's not working," I complained when they wouldn't budge any further.

He stood to his full height and shoved them down his legs. Ethan's dick sprang free and bobbed a few times before settling.

"Holy fuck, handsome."

He took his dick in hand and gave himself a few long, hard strokes. His head fell back, and he moaned. I'd never seen a man touch himself before, it was the most erotic thing I'd ever seen, and I felt a little naughty watching him.

"Scoot up the bed," he instructed.

I scrambled back, never taking my eyes off his moving hand. He reached for the table beside my bed where I'd placed a box of condoms, he tore into the box finding a foil packet. With his right hand still on his dick he used his left to bring the condom to his mouth, ripping it open with his teeth.

"Like what you see, smalls?" A sexy sly smile formed as he rolled the rubber over his long, thick length.

I didn't answer, I couldn't, and, besides, he knew I did. I might as well have been drooling. Actually, I may have been. I wanted to tell him his dick was a thing of beauty, but I thought that would sound bizarre, so I kept my mouth shut.

With his dick sheathed he reached for my panties and pulled them off before he crawled onto the bed, spreading my legs wide as he went. He settled himself into the cradle of my hips and rested on one elbow near my head. Using his other hand he cupped my cheek before moving it to my throat, then grazing my breasts, and sliding down my stomach. His hand went between my legs, and his fingers danced over my entrance before he dipped one in. Pulling out, he pushed two back in.

"Sweet Jesus," he groaned and kissed me again.

I didn't know what sensation to concentrate on, the magic he was creating between my legs or his kiss. He stroked my tongue with an urgency he'd never shown me, revealing how much he desired me—wanted me. It was unreal to think Ethan, who I'd come to understand was a strong and good man, had chosen to take a chance with me. Not to mention he was hot as hell. Women would have been lining up around the block for a chance with him if he'd allowed it.

His hand moved faster, and my hips bucked. He withdrew his hand and broke the kiss.

"I want the first time you come to be with me inside of you."

He moved and hitched my leg over his hip, the tip of his dick replacing his fingers, but he didn't push in.

He stilled and with a look of love and sincerity that made my heart swell he said, "We're going to take this slowly."

The head slipped in, and I jolted. He waited a few seconds before he gave me more. Slowly working himself in and out until we were both panting.

"Ethan," I whispered.

"I know, smalls. Nothing, and I mean *nothing*, has ever felt so good in my life."

He got that right. My inexperience didn't allow for much to compare with, but I was sure our joining was more than physical. It had to be. He finally inched his way in, our bodies fully connected he paused for a moment giving me time to adjust.

"You okay?" he asked. His voice was strained, and the sound made me smile.

"More than."

"I have to move, smalls. But if I hurt you, tell me and I'll slow down."

"You're not gonna hurt me."

"Baby, the way I'm feeling right now, I'm afraid if I let go I might fuck you so hard the bed will crash through the wall."

"We'll patch the hole later. Don't ever hold back. I want all of you."

"Fuck." He leaned down and kissed the side of my head, moving farther still until he pulled my earlobe into his mouth. Releasing it he whispered, "We haven't even started, but you feel so fucking good I want to come right now. You're hot and wet and tight as hell." My insides spasmed at his words and he groaned. "Christ."

He drew his hips back and slowly pushed in, setting a leisurely pace, his hand roamed everywhere he could reach, and his mouth explored mine. I could do nothing but wrap my legs around him and hold on to his shoulders. I was too afraid to move, scared I'd chase off the feeling he was building. I wanted to touch him like he was touching me, but I was lost, drowning in the wonder of our lovemaking.

Something started happening, and my hips bucked of their own accord.

"Honor," Ethan growled.

I didn't know if he'd said more after my name but, if he had, I hadn't heard him. A roaring had started in my ears, and I had no control over my movements. All I knew was I wanted more of what I was feeling.

The bed shook from the power of Ethan's thrusts, I had to tighten my legs around him to ground myself to him. My boobs were bouncing, and maybe I should've been embarrassed but I couldn't bring myself to care. He was relentless, pounding into me, and when his hand came to my breast and plucked my nipple, my entire soul shattered into a million glorious, euphoric pieces.

"Fucking Christ, you are magnificent." I heard him say. "So beautiful. So perfect. All of you, smalls. Perfect." His strokes became jerky and he wrenched himself up, so he was sitting back on his heels, my legs still around his waist, but my ass was off the bed. Ethan gripped my hips and helped me move with him. I now understood what "eye fucking" truly meant. His gaze was smoldering as he ate up every inch of my flesh until it landed where we were joined.

"You have no idea how hot it is to watch my cock rocking in and out of your pussy." He took a hand from my hip and started rubbing my clit in fast circles. "I want you to come with me."

"I . . . I . . . did already," I stammered out.

"No, smalls, that was just the appetizer. I want you screaming your pleasure."

His finger rubbed, and the new angle had his dick bumping the perfect spot.

"I can't, Ethan," I said but my body betrayed my words. I was already shaking, my thighs tightening, trying to ward off the new sensation that was building, bigger than before, way bigger.

"I can't stop watching your tits sway, all I can think about is how they're going to look when you're on top of me. I'll be able to suck and play with them while you fuck me."

I never imagined I'd like dirty talk, but hearing Ethan tell me what he saw, what he liked, and what he wanted to do was driving me crazy.

"Come on, Honor, let go and come with me. You feel too good, you're gonna make me come." He stopped rubbing and pinched my clit hard, a rush of heat spread over my body. "Holy shit. That's it, I can feel your pussy strangling my cock. I'm gonna come with you."

"Do it," I moaned.

"Fuck," he roared and threw his head back. Thrusting once more, he stayed still with his dick as deep as it could go. It twitched and moved inside of me, and the muscles in his neck tightened.

We stayed like that for a while before he looked down at me and smiled.

"Only you, Honor."

With my brain muddled, and my body relaxed I wasn't sure what he meant, but I was too tired to ask. Too happy. Too sated.

I'd ask later, maybe tomorrow. My eyes closed, and peaceful slumber found me.

9

A door slammed, and I was pulled from a sexy dream of Honor under me, staring at me with wonder as I pumped in and out of her until we both exploded. I heard it bang a second time and rolled out of bed. It took me a minute to realize I was back in my room, I tagged a pair of athletic shorts off the floor, yanking them up I went for the stairs.

I rounded the bottom step and looked around, no one was in the house. I glanced out the back window and caught sight of Carson running across the yard.

Fuck. What the hell was Carson doing outside? With my heart in my throat, I ran for the back door and just as I was about to scold her for going out unattended I found her and Honor lying stomach down in the grass. Honor had her camera in front of her face and Carson was holding a mirror next to her lens.

"Daddy! You're awake."

"I am. What are you doing?"

"Honor is capturing dandelions with her macro lens. That means up close. Super up close. You can see things in the picture you normally can't see."

"And the mirror?"

"I'm her lighting tech." Carson's chest puffed, taking her job seriously.

Honor finished and looked over her shoulder.

"Did we wake you?"

"No," I lied. "Taking pictures of weeds now?"

"I'll have you know, I've found great beauty in the things most people dismiss. You ready for breakfast?" Honor sat up and Carson mimicked her, both girls smiling, only Honor's eyes kept dropping to my bare chest.

"You two lovely ladies finish up out here. I'll start the coffee."

I turned and walked back into the house as quickly as I could, trying to prevent my daughter from seeing the evidence of my arousal. When had I become a horny teenager again? All it took was Honor looking at me, and I popped a fucking boner. That hadn't happened since I was sixteen. My life was segregated into two parts—before Carson and after Carson.

Before Carson, I'd bagged damn near every cheerleader and girl's field hockey player at my school. My dad was right about one thing, he taught me to treat them with respect. I'd never talked about my exploits with my friends, never bragged about who or what I'd done. But, thankfully, my dad didn't have the first clue how many I'd actually taken to bed. I'd had eighteen months between losing my virginity and Chrissy getting pregnant. One could say I'd been busy during that time. However, none of them had made my body come alive like Honor did.

After Carson there had been only a handful. Partly because I was a full-time, single dad, but mostly because I was the dad of a girl. My conscience wouldn't allow me to take a woman home under false pretenses or promises of more. I was crystal clear about what I'd wanted and needed and hardly ever approached a woman. If they were interested and came to me, we'd talk. But none of those women brought me to my knees. None of them had called to me on a deeper level. Honor checked all the boxes. Made me feel things I'd long ago set aside. I was connected to her in a way that was unexplainable.

I adjusted my cock in my shorts and wondered if I had time to run upstairs and take care of it before breakfast was ready. I could leave the girls to make breakfast and go take a shower. There was no doubt it would only take a few strokes of my hand while images from last night played in my mind; I'd finish in minutes. Remembering Honor panting under me was not helping the ache. Abandoning the coffee machine, I headed for the stairs, taking two at a time, I rushed into my room.

I pressed my forehead against the cool wood on the back of my closed door. After a moment, while I was questioning my sanity, a knock sounded.

"Ethan? We were wondering how many waffles you wanted."

Without answering, I opened the door and pulled Honor through. After shutting and locking it I pressed her back against the wall, and my mouth covered hers. What the hell was I doing kissing her without her permission? I didn't need to worry, though, her arms quickly snaked around my neck, her fingers dove into my hair, and she returned the kiss with the same desperation.

I broke the kiss and the silence stretched between us, neither of us needing to communicate verbally. Our bodies were still connected from chest to knees and the current jumping between us was more than enough.

"Sorry I fell asleep on you last night," she finally spoke.

"Don't be."

"I was so relaxed I couldn't keep my eyes open. You wore me out."

"Glad to help."

"By the cocky grin on your face, I gather you're happy with yourself."

"You have no idea how happy."

"Me, too." She closed the distance and touched her lips to mine. "Breakfast? How many waffles?"

"Surprise me."

"Are you hungry?"

"I'm hungry," I told her. "I'll be down as soon as I take care of this." I pressed my hard-on against her stomach.

"Wish I could help you take care of that." Her eyes went soft, and she pushed against me.

"There's no doubt you'll be helping." I lowered my mouth to her neck, licking my way up to her ear. "I'm gonna jerk off thinking about your beautiful tits. And when I come I'll be remembering what it felt like being inside of you. Your moans, the look on your face when you orgasmed, how good your pussy felt, how tight and wet. It may be my hand stroking myself, but it will be you that owns my orgasm."

"You can't say that to me and expect me to go down and make breakfast."

"All day, I want you thinking about me touching myself. Every time you look at me you'll know you drive me so fucking crazy I had to come up here and beat my cock into submission because you make me so goddamn hard I can't see straight. You do this to me, smalls. Only you. No one else—ever."

"Ethan?"

"Right here, Honor."

"You drive me crazy, too. I know it's too soon, but I think I'm falling for you. I just thought you should know."

My heart did a funny flip-flop in my chest. I loved how open and honest she was. I didn't want to play games and keep secrets between us. I needed honesty.

"Me, too. There's no such thing as too soon. We go at our own pace," I assured her.

"Okay." She nodded.

"Honor?" Carson shouted.

"Coming," she yelled back. "Duty calls, handsome. Hurry up and come . . . downstairs."

She gave me a shove and winked before she walked out of my bedroom.

I beelined it to the shower and promptly took my dick in hand. Just as I thought, it had taken not even a dozen hard pulls before I was exploding.

I HEARD the voices before I hit the bottom steps.

"Daddy! Gran and Pop came for breakfast. They brought donuts."

"I can see, Squirt."

It took me a moment to digest what I was seeing. Honor, Carson, and my mom were in the kitchen. Carson was standing on a chair mixing waffle batter, my mom and Honor were watching her and smiling. My dad was sitting at the table, coffee in hand.

"Morning," I said to him as I passed the table in need of my own cuppa joe. "Good morning, Mom." I kissed the top of her head then poured my morning pick-me-up. "Smells good," I told Carson and, without thinking, I kissed Honor as I passed.

Shit.

Three pairs of eyes bugged out. My mom was the first to recover. Her smile told me she approved, which should've put me at ease, but didn't. I had fucked up big time, kissing Honor in front of Carson.

"The next batch ready, darlin'?" Honor asked Carson, ignoring the gigantic elephant in the room.

"Almost," Carson answered, giving the batter another fast beating with the whisk. "Now it's done." She pushed the bowl toward Honor.

"Great job. Why don't you go set the table?" Carson jumped off the chair and went about grabbing the plates someone had already set out on the counter. Then Honor turned to me. "Go. Enjoy your coffee with your dad. Your mom and I will finish up."

Not believing it was possible, my mom's smile got bigger with every order Honor doled out.

"Are you trying to tell me I'm in the way?"

"Kinda."

"Copy that, smalls."

My ass hadn't even warmed the chair before my dad tore his gaze away from the women bustling around the kitchen and leveled one of his legendary "Dad Glares" at me. Carter and I had coined the look as legendary by the time we were teenagers. One glance and we'd spill our guts. It was good to know, at twenty-four, the look still worked; I was ready to tell him all my secrets.

"Glad to see you lowered the shield, son."

What could I say to that? If I denied it, he'd know I was lying in a red-hot-second. If I confirmed, he'd circle the waters like a shark and start asking questions I didn't have the answers to. I knew my dad wanted what was best for me. He'd always told Carter and me he wanted nothing more than for us to find good women.

"Daddy? Gran said I could go over and swim later. Is that okay with you?"

Normally, Carson and I would veg out in the house on Sunday mornings—just the two of us. Weekends were precious to me, I got to have my daughter's undivided attention. But for the first time, I wanted someone else's attention—undivided and unin-terrupted.

"Sure, Squirt."

"Really? I can go?" Carson threw her arms around my neck and kissed my cheek. "Thanks. You're the best, most wonderful dad in the world."

"All that because I said yes, to swimming?" My dad and I chuckled.

"Breakfast," my mom announced bringing over a plate stacked tall with piping hot waffles. My dad stood and took the plate from my mom, setting it in the middle of the table. I followed suit when Honor approached, taking the syrup and butter from her.

"You sit next to Daddy," Carson told Honor.

In a moment of disbelief, I stared at Carson. She always, and I mean always, insisted she got the chair next to mine. Even when her favorite uncle, Carter, was in town, she still favored me.

I pulled out the chair for Honor to sit, and Carson took the chair at the end of the table on the other side of Honor.

"Thanks," Honor mumbled and sat.

"Everything looks great. I'm happy to see my son and granddaughter are no longer starving," my dad said.

"Lenox," my mom scolded.

"What? I didn't know it was a secret Ethan's a crappy cook."

"Hush," my mom tried again.

"You don't have to worry, Pop. Honor is teaching me to cook. We made meatballs and a roast and baked chicken. She even taught me how to make homemade pizza," Carson told him.

"Is that right?" My dad looked across the table at me and realized there'd been more going on than just the kiss he'd witnessed.

Honor was now a part of our daily lives. We ate dinner together every night, the girls took pictures together, and Honor helped Carson with her reading homework. There hadn't been a day since she'd moved in that she wasn't involved in some way.

"Carter is in town next week," my mom reminded me.

"I know, I spoke to him yesterday."

"We're having a barbeque next weekend, the whole family," she continued.

"Yippy. Uncle Carter and the cousins." Carson clapped her hands.

"You'll be there, too, won't you, Honor?" My mom took a bite of her waffle as if she hadn't just dropped a bomb.

"Yeah, Honor, you have to! Everyone will be there. It's so much fun."

"I don't want to intrude," Honor told my mom.

"Nonsense," my dad cut in. "You're welcome anytime."

"See? Please. Pretty please, with a cherry on top. I want you to meet my Uncle Carter."

"Carson," I tried to dial back the begging.

"What, Daddy? I'm just asking."

"No, you're pestering. Honor may have plans or have to work," I told her.

"Do you?" Carson turned to Honor. "You don't have to work, right?"

Honor was fidgeting in her seat. I reached under the table and grabbed her hand, squeezing it before I place it on my thigh and covered it with mine.

"Thank you, Mrs. Lenox. I'd love to come."

"Please call me Lily. It will be wonderful to have you there."

"Yay. Yay. Yay. Now I get to show Honor off to the uncles."

"Honor's not a pony, Carson." She jerked back in confusion. "Saying you're going to show her off is kinda rude."

"Sorry."

Without missing a beat Honor pulled Carson into a hug and snuggled her. "Nothing to be sorry for. I'm honored you want to show me off, darlin' but I'll need you to make a list of everyone for me. There are too many people for me to remember."

"We'll practice all week. We'll start with Uncle Jasper and Aunt Emily. They have most of the cousins." Carson went on to tell Honor all about "the cousins," as she called them.

By the time breakfast was over, I was ready to be alone with Honor. My dad laughed and caught on quickly when I told my mom not to clean the kitchen and tried to rush them out the door. Carson, of course, took no urging. She was ready and dancing around the door two seconds after she'd swallowed the last bite of her waffle, completely abandoning the donuts my mom and dad had brought.

"Thank you for breakfast, Honor." My dad clapped his meaty hand on her shoulder and gave it a squeeze.

"Yes, thank you. It was wonderful getting to know you." My mom, being the hugger in the family, pulled an unwitting Honor into her embrace.

"Thank you for your help. Glad you stopped by." Then shyly she added. "Maybe we can do it again."

"We'd love that, right, Lenox?"

"Right." Once again, I got the look and I knew he smelled blood.

Well, damn, so much for keeping Honor to myself. Uncles Levi, Clark, and Jasper would know about her within the hour. I swear to Christ they're worse gossips than teenage girls. Once my uncles knew, my aunts would know shortly thereafter. And that meant, they'd converge on my house like vultures circling their prey, trying to gather any morsel of information they could.

The three of them piled into my dad's truck, and I slammed the front door.

"I thought they'd never leave."

"Ethan!" Honor giggled. "That's mean."

"Smalls, I need you naked. Now."

"Your bed or mine," she asked.

"Mine."

"Race you." She took off toward the stairs. I caught her around the waist and tried to stall her. But she wiggled her way out and, before I could reach for her again, she ripped her T-shirt over her head and tossed it at my face.

"So it's gonna be like that, huh?"

"Like what?" she asked, halfway up the stairs.

"Resorting to cheating."

"If you're not cheating, you're not trying hard enough." She unclipped her bra and threw that at me as well.

"Keep teasing me, Honor, and you'll pay for it later."

I jogged up the stairs and found her standing next to my bed pulling off her panties.

"I win," she proudly announced.

"No, smalls. I win."

"But I got here first," she pouted.

"You did," I confirmed and quickly undressed.

"Then how did you win?" She put her hands on her hips and stood there, gloriously fucking naked, giving me attitude.

"Bend over the bed, and I'll show you how I'm the clear winner."

She did as I asked, and I dropped to my knees behind her and without waiting, I licked her from clit to slit.

"Ethan," she moaned.

With my tongue in her pussy I couldn't answer. When her ass started pushing back I stood. There would be a time when I'd make her come in my mouth and by my hand, but I was greedy and wanted to feel her orgasms around my cock right now.

"You taste so fucking good," I told her and rubbed the head of my cock around her opening. She shoved back, spearing herself, my fist holding my shaft stopping her from sliding any farther.

"Honor." I panted, her heat surrounding my bare flesh. "Don't move."

"Please." She squirmed and started to pull back before sliding back to my fist.

"I have to get a condom," I tried to reason with her.

"IUD. We're protected."

She continued to slide herself up and down my cock, only having a few inches to play with.

"Smalls."

"Get one if you want, but we're protected. I promise."

"I've never . . ." I could barely form a rational thought she felt so good. "Without a condom."

"Me either. I want it. I want to feel you."

Fuck it. I pulled my hand away as she shoved back, and she took my length in a single push of her hips.

"Christ," I shouted and gripped her hips. "You're so fucking hot without the barrier. I can feel every-thing." Honor's body was still, and I could hear a hitch in her breathing. "You okay?

"Holy shit. I wasn't expecting you to move your hand. You're . . ."

"I'm what? Am I hurting you?" I started to pull out.

"No. I'm stretched, and you're really deep this way. It feels so good."

It probably made me some kind of freak, but I leaned back a little so I could see my uncovered cock sliding in and out of her. I was playing a dangerous game watching; each time I pulled out and saw my dick oiled with her excitement, drove me closer to coming. The sight and the new sensation of fucking her bare had me light-headed. There was no way I was going to last this way.

"You feel incredible," I told her.

"So do you. Please move."

"I am," I said, slowly thrusting in.

"Faster. Fuck me."

Her words sent chills over my body.

"Goddamn, Honor!" I moaned. "I can't. I'm gonna come."

"Harder," she pleaded.

"Reach down and rub your clit." Her hand moved, and so did mine. If I couldn't see her touching herself I wanted to feel it. With both our fingers on her clit it felt a little dirty and a whole lot intimate. "Holy fuck, smalls. That's so hot."

"You feel so, so, good, Ethan."

I placed my hand back on her hip and started to quicken my pace. She pushed back as I shoved forward. We were in a perfect rhythm, our bodies moving as one. Heat started in my balls and rushed up my spine.

"Oh, God," she moaned and started to tighten around my cock. I had to close my eyes and will myself not to explode.

"Hurry, Honor. I'm close. I can't stop it, you're so fucking tight around my cock. Nothing better. Slick and wet and hot."

Holy fuck, it was too much.

"I'm gonna—" she didn't finish her sentence, instead she groaned and shook. Her pussy clamped around my cock before her inner muscles spasmed.

"Honor," I shouted. "Shit. So fucking good. I'm gonna come inside of you. Jesus." I knew I wasn't making any sense, my thoughts a jumbled mess as my orgasm broke free and every muscle in my body tightened. I wasn't lying when I told her there was nothing better. I'd never had an orgasm leave me paralyzed. I couldn't move as come shot out of my cock, filling her until she was overflowing and our combined juices were dripping down my balls onto the floor. If she hadn't already drained me, the thought of that alone would've made me come.

"Holy shit," she slurred. I shouldn't have been so smug, but I loved how breathy and satisfied she sounded. "I wanna do it that way again. It was hot."

"The view of your ass is stellar," I told her. Instead of trying to cover herself or shying away like some would do, she wiggled, forcing more come to spill out.

"Glad you think so. The only bad part is I can't see and touch you. But your dick makes up for it."

I was so shocked by her statement I couldn't stop the bark of laughter.

"Happy my dick could be of service." I chuckled.

"I don't know that I'd call it service so much as pleasure."

I pulled out, and the panic started.

I had not only fucked Honor without a condom but didn't even bother to pull out. Not that the pull and pray method was reliable, but at least it would have been something. But, no, I'd buried myself and let go without thought.

Shit.

Honor couldn't get pregnant. I wouldn't survive if she wanted to give our baby away or worse, left me and took it with her.

I was uploading the last file to my client's cloud server when my phone rang, startling me.

I checked the caller ID and smiled.

Ethan.

"Hey. What's up?" I looked at the clock and noticed I'd lost track of time. It was almost dinner time, and I didn't have anything planned.

"I have a favor."

"Whatcha need?"

"Is there any way you can pick up Carson from my parents' house? I'm gonna be at least another two hours. We collared the guy who's been knocking over the liquor stores. We're still writing reports."

"Sure. I can do it now."

"Thanks. My parents have dinner plans, or I wouldn't ask."

"You know you don't have to apologize for asking me . . . or thank me. I love spending time with Carson. It's perfect timing anyway; I just finished work. Would you like us to bring you a sandwich? If you made an arrest, I bet you skipped lunch."

"Yeah, we did." he chuckled. "If it wouldn't be too much trouble, I'd love one. Let me check with Lorenz and see if he wants something. I'll text you."

"Okay. I'm leaving now."

"Thanks, Honor."

To say Ethan had pulled back may have been an overstatement, but something had changed. Sunday, everything was perfect. We'd made love three times before Ethan went to pick up Carson and a pizza. We'd eaten together, laughed, heard all about Carson's day, and then he'd kissed me good night and went up to his room. I'm not sure what I'd been expecting but a quick kiss and a goodnight wasn't it.

As the week had progressed, things had become, for a lack of a better word, strange. He was still engaging in small talk, and we ate dinner together. We'd even gone back to my room every night and made love, but it was different. It had lacked the passion and raw need he'd had Sunday. The sex was still great, but it was like mentally he'd checked out. I wasn't sure what I was supposed to do.

Carson was waiting for me when I arrived at Ethan's

parents' house. As always, she was bouncing up and down and happy. Lily apologized, explaining they had dinner plans with Levi and Blake. When Lenox came into the living room in a pair of slacks and button down, I noticed again how much Ethan and he looked alike.

"Honor," Lenox stopped me as Carson and I were headed for the door. "I found this the other day and wanted you to have it."

Lenox handed me a photo. A group of men all dressed in Army fatigues stood in front of an American flag. I scanned the picture and picked out my father immediately.

"How did you get this?"

"That's me," he pointed to a much younger version of himself. "Levi, Clark, and Jasper." He moved his finger over the picture pointing out each man.

"Where were you?"

"That's top secret," he chuckled. "I thought you'd like it."

"Yes. Thank you. I only have one picture of my dad."

"Well, now you have two. I'll see if I have anything else."

"Really, Lenox. Thank you."

"My pleasure. You beautiful ladies have a nice evening."

Without thought, I moved toward him and hugged him as tightly as I could. Much to my surprise, he hugged me back. Carson tugging on my hand, eager to get going, ended the embrace, but not before Lenox graced me with a smile. Holy hotness, it was easy to see where Ethan had inherited his grin. Lily was a beauty and had contributed to some of Ethan's good looks, but he was his father's son.

Ethan had already texted me to tell me he'd called in an order at a sub shop around the corner from the station. All I could think about on the drive to the restaurant was the picture Lenox had given me. I was dying to get home and study it more carefully. I didn't know Buck Sully all that well, and depending on who you spoke to, they'd tell you he was a great hero or an absentee husband and father. My guess was he was somewhere in the middle. I glanced in the rearview mirror and looked at Carson. I was happy she had a great dad.

With sandwiches in hand Carson and I walked into the station. The desk clerk buzzed us through and gave me directions to Ethan's desk. Not that she needed to, Carson led the way, telling me all about her Uncle Lorenz and Aunt Maria. She told me they had dinner over there all the time, and I wondered if that was part of Ethan's problem. I'd barged into his life and disrupted his routine. Not only with Carson but with his friends too.

"Daddy," Carson called out, and before I could stop her, she took off across the room.

"Hey, Squirt." He swung her up into his arms, and she immediately started to wiggle out.

"Ouch. Your stuff is poking me."

He set her on her feet, and a tall, dark, and handsome man cleared his throat before she beelined it towards him. Whoa, what was it with all the good-looking men in this town?

"Hiya, Princess Rose, long time no see. What, did you forget about your old Uncle Lorenz?"

"No, silly. Meet Honor." She pulled his hand forcing him to turn in my direction.

His head swiveled between me and Ethan before landing on me again. He pushed his hand in my direction.

"Oscar Lorenz," he offered.

"Nice to finally meet you, Oscar. I've heard a lot about you."

"Same here, but it seems our boy here has been keeping secrets from his partner." He shook my hand, and I wasn't sure what his comment meant. He threw an accusatory glance in Ethan's direction. "Just all right, huh?" Lorenz shook his head and turned back to me. "Thanks for coming all the way down here with our dinner."

"No problem."

Ethan was still staring at me with the same funny look he'd had all week. I was beginning to feel like a lab rat.

"I guess we'll be on our way," I announced to no one in particular.

The look of indifference had changed, and Ethan's gaze went over my shoulder and looked pissed, really, really pissed.

"What do we have here? Officer Shit-For-Brains has a hot wife and a cute little girl."

I quickly shoved Carson behind me, shielding her from the handcuffed man's view. The venom in his tone sent a chill down my back.

"Keep walking, asshole," Ethan said to the man, then to the officer guiding the suspect. "Take him away."

"Too late, Officer Ethan Lenox. I already saw them and I'll be out of lock up in under forty-eight hours."

Ethan moved with lightning speed and was in the man's face in a heartbeat.

"You threatening me, motherfucker?"

Carson stiffened behind me, and I reached back, anchoring her tightly. I was stuck in place with nowhere to go.

"Not a threat, officer. Just telling you, I'll be walking out of here soon."

"This is your only warning. Stay the fuck away from my family."

"Or?" the man taunted.

"Or you'll find yourself not breathing."

"You threatening *me?*" The asshole had changed the tone of his voice, trying to sound like a victim.

"Goddamn right I am."

"We'll see, copper."

"Get this fucking dirtbag out of my sight," Ethan instructed.

When the officer behind the shit-talking perp gave him a shove, he stumbled forward and disappeared around the corner. As soon as the men were out of sight, Ethan stalked straight to me and grasped my face, bringing his just inches from mine.

"Are you okay?"

"Yeah, yeah, I'm fine," I dismissed his question.

"Thank you." He closed the distance and for the second time he kissed me in front of Carson. Only this time it was on my lips.

He released my cheeks and bent down, grabbing Carson from behind me. "Are you okay, Squirt?"

"Yes. Honor hid me. Someone needs to wash that bad man's mouth out with soap for saying those bad words."

I wondered if Carson realized it was Ethan who'd done the cursing. I gathered not, considering I was looking right at him while he spoke and I'd barely recognized his voice.

"I'm sorry."

"Gran and I baked a cake today. But we couldn't eat it. She said it was for Aunt Blake because it's her favorite."

And just like that, the bad guy was forgotten.

"I'm sure you ate plenty of other treats."

"I cannot confirm nor deny that, Daddy. It's top secret."

Lorenz let out a belly laugh before he recovered and told me. "Princess Rose, here, has the entire Lenox family wrapped around her finger."

"That she does. We'll let you two get back to work. Your mom said Carson still had spelling homework. We'll throw dinner together then work on it."

"Thanks." And Ethan smiled the first real smile I'd seen since Sunday.

"Anytime, handsome. Let's go, darlin' we have bacon wrapped chicken to make and spelling words to study."

"Do I get a cookie if I get all my words right?"

"No. You already had a ton at Grans. You'll get a high five and you'll get to pick the before-bedtime movie."

"Deal." Carson nodded.

"Deal," I repeated. Ethan's face was funny again. "What?"

"Nothing. I'll see you at home. Love you, Squirt. Be good."

"Always am. Love you, too, Daddy."

I felt Ethan's eyes boring into the back of my head as we made our way out of the bullpen.

Hot and cold. Fine one minute, pensive the next. I had to talk to him tonight. Good or bad something had to change.

DINNER WAS A HIT. Carson cleared her plate and told me how much she loved bacon wrapped anything. I had to agree, bacon made everything taste better. She aced her spelling words and we watched Frozen until she fell asleep on the couch. It wasn't a moment too soon. If I had to listen to Elsa sing one more time I was going to find ear plugs.

After I carried Carson up to bed and tucked her in, I finished cleaning up the kitchen and set the coffee for extra early tomorrow. I'd been slacking on my runs and needed to get back to it. I was finding I didn't need the stress relief pounding the pavement had always provided now that I was getting a different kind of pounding. The thought made my cheeks heat and my panties dampen. Even with Ethan's current mood fluctuations he was still phenomenal in bed and always made sure I went first.

I'd sat on the couch, planning on waiting up for Ethan, but within minutes my eyes were heavy and a nap until he got home sounded good.

"Honor. Wake up."

Ethan.

"I was having such a good dream."

"What were you dreaming about?"

"We were on an island, just the three of us, and we were playing Frisbee. I was winning."

"Is that why it was a good dream, because you were winning?" I heard him laugh and opened my eyes, not wanting to miss him smiling.

"No. It was a good dream because I was with my two favorite people and no one else was around. Just the three of us."

His smile faded, and I'd had enough.

"What's wrong?" I asked and sat up.

"Nothing, smalls. It's been a long day."

I checked the clock, it was after ten, and he'd left the house at seven to take Carson to school before he went to work. It *had* been a long day, but that wasn't it.

"I'm not talking about right now. I'm talking about all week."

"Nothing's wrong."

"Ethan, if this is going to work, we have to be honest with each other. Even the uncomfortable stuff. And don't treat me like I'm stupid. You've been retreating since Sunday. What happened? Am I doing something wrong with Carson?"

He sat down next to me and was quiet for a long time.

"No. You're great with Carson."

"I feel like there's a but attached to that sentence. Is that a bad thing?"

"Kinda."

His answer was like a physical blow straight to my stomach. I loved what Carson and I were creating. It was going to kill me if I had to pull back from her.

"Shit, Honor. No, it's not. I don't know. I can't find the right way to say it."

"So why don't you just blurt out what comes to mind."

He thought for several moments before he answered. So much for blurting it out.

"It's always been just Carson and me."

"I know," I cut in.

"I thought it always would be. Now she has you, too. I'm struggling with what to do with that."

"What?"

"It's not jealousy. I love watching the two of you

together. I love that she's comfortable around you and asks you to help her. I think that's what's hard. I love it, but at the same time it scares the fuck out of me. What if something happens and you leave?"

"Leave? I don't want to leave, Ethan."

"You say that now, but it could happen. And we haven't used protection since Sunday. What if you get pregnant?"

"Is this what the problem is? You're afraid of me getting pregnant?"

"No," he emphatically answered. "Not because of the reasons you're thinking."

"First, I told you I have an IUD. Of course nothing's infallible, not even a condom." I raised my eyebrow as a reminder. "But if I were to get pregnant. We'd deal with it."

"Deal with it?"

"Ethan. Tell me what's wrong. Right now. You know I didn't mean deal with it as in not have it."

"You'd keep it?"

"Yes. I want kids."

His whole body relaxed, and right before my very eyes a weight lifted from him.

"So, you've been acting weird because you were worried I *could* be pregnant. And thought that if I were pregnant, I'd run like Chrissy did. Either I wouldn't have it, I'd leave it with you, or I'd take it and you'd never see it."

"Something like that."

"I cannot believe you'd compare me to her."

"I wasn't. I just—"

"Yes, you were. I am not her. We are not sixteen. I don't pretend to know what the two of you went through. I can't pass judgement on her because she left you with the best gift in the world. But I can tell you with my whole heart, I would never leave my child. Not at sixteen, not at twenty-three, not at thirty. So, Ethan, don't you ever compare me to Chrissy again. And next time you want to know something, ask!"

"I'm sorry. I was wrong."

"Goddamn right you were. Now let's talk about condoms." His lips twitched, and I felt my temper rise. "You think this is funny?"

"No." He smiled.

"I'm not smiling, Ethan. I've spent the last few days worried I'd done something wrong. Afraid you were done with me and didn't know how to tell me."

Ethan grabbed me, and I shrieked. Once he had me straddling his thighs and we were face-to-face he started. "I'm sorry I worried you. I told you when we started this I'd fuck up. I did, and I'm apologizing. I should've talked to you but, honestly, I couldn't under-stand what was going on in my head, so I couldn't explain it to you. I don't want you to change a thing. You're perfect and that in itself scares me. I can't lose you, Honor. I don't want to use condoms. You want the truth?" I nodded my head and braced. "I don't care if you get pregnant. Part of me has been hoping all week your fucking IUD will somehow fall out, or break, or however the hell an IUD can fail. I know that's fucked up and irresponsible, but I never wanted Carson to be an only child. I just assumed she would be. When I was younger, I'd always wanted a big family. I saw my parents and my aunts and uncles with their kids and I wanted the next generation to have what we all had. I was never lonely growing up, there was always a cousin around to play with. It kills me because I had Carson so young she's missing out on that."

"She's not missing out on anything. She has all the cousins."

"Honor, my youngest cousin is ten years older than her."

"So? They obviously give her plenty of attention because all she talks about are them and your brother."

"Out of everything I told you all you picked out was what I said about Carson."

"Because that was the only important part."

"You've got nothing to say about me wanting to get you pregnant?"

I had plenty to say but nothing I was willing to

verbalize. I should've told him he was nuts and anytime in the future we had sex he was going to double up on the condoms, but that wasn't the way I felt. Maybe I was the one that was nuts. Totally and completely off my rocker. We needed to pump the brakes on the baby talk; however, I would be lying if I said I didn't like the fact he wanted me to be the mother of his future children.

"Sorry to say, that is a non-topic, handsome. It can't happen, I've been assured by my doctor my IUD is exactly where it needs to be and is good for another few years yet."

"We should test it out, check the accuracy of the device."

He lifted his hips and pressed his hard-on between my legs.

"Maybe we should." I said returning his smile.

"We good?" he asked.

"I am as long as you are. And you promise never to compare me to Chrissy again."

"Promise," he replied.

"Then take me to bed, handsome. Seeing you in your uniform does crazy things to me."

He stood, and I wrapped my legs around his back.

"You have a thing for men in uniform?"

"No. Just you in yours."

"Good answer."

He walked us to my room, kicked the door closed, locked it, and tossed me on the bed.

"I love coming home to you."

"It's the best part of my day."

While I undressed I watched as he stripped out of his uniform. I was sorry to see it come off, but the more flesh he exposed the less sorry I became.

He crawled into bed and was kissing me when it dawned on me, he hadn't asked about Carson. He trusted me with the most valuable thing in his life—his daughter.

11

"We don't have to stay long," I told Honor.

"Ethan, I'll be fine. Are you sure you want me to go?"

Of course I wanted her to go. To use Carson's words, I wanted to show her off to my family. More than that, I wanted her to get to know everyone. But there were a lot of us, and it was going to be overwhelming.

"Yes," I answered.

"Then stop worrying. Carson has given me the rundown and she even quizzed me on who's who." Honor laughed.

"How did you do?"

"Not well. You have eight cousins and two of them are married. Plus, your three aunts and uncles, your parents, and your brother. I think I have everyone's names down but once Carson started with ages and occupations I failed."

"If it gets to be too much, just tell me."

I didn't know why I was so worried. My family was cool, they'd pull her into the fold and make her feel right at home. Maybe that's what I was afraid of. Either they'd scare her off, or she'd be another level deeper into my life. Making the pain even more unbearable if she left.

The other night when Honor had called me out on my shit, she'd smoothed the rough edges, but I still felt out of sorts. It was like I was waiting for the other shoe to drop. My gut was screaming at me that something bad was going to happen. It was only a matter of time before my life was pulled out from under me. I couldn't shake the feeling.

"Stop worrying. I won't embarrass you, I promise."

"Smalls, you've met my parents. There's nothing you could say or do that would embarrass me. My family is loud and the best group of people I know."

"What in the world is taking Carson so long? Carter's already at my parents' she's normally bouncing off the walls, begging to go."

Honor took my hand in hers and looked from the stairs to me.

"She'll be right down. She's finishing a surprise for your parents."

"A surprise?"

"Just a little something she wanted to put together. It's more for your mom, really."

"Did you have something to do with this surprise?"

"Maybe."

I stepped closer and took advantage of our rare moment of privacy and kissed her. "Thank you."

"Wow. If I get kissed like that every time I help Carson with a project, I'm helping more."

"Honor!" Carson yelled. "I need help. Come quick."

"Duty calls, handsome."

Honor jogged up the stairs to help Carson, and, not for the first time, I was stunned. My daughter had called for Honor—not me. Even after Honor and I talked about it, I still couldn't find the right words to express how I felt. I certainly wasn't jealous of her. I wanted Carson to forge her own relationship with Honor. I wanted them to have something special between them. But it didn't make the twinge in my heart any easier to take.

My phone beeped in my pocket, and I pulled it out to find Carter had texted.

Carter: Where the fuck are you, jackass?

Me: Christ you're impatient. Be there in 20.

Carter: Hurry up. I'm dying to meet your woman. Fair warning, Mom is planning a full-court press.

She's pulled out all the stops to cement Honor to the fam.

Me: Fucking hell. What's she up to? Will there be a minister to marry us too?

Carter: Marry? That was a jump, brother. Something you're thinking about?

Me: Fuck off. See you in 20.

Marry Honor?

It was way too soon to even think about marriage. I grabbed a water from the kitchen and thought about it some more. Why was thinking about marrying her so crazy when a few days ago, I admitted I wouldn't mind if she got pregnant. I was so confused, I needed my head examined and I needed to stop allowing my brother to crawl in my mind and play his games.

"Ready," Carson announced.

On the drive to my parents' house Carson continued to give Honor a rundown of our family. By the time Carson was done even I was confused about who was who and I knew all of them. I had no idea Carson knew so much about our family history. She even knew my mom had been taken by bad guys, and my dad had had to save her. When the hell had my mom or dad told her that story? They didn't tell me and Carter the story of how they met, separated, and reunited until we were teenagers.

The block was full of cars by the time we pulled up.

My cousin Nick was getting out of his truck, helping his wife Meadow down when he noticed and waved.

"That's Nick," I told Honor. "His wife is Meadow."

"Meadow has a scar on her face," Carson added. "She's so brave. A bad, bad woman hurt her really bad, and Cousin Nick saved her. He's brave, too. He's a Special Agent."

Honor fidgeted for a moment before she turned to me.

"FBI, right? He was working a serial case and Meadow was a victim, turned witness, turn victim again. They used to live in Virginia."

"Correct."

Honor turned in her seat and gave Carson a high five.

"Bam! I remembered."

Both of my girls giggled, and I cut the engine.

"Ready?"

"Yep."

"I am. I want to go swimming," Carson added.

Nick and Meadow were waiting for us when we made our way to the front porch.

"Ethan. Good to see you. I heard you made an arrest on the liquor store robberies."

"We did. Caught him on his seventh hit. His

sheet's a mile long, he shouldn't have been walking the streets."

"No work talk," Meadow said.

"You got it, Red." Nick smiled at his wife.

"Nick. Meadow. This is Honor Sullivan."

The three of them exchanged pleasantries before Nick scooped up Carson and walked to the door. When I'd announced to the family I was going to have a child, I'd been most worried about Nick and Meadow's reaction. They'd wanted kids, but due to Meadow's attack she was unable to have children. And there I was, way too young and in no way ready, but I was having one on accident. When they moved to Georgia, they'd started talking to adoption agencies after I'd explained I couldn't and wouldn't give up Carson. Neither of them had been anything other than supportive, but I still wonder if the timing was like a slap in the face.

We stepped into the foyer, and I pulled up short, stopping Honor in the process. The house was utter chaos. I let the sight of my family wrap around me. I lived for these barbeques. We'd been having them for as long as I could remember. Normally, they were for no special reason. But today, I was nervous. I'd never brought a woman to a family gathering. They were sacred, my time to connect with the people who meant the most to me. I'd never met anyone I'd wanted to bring into the inner circle—until Honor.

"There are so many people here," Honor murmured.

"If you get overwhelmed, tell me."

"There you are," Carter said. "Why the fuck are you standing in the doorway?"

"Nice. Honor meet my brother, Carter."

Carter stood an inch taller than me but other than that we were matched in size. And no one would doubt we were brothers. Much to my mother's delight, we both looked just like our father. Lily Lenox always bragged about how she had the best-looking men in Georgia. I'd always thought she had to say that about me and Carter because we were her sons. Then middle school came, and both of us got our share of attention. But high school was when I'd realized the opposite sex appreciated the Lenox genes.

He was sizing Honor up, and if I didn't know his secret, I would've warned him to take his eyes off my woman. But I knew something the rest of the family didn't know. I was about fifteen when he told me, making Carter around seventeen. He made me promise to never tell. To this day, I think the secret is stupid. No one would care. There is one thing this family wants and that is for everyone to be happy. And the thing Carter isn't, is happy. He had a bad ass job as a Navy SEAL, had great friends, but had zero personal life. And if the same thing rings true at twenty-six as it did when he was seventeen, he was a choir boy. Considering his SEAL platoon calls him Church, I'd bet it was still the case.

"Nice to meet you," Honor broke the silence.

"You, too. Come on in, Mom's been waiting for you," he told her.

Mom?

Not my *mom, not our mom—just Mom.*

"There you two are. I thought I saw Carson running down to the basement."

And, it was too late, my mom had found us.

"Hi, Lily," Honor beamed. "Do you need any help?"

"Yes. Come on and leave the boys to catch up; I'll introduce you around."

"Okay."

Before my mom could led her away I stopped her, looked around, and not seeing Carson, I brushed my lips against hers. "Please don't let them scare you away."

"I'll be fine."

I let my mom steer her in the direction of my aunts, Emily, Regan, and Blake, and sighed. Nothing like baptism by fire.

"You're fucked," Carter said.

"Come again?"

"You won't see Honor the rest of the day. Mom thinks she's hit the jackpot. One of her sons has finally given her a daughter."

"I think you're exaggerating a little."

"Am I?"

"You realize I've known her like a minute, right?"

"And?"

"It's a little too soon."

"Do you remember the stories the uncles told about meeting their women?"

"How could I forget?"

My uncles told those stories any chance they could. There was a lesson about bravery, family, and love in each union.

"So then you know it is not too soon. Ethan, the fact she's here, and you allow her and Carson to spend time together tells me you already know. If you'd get out of your own head for two seconds, you'd see it. Mom and Dad do. I do."

"You met her for like two seconds," I reminded him.

"That's all it took. Two seconds and I knew."

I wondered if he was talking about him or me. He'd been in love with Delaney Walker for nearly ten years. I understood why he hadn't said anything when he was seventeen and she was fourteen, but now? He refused to believe the family would accept it. His excuse being she was our cousin. But she wasn't—not really. Not by blood. Just because we grew up with Jasper, Clark, and Levi as our honorary uncles didn't mean we were related in any way. And he was crazy if he thought we all didn't know she returned his feelings.

"You know she loves you, right?"

"We're not talking about me," he deflected.

"Why not? You never want to talk about you. It's time we do."

Over the years there'd been a lot that had changed about my brother, one of those things was his carefree personality and another was he'd perfected my father's glare. He could bring a man low with just a look.

"I'm leaving in a few days," he told me.

"Fuck. Where?"

"Back to Africa."

"How long?"

"At least six months."

Fuck. The news was going to kill my mom.

"Mom?"

"I haven't told her yet. Dad knows. I'm sure he's told the uncles. But I wanted Mom to have her day before I dropped the bomb."

"And Delaney?"

"She knows, too."

So, Carter was still in contact with her, more so than he wanted me to know.

"How is she?"

"Same as she always is when I leave. Scared, upset, crying." Carter faced me and for the first time he tore his mask away and let me see his pain. "It fucking guts me. Every. Single. Time. Now do you understand why I can't have her? I want her happy and smiling every day. Not worried if her man is coming home or waiting for months to hear from me. She deserves better."

"That's her choice, Carter. She's loved you since she was fourteen. And I can't think of a better man for her."

"Wrong. It's my choice. I told her yesterday it was time to move on. She needs to stop wasting her life waiting on something that's never going to happen."

"Wait. Have the two of you . . ."

I wasn't sure how to phrase my question without sounding crude.

"Yes."

"Holy fuck," I whispered. "You never told me that. How long?"

"Years."

"Boys," my dad interrupted. "You tell him?"

"Yeah," Carter answered.

"Not a word to your mother. I want her to enjoy introducing Honor to everyone."

"Why does everyone keep making a big deal out of this?"

"Because, it is a big deal. My future daughter is meeting the family for the first time."

Carter chuckled and pounded my back a few times before he walked away to mingle with the crowd. I caught Honor across the room talking to my Aunt Emily. They were laughing but that's not what had my attention. My gaze went lower to Carson's hand in Honor's.

The love that had taken root and had started to blossom, exploded in my chest. I was no longer able to deny it. Honor was mine.

12

"What's this?" Lily asked.

"Open it, Gran, it's a surprise," Carson told her. "Honor helped me make it."

"I'll take this out to the table," Emily said, picking up a tray of burger fixings.

"Thanks, Em." Then Lily took the surprise from Carson and inspected the wrapping. "Did you do this all by yourself?"

"Yep." Carson stood a little taller. "All Honor did was hold the sides, so I could tape it."

"Is there any tape left on the roll?" Ethan asked, joining us in the kitchen.

"Yes!" Carson declared, and I shook my head in the negative.

"What's the occasion?" Lenox asked.

"Honor said you don't have to wait for birthdays to

give presents. Sometimes you can do it just because. To show someone you love them. So I made Gran a just-because surprise."

"That was nice, Squirt."

"I thought so, too." Carson proudly smiled.

The gift had been her idea, I only helped with the execution.

Lily tore through the paper and gasped.

"Carson Rose!"

"Do you like it, Gran?"

"I couldn't love it more."

"Do you see? It spells love."

Lily held up the sign for Ethan to see.

"Are those pictures from Savannah?" Ethan asked inspecting the letters.

"Yep. Honor printed them out. She taught me how to mod . . ."

"Mod podge," I reminded her.

"We mod podged the pictures to the letters and painted the wood. Honor said she had to glue the letters to the wood because the glue was poison and I couldn't touch it. See?" Carson proudly pointed to the piece of wood then to the black and white photos of her and Ethan that covered the L-O-V-E. "It's me and Daddy."

"This is the best present I've ever received," Lily announced with tears in her eyes.

"I take exception to that," Lenox said. "You told me the diamond earrings I gave you last Christmas were the best present."

He winked at Carson.

"Well, now this is," Lily huffed. "Lenox get a hammer I know just where I want it."

"Now? We have a house full of people, woman."

"Yes, right now."

Lenox tromped out, muttering something under his breath. He wasn't fooling anyone. He'd do anything to make Lily happy, including hanging a photo collage in the middle of a party. By the time Lenox returned Ethan still hadn't said anything, and I worried I'd overstepped. Lenox and Carson followed Lily into the living room.

"Do you like it?"

"No." His answer wiped the smile off my face.

"No?"

"There are no pictures of you."

"Me? Why would I put a picture of myself on the sign? It's supposed to be about family."

"I want you guys to make a new one. With pictures of you included."

"Ethan, I don't have any pictures of myself."

"I do." He pulled his phone out of his pocket, unlocked it, tapped the screen. "Here," he said, handing it to me.

There was a picture of Carson and me with our heads together looking at the back of my camera. We were in Savannah.

"I didn't know you took that."

"There's more," he told me.

I scrolled through the images and there were dozens and dozens of pictures of me with Carson. Us cooking, me showing Carson how to use my camera, us reading, some images I didn't know what we'd been doing but we were smiling at each other. Then there were the ones of me alone, I was never looking at the camera. He'd captured me doing everyday things around the house, including vacuuming.

But there were none of Ethan and me.

"Why did you take these?"

"I remembered what you said at the park the first day I met you. I'll never forget those moments but I still wanted the reminder. I like knowing I can pull up one of those pictures and see your beautiful face and remember how happy you make Carson and me."

"Thank you. I want these, all of them. I don't have any of Carson and me."

"I want those on a new sign for our home."

"Okay," I whispered, afraid if I spoke any louder my voice would give away how much it meant to me that he wanted to include me in his family pictures.

"Will you go out to dinner with me tomorrow?" he

asked.

"Of course. We should go to the pizza place with the Pac Man game. Carson loves it there."

"Just the two of us. I want to take you out."

"Like, on a date?" I laughed.

I lived with him, we'd been sleeping together for weeks, and we'd already talked about both of us wanting to keep moving our relationship forward. Wasn't it a little late to start dating?

"Exactly like a date. We've never been out just the two of us."

"I appreciate you offering. But we get time alone together every night." Ethan smirked, and I continued. "You know what I mean. With you comes the awesome bonus of Carson. We don't need to leave her out."

Ethan stalked toward me and I retreated until my back hit the fridge. His hands came to my face like they always did when he wanted my undivided attention.

"Will you please do me the honor of going on a date with me?"

"Since you asked so sweetly, handsome, I'd love, too."

"Smartass."

Then in his parents' kitchen he kissed me. He hadn't looked around to see if anyone was watching or where Carson was, he simply devoured my mouth.

"Get a room," Ethan's cousin Jackson said.

Ethan slowed the kiss and pulled away, flipping Jackson off he stepped away from me.

"Did Quinn leave?" Ethan asked.

"Yeah. She had a date." Jackson's face turned to stone.

I'd already been told that Jackson Clark and Quinn Walker were the best of friends. They had been since they were in diapers. By the look on Jackson's face I guess he wasn't happy she was dating someone. Ethan had told me he was overprotective of her, but I hadn't fully understood just how much.

"With whom?" Ethan joined in Jackson's distaste.

"Bobby Reynolds."

"Bang 'em Bobby?" Ethan asked.

"One in the same. I already warned him I'd break his fucking legs he tried any of his normal shit with Quinn."

"Who's trying what with my daughter?" Jasper Walker asked.

"Banging Bobby Reynolds," Jackson told him. The name alone told Jasper the who and the what. Everyone in the area knew Bobby's reputation.

"Did you give him the talk?" Jasper asked.

"Abso-fucking-lutely." Jackson sneered.

"Good man. Thanks for always watching out for her." Jasper clapped Jackson on the shoulder and opened the fridge. "Honor would you like a beer?"

"Yes, please."

He twisted the top off before he handed it to me.

"Em told me she invited you and Ethan over for dinner next week."

"She did. I haven't had a chance to talk to Ethan about it yet."

"Ethan?" Jasper lifted a questioning brow.

"We'll be there," he answered.

"Good. We'll see you guys outside."

"What, you're not gonna offer us a beer, Uncle Jasper?" Ethan laughed.

"You got two arms."

"Funny how 'the look' works just as well now as it did when we were kids," Ethan joked.

"Damn right. I'm going to eat before there's nothing left." Jackson made his way to the back door.

"He's right. We better hurry."

I WAS SITTING on the back deck, beer in hand, watching the guys throwing a football around, Carson chasing whomever had the ball. I don't think she cared much about what team she was supposed to be on. As long as she could jump on whoever caught it, she was smiling.

Lily, Emily, Reagan, Blake, and the Walker girls, minus Quinn, all sat down at the table I was sitting at.

"This feels familiar," Lily commented.

"It does. Only the first time we sat on this deck together we were watching the guys put together a swing set," Emily mused.

"It was a nice sight wasn't it? If I remember correctly, Jasper had his shirt off and was flexing, trying to get your attention," Lily continued.

"He got it all right. It was hot as Hades. Jasper had sweat . . ."

"Gross. Please stop," Delaney Walker complained.

"My ears are bleeding, Mom," her sister Hadley added.

"I'll need therapy for many years if I hear how hot my father is," Adalynn Walker put in.

"Sorry, girls, but your father is pretty hot," Emily poked.

The older women all laughed when the Walker girls groaned.

I had to agree with Emily, Jasper was hot. So were Clark and Levi. If the men looked this good in their fifties I couldn't image what they'd looked like when they'd met their wives.

"Kayla's cancer is back," Emily whispered.

"No!" Lily gasped. "How long?"

"Awhile. They told us last night, but they've

known for a bit. She's decided not to do treatments this time."

I heard the Walker girls sniff, and I felt like I was encroaching on a very private family discussion. When Carson gave me the CliffNotes version of her family as she knew it, she'd mentioned that Jason Walker's wife, Kayla, was very sick when they got married, but she'd gotten better and all was well. Sadly, Carson's intel was out of date.

"What? Why? She fought so hard the first time," Blake said.

"And second," Adalynn reminded them.

"That's exactly why. The doctor told her that at this point there's nothing left to do," Emily informed them. "She wants what time she has left not to be spent in the hospital."

"How long?" Reagan asked.

"Not long. Maybe a couple of months. Tops."

Tears pricked the corner of my eyes, and I mentally went through the pictures I'd taken today. I knew I had some of Jason and Kayla but made a note to take more.

The women continued to talk, however I'd gone back to watching the football game. Carson was slowing down, the ball was being passed, and she was no longer running after the receiver. When she looked over at me I knew something was wrong.

I stood but before I could go to her she was running straight for me.

"Honor," she panted.

"What's wrong?"

"I don't feel good," she whined.

"All right. Let's go sit down."

That's when it happened, my introduction to motherhood—sort of.

Carson sat on my lap, cuddled in, and then threw up all over me. All. Over. Me. Everything she'd eaten all day was on my chest and lap. Pieces of vomit were in my hair as well.

She retched again, and I was able to move her to the side, and, luckily, most of it hit the concrete, but my shoes were now covered as well.

Chairs scraped all around us. The Walker girls bolted before they got hit. Someone ran inside the house, and Lily stood beside me.

"Shit," Ethan mumbled when he got to us. "I'm so sorry, Honor."

"You feeling better, darlin'?" I asked Carson, ignoring Ethan.

"A little."

"Good. We'll sit here a second before we clean you up."

"I'm sorry," she cried.

"Nothing to be sorry about."

I couldn't hug her without smooshing the vomit covering us but I wanted too. I hated that she was crying.

"Here," Lily handed me a wet wash cloth, and I wiped Carson's face.

"That was for you." Lily chuckled.

"You wanna come with Gran, and I'll get you in a bath and all cleaned up?"

"No. I want Honor to do it."

Lily recoiled and placed her hand on her chest as tears started rolling down her cheeks. Lenox came to her side and tucked her in close. But through her tears she was smiling. Ethan looked from me to Carson and to his parents. A look passed between him and his dad.

And in some weird Lenox language only they knew, Lenox said, "Bone-deep."

Lily buried her face in Lenox's chest and her body shook. I felt like I was missing something big and maybe if I hadn't been covered in vomit, I would've been able to decipher their family code, but I was, so I couldn't.

"Bone-deep," Ethan echoed.

AFTER I'D CLEANED up and changed into gym clothes Delaney had in her car, I gave Carson a bath and helped her into a pair of jammies and we called it a night.

I said goodbye to everyone and was overwhelmed by their kindness. Ethan was lucky he had such a great family.

We were finally at the door when Lily pulled me in for a hug and held on tightly.

"Thank you."

"I didn't do much."

"You, sweet girl, have done everything."

Before I could answer she pulled away and moved into her husband's embrace.

"Thanks, guys. We'll see you later. Sorry for the mess."

"Not the first, won't be the last," Lenox responded.

"Ready to go home?" Ethan asked Carson.

"Yes."

But instead of taking Ethan's hand she grabbed mine.

"Will you lay down with me when we get home?"

"Sure will, darlin', right after you drink down a special cup of tea to make your tummy feel better."

Lily sniffed, Ethan cleared his throat, and Lenox smiled.

There was something in the water, they'd all gone batty.

13

"You sure you still want to do this?" Honor asked.

"Carson is fine," I told her for the tenth time. "No fever. She hasn't been sick since yesterday. It was all the crap she ate then the running around."

"Okay. If you're sure. You know better than me."

"I'm sure. Carter will be here any minute and he wants time with Carson, anyway."

With all the commotion last night I hadn't been able to tell Honor why my brother wanted some one-on-one time with his niece.

I still wasn't sure what to make of last night and how Honor had handled everything like a rock star. She hadn't missed a beat. Most women who'd just been thrown up on would've had a fit. Not, Honor. She calmly sat with my daughter on her lap and comforted her. Even though I knew she probably wanted to gag.

God knew I did. That shit was gross, and had been everywhere.

As soon as Carter walked in the door I'd ushered Honor out. Part of me had been afraid I was going to be stood up, and she'd opt to stay home to make sure Carson was okay. That wasn't happening, though. Honor had disappeared into her room about an hour ago and had emerged looking stunning. She always looked great, but, tonight, she had on a little extra makeup and her hair was pulled up in a fancy twist, showing off her sexy neck. It would be a bloody miracle if I could make it through dinner without sporting a hard-on. She even wore the bracelets Carson had given her to wear for our date.

I'd been scared shitless to tell my eight-year-old I was going out with Honor. It would've been laughable the way I'd stumbled over my words had the situation not been so serious. Carson had simply shrugged like it was no big deal. When I'd asked her if she had any questions, she'd asked if we'd bring home ice cream if she was good. Against my better judgement, I said yes. Call it guilt for going on my first date since she was born.

"This is really nice, Ethan." Honor noted when I pulled up to the valet.

"Let me open your door," I warned when she went for the door handle.

The valet opened my door, handing me a ticket, and I rounded the hood to Honor's side.

"Thank you, handsome."

The lighting in the restaurant was dim, the dark blue walls making it even more so.

"Have you been here before?" she asked.

"No."

After a quick exchange with the hostess we were seated and greeted by our server, an older gentleman, who'd flirted shamelessly with Honor. He took our drink order, and we looked over the menu.

"Ethan—"

"Don't, Honor. Don't look at the prices, just order what you want. And I swear to Christ if you order a salad because it's inexpensive I'm introducing you to spankings when we get home."

The thought of my hand smacking her ass had me inhaling through my nose, trying to calm my very perverted thoughts.

"You can't say that to me."

"I just did."

"But—"

"Honor." I heard from behind me. Her eyes left mine and she directed her gaze over my shoulder. The color drained from her face, and she sat up straighter. "If it isn't my wayward daughter."

Daughter? Honor's father was dead. I scooted my

chair back and stood. I couldn't have been more shocked if Buck Sully had come back from the dead and was standing there himself.

Standing I said, "Congressman Harris." When I noticed his son standing beside him I added, "Sam."

"Officer . . ."

"Lenox," I supplied.

"That's right. Officer Lenox. Honor, aren't you going to come say hello to your father?"

What the fuck? I shot a look at Honor and she looked worse than Carson did last night after she'd puked all over my parents' patio. She stood, nearly knocking her chair over, then walked around the table and stopped by my side.

"Hello, Frank," she offered.

"You know, your fiancé has been trying to get a hold of you. I must tell you, I'm disappointed in your behavior. I thought you'd have more class than to abandon your duties.

"Don't you ever call him that again."

Congressman Harris's eyes narrowed to slits. "You seemed to have forgotten your place, young lady."

He stepped closer, and I pulled Honor back. "I think it's time you leave, Officer Lenox. This is a private family matter."

"I'm not going anywhere," I informed him. Sam

was still standing in the same place; his eyes had not moved from Honor.

"You will if you don't want me calling your captain."

"You can call whoever the fuck you want, but I'm not leaving here without my woman."

"Your woman?" Sam spoke for the first time.

"What are you, a Neanderthal?" the congressman asked. "Disappointed, indeed, Honor. This is the type of man you consort with?"

"Please leave, Frank. I made myself clear when I moved out. I want nothing to do with you. Ever."

"You mean, ran away. Leaving your poor fiancé to worry about you."

Honor's face went from white to red, and she snapped. "I told you to never to call him that again. I never agreed to marry that man. That was your plan. I told you then, and I'm telling you now, I will never, ever marry him. I don't care about your political games. I don't care about you, and I never cared about your son. Leave me alone, Frank, or I swear I'll scream from the rooftops about what a piece of shit Congressman Franklin Harris really is. If you think I don't have pictures of you sneaking your whores in before my mom was dead, you're wrong. What do you think your adoring public would think about the hookers you brought home the night you buried my mother?

"Consider this our final goodbye."

"You'll be sorry."

"The only thing I'm sorry about is that my beautiful mother married you. Stay away from me. Please take me home, Ethan."

"I'll give you twenty-four hours to rethink your position."

"You're done." I stepped between Frank and Honor. "She's made herself clear. She doesn't want to hear from you or your son again. You will respect that."

"Ethan Lenox. I know all about you—low-class trash. You knocked up your high school girlfriend, dropped out of school shortly after, and later joined the police force. You do not want to go up against me. Cut your losses, kid, and move on. Honor has an obligation to this family. One she will fulfill."

"Like hell she will. Now move out of the way and don't contact her again. She doesn't need twenty-four hours to think about anything."

"We'll see." The smug bastard crossed his arms over his chest and stepped to the side.

"Yeah. We will."

I reached behind me and Honor took my hand, when I brought her to my side and tucked her under my arm she pushed close and tried to hide her face. I wished like hell we were someplace private and not in a restaurant full of people. Frank needed to be taught a lesson, one I was more than happy to teach him. But nothing good would come from me delivering the ass whooping he deserved in a crowded room full of witnesses.

I didn't know what the fuck family obligation meant, but I didn't like the way my woman was shaking and was so scared she was trying to disappear.

My truck was pulled around, and I had to peel her arms from around me to get her into the Yukon.

"I'm sorry, Ethan. I'm so sorry."

"Let's just get you in, smalls."

"Ethan—"

"Give me a minute."

I was trying to get my temper in check. I didn't want to say something I'd regret later and with how angry I was, nothing nice was going to come out of my mouth. Not wanting to go home yet, I drove around until I found a semi abandoned parking lot and parked.

"I'm sorry," she said again.

Fucking hell, she obviously wasn't going to respect my need for silence.

"Wanna tell me what that was about?"

"No."

"Right. So, all the talk about honesty, even the uncomfortable stuff was bullshit. You want the truth from me while you keep secrets, like the fact you're fucking engaged."

"I'm not engaged. I said I didn't *want* to talk about it, not that I wouldn't."

"Let's have it, Honor. Tell me why Harris said you were engaged. And don't fucking lie to me. I want the whole truth."

"I didn't tell you because I didn't think he'd ever be a problem."

"So, there is something to tell?"

"No. My mom married Frank. From the beginning I didn't like him or Sam. At first, I thought Sam was gay, then I caught him watching me. It was weird and gross. I told my mom about it, but she blew it off and said he was just a spoiled, lonely kid who had a crush. I knew he went into my room when I wasn't home. I could never prove it, but I just knew. We were teenagers, and I didn't want to think about what he did in there."

"Your mom never talked to Frank about Sam's behavior?"

"Not that I knew of, and even if she did, it wouldn't have done any good. Sam was perfect in Frank's eyes. He has been grooming him for politics since he was a kid. What Sam wants, Sam gets. No one will stand in Frank's way when it comes to giving him anything and everything."

As a police officer, I didn't like what Honor was telling me. I'd witnessed firsthand how Sam looked at

Honor, and it was creepy as fuck. Adding that to what I already knew about him from my shifts on his protection detail, I had a bad feeling.

"And the man who you're supposed to marry? Who is he?"

"Greg Wells is a city council member in Atlanta. Frank says he has potential and he's friends with his father. I don't know whose idea it was, but one day Frank announced I was going to marry Greg. I said no. He pushed and threatened to kick me out if I didn't agree. It was a no brainer, I was leaving. I should've left right after my mom died but I didn't."

"Tell me about when your mom died."

The hurt that crossed her face was maddening. I hated that I had to make her talk about something so painful, but I didn't have a choice. Her mother had obviously played a part in the story.

"My mom was alive one day, and the next she was gone. Literally and figuratively. We hadn't even buried her yet and Frank ordered the staff to get rid of all her belongings. I was so fucking sad and broken I didn't have it in me to stop them when they packed up her clothes and got rid of them. In a moment of defiance, I went into my mom's room and went through what was left of her stuff, taking things that meant something to me. Earrings she'd had before Frank, her favorite lipstick, silly stuff really. None of it had any monetary value. But I knew Frank would be mad I'd taken it. He was trying to get rid of any evidence my mother ever lived there. I also found a small box in the attic with my mom's name on it. I should've moved out that day, but I couldn't.

"If you hated him so much and Sam made you uncomfortable why would you stay in the house?"

That was the part that had me confused. She'd been over eighteen and had graduated high school, she didn't have to stay there.

"Ethan, you'll never know what it feels like to have no one. I had nothing. No family to help. My friends were not in the position to offer assistance, not that I would've asked. I had to suck it up if I wanted to finish school. I needed time to plan. After paying tuition I had no money left to move out. And as strange as this sounds, as much as I hated Frank and that house, I could still remember my mom there. Us in the kitchen, her in her sewing room, I wasn't ready to give up the last place I'd seen or spoken to my mom."

She was right, I didn't know what it was like not to have my family in my corner. Mine had always been there to support and guide me. And not just my parents, my extended family as well. I couldn't begin to imagine what I would've done at sixteen if my parents hadn't been around.

"You paid your tuition? Harris is loaded, why didn't he pay?"

"Control. He would've, but there were strings, and lots of them. I wanted no part of his demands. So, I paid, and he and Sam sat back and laughed as I struggled, dangling money in front of me, trying to get me to cave. I never did. The only thing I took from Frank was the roof over my head."

"Why did you finally leave?"

A look of disgust crossed her face, and I braced for the answer.

"One night, Frank came home red-hot pissed and said he was tired of me stalling. Greg wanted to announce our engagement, and I had twenty-four hours to get my shit together and meet with the Wells family. And if that wasn't bad enough, he had a contract outlining my wifely duties."

"I'm afraid to ask what the contract said."

"It listed, in detail, what my duties were as a wife." Her voice had gone flat. "How many times a week I was to provide sex, oral and vaginal. Birth control was at Greg's discretion. The list was disgusting. Who the fuck has to order their wife to have sex with them? I would be given a monthly allowance; however all bookkeeping was to be done by the family's accountant and every penny was to be accounted for. I had no right to exit the marriage. Reading it made my skin crawl."

"What the fuck?"

I wished I could turn back in time and beat the holy shit out of them both. Witnesses be damned.

If I'd thought this situation was bad before, it had just crossed the line to fucked.

14

My head was spinning from seeing Frank and Sam. Adding to my discomfort and embarrassment was having to tell Ethan about Frank's plan. To Frank I was nothing more than a whore he could trade for political gain. And Sam, desperate for Frank's approval, went along with anything his father said.

"What did they say when you told them you wouldn't agree to marry Greg?"

"The same thing he said in the restaurant. It was my obligation to my family."

"What did he say when you left?"

"Nothing. I just packed my stuff and drove off. I had no reason to say goodbye. I'd already given him an answer and I didn't owe him any further explanation. I only took what belonged to me and my mom and walked out the door."

"The bed," he mumbled.

Shit on a shingle he was putting it together. I supposed it didn't make a difference at this point, I'd already been completely humiliated, but it still stung having him know how destitute I'd been. Not that I was that much better off now, but I did own a bed, nightstand, and dresser. Furniture I'd purchased with money I'd earned. I was able to pay my rent and still save money. I wasn't swimming in it, however, my prints were selling and my design business was growing. I was proud of what I'd accomplished.

"Why didn't you tell me?" Hurt shone on his face and I didn't know how to explain it had nothing to do with me not trusting him and everything to do with me not wanting to admit I was worthless. According to Frank and Sam my only value as a person was an indentured sex slave for Greg. That was what they thought of me. Frank thought I owed him a debt and he was going to collect.

"Because I never wanted to think about it again. I didn't think it was a big deal."

"A big deal? Did you really think Frank was going to let it go?"

"Yes. I figured he'd move on."

"Clearly you were wrong. You understand that now, right?"

"Clearly. I'm not stupid, Ethan. I know a threat

when I hear one. That's why I think I need to move. Leave Georgia all together. I thought I'd moved far enough away I'd never see him again. I was wrong."

I don't know why I'd said I should move. It wasn't something I'd planned on saying. It just spewed out before I could think about the ramifications of my words.

"Move? Are you fucking serious?" Ethan was pissed, really pissed.

"I don't want my problems touching you or Carson. He's right, his reach is long. He could cause a lot of problems for you at the station. We have to think about Carson."

"I'm not worried about my job, Honor. Fuck my job. I'm worried about you."

"He can't do anything to me. I don't have anything to lose. What do you think he'll do? Kidnap me and hold me hostage until I agree to marry Greg? He's not that crazy."

"He's not? He had a goddamn contract drawn up outlining when you were to fuck Greg. If that's not crazy I don't know what is. I wouldn't put anything past that lunatic. And I don't like the way Sam looks at you. There's something wrong with him, he's fucking nuts, too. There's no way you're going anywhere. I'll talk to my dad and Lorenz, and we'll go from there."

"No! You can't tell your dad."

Panic clawed at my chest, and the oxygen was ripped from my lungs.

"Why not?"

"You don't get it. I never wanted *you* to know what was going on in Frank's house. I didn't have the picture-perfect family you have. I didn't grow up with loving parents. I had a philandering stepfather who fucked whores in his study while his wife slept in the room above. I had a stepbrother that more than likely jerked off on my bed or went through my clothes hamper and smelled my panties. Do you think I really want your dad to know where I come from?"

"Where you come from? Do you think that little of my family?"

"God, no." What could I say to make him understand? "I'm embarrassed. Can you put yourself in my shoes for two seconds and think about how humiliating it is? I want them to think I'm good enough for you."

"Good enough for me? Jesus, Honor. You realize I am exactly what Frank said I was. I knocked up my high school girlfriend. I dropped out and had to finish my education at home because I was taking care of an infant. I didn't walk across some stage and graduate. I had to go to a testing center and take the high school equivalency exam. I don't even have a regular diploma. Do you think less of me because of my past choices?"

Was he crazy? I respected him for all he'd sacri-ficed and done for Carson.

"No!"

"Then why would anyone think less of you for something that wasn't your choice? Everything that is happening is on Frank. Nothing's your fault."

"It sure feels like it is. Not to mention I brought this shit to your doorstep."

Ethan sighed and grabbed my hand.

"You didn't bring anything. They did."

"I'm sorry I didn't tell you."

"I understand why you didn't, but, in the future, don't hide shit from me. A very smart woman once told me the only way to make a relationship work is by being honest. Is there anything else you need to tell me?"

"No. That's all."

"Okay. Are you hungry?" he asked.

"Do you forgive me?"

"There's really nothing to forgive. I wish you would've trusted me enough to tell me." I started to protest but he silenced me. "But I get it. We're still working out the kinks, getting to know each other. How about we try another restaurant and finish our date?"

"Sounds perfect."

MUCH LATER THAT NIGHT, after Ethan had made love to me, sweetly we were lying in bed and I was tucked into his side, my arm over his chest and my thigh over his, I thought about his question from earlier.

"I lied in the car when you asked me if there was anything else I needed to tell you." His body stiffened under mine, and I quickly continued. "There *is* one more thing; I love you."

He didn't relax like I thought he would but instead he rolled me to my back and loomed over me.

"Say it again," he demanded.

"I love you." This time he closed his eyes and smiled.

He settled over me and hitched my leg over his hip.

"I love you, too."

"You don't have to—"

My words were silenced when he kissed me. And when he slid inside of me I gasped at the force of his thrust.

"Guess I should be ashamed about how easy I gave it up on our first date, huh?"

Ethan slowed his pace and, in a magical moment I'll never forget, threw his head back and laughed. His body shook with hilarity and it was one instance I didn't need a photograph to always remember the beauty he'd given me.

I'd never, ever, forget it.

15

"Daddy, did you sign me up for cheer camp?" This was the third time Carson had asked in as many days.

"Yes, Squirt, I did. What's wrong?"

"Um, nothing . . ."

"Was that a question? It sounds like something."

"Sorry. Sorry I'm late. It's so hot out there already, the last half-mile was brutal," Honor said, shutting the front door behind her. "Give me one second and we'll start the pancakes."

"Gran and Pop will be here in ten minutes," Carson reminded her.

"I know. I'll be right back."

Honor scurried off to her room, leaving me with a worried Carson.

"Are you going to tell me what's wrong?"

"Is Honor going to be my mom?"

"What?"

Fuck. Fuck. Fuck.

I was not prepared to have this conversation with my daughter. The last time we talked about moms she was five and had come home from kindergarten in tears because someone had teased her about not having a mom like everyone else. I'd never wanted to kick a five-year-old's ass so badly. That was a hard talk to have. I went with my gut and explained as gently as I could why Chrissy had left. I made sure to tell Carson that while Chrissy wasn't ready to be a mom she loved her so much and wanted her to have the best life possible. Maybe it was odd, but Carson never asked about Chrissy after that. And I'd watched for any signs Carson might have needed to talk about it. My parents did as well. However it never looked like it'd bothered her.

"I was thinking . . ." she started. I didn't say anything, I simply waited for her to gather her thoughts. "Now that we have Honor I don't need to go to cheer camp."

That was a change of subject.

"Why's that?"

"Cheer camp is summer camp. I have to go to summer camp because school is out, and you work. *But now we have Honor.*" She said the last part like I was dumb, enunciating her words.

"Squirt, Honor isn't our live-in babysitter, and she works too."

"That's why I asked if Honor was going to be my mom. Mom's don't babysit their own kids, do they?"

Fuck.

A clatter behind me had me flying out of my chair, turning to see what'd happened.

"Hi, Honor. Ready to make the pancakes?"

Honor looked . . . freaked out. Carson was giving me whiplash. Not to mention she'd dropped a nuclear bomb big enough to take out all the European Continent and was now talking about pancakes. And there was a knock on the door. Jesus!

"I'll, um, get the door. Sorry. I didn't mean to interrupt." Honor picked up the brush she'd dropped and practically ran for the front door. Not that I blamed her. I'd be surprised if she returned.

My dad came into the dining room and looked between Carson and me. "What's going on? Why does Honor look—"

"Nothing." I cut him off.

I thought I'd been spared any further questioning, but when my mom and Honor came in, holy fuck, had I been wrong.

"You ready to make pancakes?" my mom asked.

"Yep."

"Good." Then my mom, being a super-sleuth-female, sniffed something was amiss with her tribe and had to ask, "What's wrong? What are you guys talking about?"

"Nothing's wrong, Gran. We were just talking about how I didn't need to go to cheer camp this summer if Honor is going to be my mom."

I thought all the air had been sucked from the room when both women inhaled like it was the last breath they'd ever take. My father was stone-faced. And Carson was smiling, like she'd simply solved this summer's issue with where she would go while I was at work.

"What?" Carson asked looking at all the adults in the room like we'd grown three heads.

"Nothing, darlin'. Let's hurry and mix the batter up. I'm starving."

"Okay. I set everything on the counter like you asked."

"Perfect. We'll have them whipped up in no time, and Gran can man the griddle."

"What's a griddle?"

"Let's go into the kitchen, and I'll show you." Honor's hand shook as she reached for Carson. "Ethan. Lenox. Would either of you like a cup of coffee."

My dad just stared, Stunned, I swallowed the lump in my throat, but Honor didn't miss a beat. Neither of us answered, but she forged on like we had. "Great. I'll bring you both out a cup."

Honor and Carson went into the kitchen, however, the rest of us were glued in place.

"What the fuck just happened?" I whispered.

"I think you know what happened," my dad answered.

"No, dad. I don't know. What am I supposed to tell Carson? Honor is freaked the fuck out, not that I blame her."

"Tell Carson the truth. And the last thing Honor is, is freaked out."

"And the truth is?"

"That, yes, one day Honor will be her mom," my mom answered.

"Seriously? That's all you have? She's eight," I reminded them. "I can't tell her that."

Honor came back and placed two cups of coffee on the table, sliding the cup of black coffee toward my dad, and the slightly blonde one in front of me.

"Already put your sugar in it, Lenox."

"Thanks."

"Hey." I grabbed her hand before she could walk back into the kitchen.

Honor looked down at me and shifted her head to the side, and, suddenly, I wasn't sure why I'd stopped her or what I wanted to say.

"Yeah?"

"Thank you."

"It's just coffee, handsome."

"No. Thank you for not freaking out and running a mile."

"Lucky for you I already did three this morning." Honor winked and walked back into the kitchen leaving me with my chuckling dad.

"I'm gonna help the girls." My mom excused herself.

"I see it's starting to sink in," my dad said.

"Please don't start talking in riddles. I haven't even finished my first cup of coffee."

"Fine, I'll lay it out for you. That woman in there loves you and loves your daughter. Straight up, Ethan, she's not freaked out, she's not gonna run out on you and Carson, but she's looking to you for direction. So the question is, how are you gonna play it? Sit on the fence and twiddle your thumbs or are you going to claim it and fight to keep it?"

There was another knock at the door, and before I could get up Honor yelled out. "I'll get it."

Now was not a good time for someone to come to my door and try to sell me something. I didn't want to buy Girl Scout cookies, I didn't want to find God, and I didn't want to install solar panels. What I did want to do was figure out how I was going to have a very important conversation with my daughter and woman.

"Ethan. There's a woman at the door who would like to speak to you. She said her name is Christina," Honor told me and walked back into the kitchen.

"Did she ask for me or the homeowner?"

"You. Ethan Lenox."

Christina? I didn't know anyone named Christina.

With my irritation at an all-time high, I stomped to the door like a two-year-old, pouting. I opened the door and my irritation morphed into red-hot rage.

"What the fuck?"

I stepped onto the porch, closing the door behind me.

"That's the greeting I thought I'd receive," she said.

"What the hell are you doing here, Chrissy?"

"Wow. No one's called me that in a long time." Her lips tipped up in a tentative smile.

"Did you come all this way to talk about what people are calling you now?"

"I need to talk to you. May I come in?"

"Hell no. And there's nothing we need to talk about."

"There is, Ethan. We need to talk about our daughter."

Was she out of her fucking mind? I knew this day would come. I fucking knew it. It didn't matter that

Chrissy had signed away her parental rights, that she'd refused to hold or even look at Carson, I knew the day would come when she'd have a change of heart and show up. In actuality I was shocked it had taken this long.

"You mean, my daughter. The child you signed away your rights to," I reminded her.

"You don't need to be so cruel."

"Cruel? I'm not telling you anything you don't know. You were there, remember?"

"I was sixteen." Chrissy began to cry.

"So was I. Yet, I stepped up. I took responsibility for my child. I took her home by myself and learned how to be a parent, both her mom and dad. I stayed up nights with her. I've raised her. You chose to leave. It's been eight years. You're too late."

"You had your family. My parents told me they'd disown me, I wouldn't have had any help."

"Bullshit. I asked you to marry me. I offered you a way to keep her. You knew damn well my parents would've never turned their backs on us. We could've made it work. But that's not what you wanted."

The tiniest part of me felt bad for her. I couldn't imagine what she'd felt all these years, knowing she had a daughter she'd never know. That was one of the many reasons I couldn't have given Carson up for adoption. I wouldn't have been able to live knowing my daughter was out there somewhere.

"What do you want, Chrissy?"

"I want to see her." She was still crying, as a matter of fact, she looked like she'd been crying before I'd even opened the door.

"Why?"

"I just want to see what she looks like."

"And then what?"

"I'll go back to California."

The empathy I'd felt for her quickly dissipated. It wasn't bad enough she'd left Carson once, now she was willing to do it again. Only this time it would have lasting implications.

"Are you fucking serious? Anywhere in your thought process did you think about Carson? What it would mean for *her* if she saw *you*?"

"Of course. I thought she'd like to know who her mom is."

"Jesus H. Christ. Really? Never gonna happen, Chrissy, go home."

"I came all this way, and you won't let me see her? Why not?"

"The fact I have to explain this to you is the very reason I won't let you see her."

"Why are you being so unreasonable?"

I thought I was being perfectly reasonable. I was

standing outside having a conversation rather than just slamming the door in her face like I should've.

"Do you have children?"

"No."

"Right. I figured, because if you were a mother you wouldn't be standing on my porch on a Sunday morning asking if you can just see her then leave and go on your merry way without a care or concern what it would do to her after you left. The questions she'd have, the abandonment she'd feel, the hurt. No, if you were a mother, you'd understand how incredibly selfish you're being."

"I have a right to see her."

"No, you don't. You signed that away. And, had you started this conversation differently, I would've at least entertained the idea of you meeting Carson. But she's not an object you look at, ooh and ah over how pretty it is, and then set back on the shelf and leave it. Don't come back here, Chrissy, you won't like what happens next."

"Please!"

"I'm serious, Chrissy. Leave. Go back to your life and don't ever knock on my door again."

"I can't. I wonder about her. Is she okay? Is she happy? Does she miss me?"

I took a deep cleansing breath and looked at the woman in front of me. Christina was very different from the carefree Chrissy I'd been infatuated with. She was still a beautiful woman, but the brightness had dimmed. I didn't know from what and I didn't care enough to ask. There had been a time when I would've pulled her into my arms and comforted her. However, she'd killed any of those feelings when she shut me out after she told me she was pregnant. A little over eight-years ago I'd asked her to marry me and now I felt nothing for her.

I wondered if it would've gone differently if she'd knocked on my door before I'd met Honor. Would I have been more receptive to Chrissy showing up? Hell to the no, I would've been doing the same thing, telling her to pound the pavement and never darken my door again.

"She's happy. She's loved. She has a good life and a large, adoring family. She wants for nothing, emotionally or otherwise. That's all you need to know."

"If you change your mind, I'm staying a few days."

"I won't."

"But—"

"No buts. I told you everything I'm going to." Then I found myself repeating the last words I'd spoken to her in the delivery room. "Take care of yourself."

I didn't bother to wait for her response or for her to plead with me to see Carson. I walked back into the house and closed the door.

Not surprisingly, my dad was standing there waiting for me. His demeanor matching my own —furious.

"Did you hear?" I asked.

"Every word."

"Did the girls?" I prayed my dad had shielded them from knowing who was at the door.

"No. Pancakes are on the table. We'll talk after breakfast."

I'd like to say that walking into the dining room and seeing Carson and Honor already at the table smiling and happy soothed my anger, but it didn't. What had been a great source of joy for me had now changed into dread.

This was the beginning of the end. I could feel it, something was very wrong.

16

Lily was closely watching every move Ethan made. He'd barely eaten his breakfast and snapped at her when she'd asked if he was on nights this week, which earned him a warning growl from Lenox. Carson had chattered away throughout the meal but for the first time, Ethan wasn't paying attention to her. She'd even had to call his name and repeat her questions.

That was unheard of; Ethan was present. Always. Whoever had been at the door had shaken him. I wondered if it was an ex-girlfriend. She was beautiful, maybe he was now having seconds thoughts about us. Logically I knew she couldn't be an ex, he'd told me he hadn't dated since Carson was born, but some women saw sex as a relationship. Then there was the possibility he'd lied. I didn't know what the problem was, but the house felt stifling.

"He'll be fine," Lily whispered, rather unconvincingly.

"Who was at the door?" I asked, handing her the dish I'd washed so she could dry it and put it away.

She placed the plate in the cabinet before turning toward me, resting her hip against the counter. I should've known from the look that crossed her face it was going to be bad. However, I could never have guessed how bad.

"Chrissy."

"What?" The glass I'd been washing slipped from my hand, landing in the sink with a clatter. "*Chrissy Chrissy?*" I whispered.

"Yes."

This wasn't happening. Chrissy was worse than any made up girlfriend I'd pictured in my mind. Chrissy showing up was the worst possible thing that could have happened. Did she want Carson?

"Where's Carson?"

Before I could go in search of her, just to see with my own eyes she was in the house and fine, Lily stopped me.

"She's out back with Lenox and Ethan."

"Should they be outside? What if Chrissy tries to take her?"

"Chrissy may be a lot of things, what she isn't is

stupid enough to jump the fence and take on Ethan and his dad."

I was being silly, but fear had wound around my heart and was threatening to stop it from beating.

"You're right. I'm over reacting."

"No, you're reacting exactly how a mother who's protecting her child would."

"But I'm not her mom, Chrissy is."

Lily sighed and grabbed my hand, abandoning the cleanup. She led me to the couch and pulled me down beside her.

"I think you know how much you mean to our family. So it won't come as a shock to you that we are thrilled to have you in our lives—in Ethan and Carson's lives. I want you to remember that when I tell you this story. Neither Ethan nor Lenox know this, it's the only secret I've ever kept from my family." Lily checked over her shoulder before she started. "After Ethan told us Chrissy was pregnant and she wanted to give the baby up for adoption, I went to the Krier's house to talk to Chrissy and her mom. I told Chrissy if she wanted to keep the baby, Lenox and I would help them financially. Mrs. Krier had a fit. The woman was in hysterics, saying she wanted her daughter to go to college and a child would ruin her life. She was having no part of Chrissy and Ethan keeping the baby. She stormed out of the house leaving me alone with

Chrissy, who was really the person I wanted to talk to anyway. They may've been sixteen, but the decision was theirs, not the Krier's nor mine or Lenox's.

"After Chrissy calmed down, I asked her what she wanted. I told her flat out we would welcome her into our home if she wanted the baby. She admitted adoption was her choice. She was very adamant she didn't want to be a mom. She also confided in me, she didn't want children when she grew up either. She wanted to be a doctor and was very passionate about medicine. She is one, by the way. She was awarded a full scholarship and completed her undergrad in three years. She finished medical school and went on to do her residency in a research hospital. I don't know why she was here, but I don't think it's because she wants to take Carson."

"Ethan?"

"No. With Ethan comes Carson. This may not paint Ethan in a very good light, but he didn't love her. He thinks I don't know this, but Chrissy told me he asked her to marry him. I wanted to smack my son but at the same time I was proud he was trying to do what he thought ewas right. They could've raised Carson as friends, he didn't need to marry someone he didn't love."

"She said no," I told her something she obviously knew.

"She did, because she didn't want to be tied to him or the baby. Chrissy just wanted out."

I glanced out the window and saw Ethan and Lenox headed for the back door.

"Thank you for talking to me," I said, knowing our time was running out.

"Anytime, sweet girl, and we'll talk about what Carson asked when this latest shit storm blows over." I smiled at Lily's choice of words. It sounded like something Lenox would say. "But I have to know, is that something you want? To be Carson's mom."

"Very much, yes."

"That's what I thought." She patted my knee and stood. "Let me help you finish cleaning up before we head home."

We were entering the kitchen when the back door opened, and Carson came running to me.

"Are we gonna go to the park and take more pictures of the giant magnolias?" Carson asked.

"As soon as we're done—"

"Not today, Squirt. Something came up at work, and you're gonna go with Gran and Pop to their house."

"But, Daddy. Honor was going to let me take pictures today. Can't she watch me while you're at work. I always go to Gran and Pops."

"Not today. I'm sure Honor is busy later." Ethan

turned to me, and I was brought back to the day I'd met him in the park. The stare was the same, full protective mode and a whole lot pissed off.

"We'll do it another day, darlin', promise. But we have to follow daddy's rules, and he said today he wants you to go to Gran's house. We'll take pictures another day."

"Fine." Carson stomped off to the stairs.

I bit my tongue until she was out of sight, then, uncaring Ethan's parents were in the room, I let him have it.

"Don't you ever do that shit to me again," I seethed.

"What shit?" he shot back with the same irritation I'd given him.

"You know what you just did. I had plans with her today. You changed your mind about letting me take her to the park. Fine. You're her dad. But don't blame that on me and tell her I'm busy. I'm never too busy for her, and what you did was total bullshit."

"Bad move, son." Lenox added.

"It seems to me everyone has forgotten I'm her father."

Shit on a shingle, that hurt. It hurt so badly and so deeply, I couldn't stand to be in the same room with him.

"Don't worry, Ethan, I'll never forget that *you* are

her father. Lily, thanks for your help cleaning up. Lenox, it was nice seeing you."

I hightailed it to my room and gently shut the door as the first tear fell.

Screw him!

A little while later there was a knock on my door and I was debating whether to answer it when Ethan opened it.

Ass.

"I'm leaving. I don't know what time I'll be home, so don't bother waiting for us to eat. My parents are taking Carson to dinner."

Jerk.

"You have time to explain to me what's crawled up your ass?"

I wanted to kick him in the balls when he looked at me as if I was annoying him by asking.

"Nothing's crawled up my ass. I made a decision about where I wanted my daughter to go while I was at work and suddenly there's a problem with it."

"Seriously? The problem was you told your daughter I was too busy for her. How the hell do you think that makes her feel? Huh? Especially after what she asked about this morning."

"So, that's what this is about? I'll be talking to Carson about that tonight."

"And what are you going to tell her?"

"The truth. I'm her dad. And I'm not ready to entertain the idea of anyone being her mom."

"Entertain? You're unbelievable."

"Listen, Honor, this is moving way too fast. We need to dial it back and slow down."

The tears that had stopped were now welling up again. My whole life I'd sucked at hiding my emotions and anger was the worst.

"Why?"

"We just need to slow down. I'm not ready for this. Everything is moving too fast. I was wrong, I can't do this."

"This? You can't do this? You mean you and me? You were worried about me leaving you and now you're the one running."

"I'm not doing anything but saying we need to slow down."

"Why was Chrissy here?" I changed the subject.

"It's not important."

"I think it is. Everything was great until she showed up. No secrets remember?"

"That's rich coming from you, don't you think?"

Dick.

"Have a good shift, Ethan. Be safe."

I laid back down and gave him my back, effectively ending the conversation. Nothing good was going to come from us talking anymore. He was . . . whatever he was, and I was hurt. If we moved forward one day, I may regret my next words no matter how good they'd feel to say at that moment.

"See you tomorrow."

Ouch!

He closed my door, and I heard him leave.

I didn't see Carson or Ethan that evening. Instead I went to bed alone in the house, devastated, and completely heart-broken.

17

"You've got a bad attitude tonight," Lorenz told me.

We'd had a shit shift. One call after another had come in, and we'd skipped taking a dinner break when a disturbing the peace call came through. The guy was a jackass. All he had to do was turn down the music. Instead he wanted to give attitude, which made me think of Honor, and that pissed me the fuck off. Over the last eight hours she was never far from my thoughts, and that pissed me off, too. I should've been thinking about Chrissy and what her surprise appearance meant for Carson. But, instead, I was more concerned with what I'd said to Honor and the look of anguish I'd caused. Fuck, I was an asshole. Even knowing I'd been a dick, I couldn't bring myself to call her and apologize.

"Me? He kicked the fucking speaker at me."

"Don't you think you're exaggerating a bit? He didn't kick it at you, he kicked it, and it happened to land near you. You turned a desk appearance into an arrest."

"Whatever. He kicked the fucking speaker. He should've turned it down when we asked."

"Christ, what's twisted your nipples tonight? Trouble in paradise?"

"Funny."

"Nothing's funny from where I'm standing. Something happen with Carson?"

Lorenz was a good friend, always looking out for Carson and me. He was a father, he'd understand.

"Carson asked if Honor was going to be her mom."

"And? That's got you jamming some poor guy up on resisting arrest when he didn't turn his radio down fast enough? Not tracking, friend."

"Then not even two-fucking-minutes later Chrissy Krier shows up at my house. Asking if she could see Carson. Just see her. Not be a part of her life. Not spend time with her. No visitation. She wanted to see her then bolt her ass back to wherever she lives."

"You're shitting me? Tell me you're fucking shitting me."

"Wish I were."

"What'd you tell her?"

"Who Carson or Chrissy?"

"The bitch," he replied.

"Told her to beat rocks and never come back."

"You think she'll listen?"

Lorenz had asked the million-dollar question. My deepest fear was Chrissy would come back and upend my daughter's life.

"Got me."

"What did Honor say?"

"About Chrissy?"

"Jesus. Yes, about Chrissy showing up."

"Didn't talk to her about it."

"Come again?" He rocked back on his heels and gave me a dirty look. "Let me see if I understand this. Honor's been in your house two months—give or take. You've been sleeping with her nearly that long, you're in love with her, and your daughter is close to her. Close enough, she's asking if Honor's gonna be her mom. The woman who donated her eggs in the creation of your child shows up at your house, and you didn't talk to Honor about it?"

"Nope."

"What the fuck is wrong with you?"

"Not a damn thing. I need to wrap my head around what's going on before I talk to anyone. Besides, I told Honor we need to slow this shit down. Things are moving too fast, Carson could get hurt."

"This shit," he spit out. "You mean, Carson or you?"

Both. Me. Fuck. I didn't know how to answer that.

"Hell if I know."

"You have a thirty-minute drive home. I suggest you figure this shit out. And by that, I mean, pull your head out of your ass. I'm dog tired and goin' home. Let me know if you need any help getting Chrissy gone."

"Thanks."

Ten minutes later I was heading out the back door and found my dad leaning against the side of my Tahoe, like I was a teenager needing a ride home.

What the fuck?

"Dad," I greeted when I made it to my car.

"We need to talk."

"Can it wait? I just had my ass handed to me by Lorenz, and my shift sucked. I just wanna go get Carson and go home."

"I never took you as a quitter."

Guess we were talking about this now.

"I'm not quitting anything."

"Right. If I were a betting man, I'd put my house up that today, after we left, you ended things with Honor or something just as stupid."

"Good thing you don't bet then, because you would've lost your house." My dad held my gaze, not believing me. "I didn't end things. I told her we needed to slow down. Carson's getting too attached, and I have to figure out what Chrissy's up to."

"Right, that falls into the "something equally as stupid" category. I see you've found your shield."

"I'm not fucking hiding. Carson is—"

"Just fine. Happy. Healthy. Thriving. She loves Honor. What more do you want?"

"That's just it. She loves Honor. What if something happens, and she bolts?"

"Then you fucking fight to make her stay."

Why the hell was everyone on my case? Couldn't they see I was trying to do what was best for my child? I thought my parents would be happy I was being responsible and putting my daughter's needs before my own. I was right.

"It's not that simple, Dad."

"It is. Besides, she's not bolting–you are."

"I couldn't even make the girl who was carrying my child stay. There was supposed to be some sort of bond between us. Fuck!" I pulled at my hair until pain radiated over my scalp. "Goddamn it. We love her. If she leaves us, we'll break. Both of us. Chrissy showing up today reminded me I fucking failed. I couldn't even give my kid the one thing all children should have—a mom."

"Honor is not Chrissy."

"I know that. She's more. She's the woman I could

love for the rest of my life. She's the mom I want Carson to have. She's my bone-deep, I know it. But if she doesn't feel the same way, Carson will be crushed, it will rip my heart out, and I won't survive."

"It's called trust, Ethan. You need to learn to trust her."

"I do."

"No you don't, not the way you should. I trust your mother with my life. I trust that she'll never leave me. Love is a choice, son. I wake up every morning and I choose to love your mom. And every night when we go to bed, I choose her again. The thought of her not being there doesn't cross my mind; it's an impossibility."

"I need time."

"No, you don't. The longer this festers the worse it will be, the deeper the hurt, the harder to fix. I didn't drag my ass all the way across town and stand outside for an hour because it can wait. Honor Sullivan will love you and Carson until her dying breath if you let her."

"How do you know?"

"Because I see it in all the little things she does. I see how she searches you out. How she watches Carson. I see how she's always got her finger on the pulse of her family. The girl is as see-through as they come."

"Appreciate you taking the time to come down here. I'll think about what you said."

"Ethan—"

"Dad. I'll think about it. Thank you for always having my back, but I have to work this out for myself. I need to think."

"Fair enough." My dad clapped me on the shoulder and made his way to his truck.

I had thirty minutes to think about what my dad and Lorenz had said before I had to face my mom. On the drive over, I'd tried to devise a plan where my dad brought Carson out of the house for me, so I could hide like a pussy. My mom had no issue giving me the hot side of her tongue if I pissed her off, and her guilt-trips were second to none. I'd told my dad I'd think about what he'd told me, but the truth was, I didn't want to think about anything. I wanted to go home, fall into bed, and stop thinking altogether. Everything was a mess. If I tried to sort it out tonight, I'd get nowhere.

All too soon I pulled into my parents' driveway. My dad met me at my truck, and we walked in together. My mom's eyes came to mine, and she brought her finger to her mouth shushing me. Carson was asleep on the couch next to her. Perfect. That meant we couldn't talk.

I picked Carson up and when my mom stood I kissed her cheek.

"Thanks, Mom."

She reached up stroked the side of my face.

"I hope you know how much I love you, Ethan. I want nothing but happiness for you," she whispered.

"I do, Mama."

"Then you'll know how much it pains me to say this, to my baby boy—you're an ass. Let Honor in. And don't let Chrissy steal the rest of your life. There was nothing you could've done to change her mind. She didn't want my beautiful granddaughter then, and she doesn't want her now. Do you know anything about her? Ever looked her up?"

I assumed my mom was talking about Chrissy, so I answered in the negative. I'd never been curious enough to do an internet search.

"She didn't stop living, Ethan. She's a doctor and doing well for herself."

"Why are you telling me this?" I couldn't give a rat's fucking ass how well Chrissy was doing.

"When are you going to start living yours? You had a child, you weren't sentenced to a life without love and happiness. Go home and make things right with Honor."

Despite my mom's harsh words her hand had never stopped gently rubbing my face. Where my dad could pin me with a hard stare, my mom's eyes always softened when she delivered her lectures.

"I appreciate your concern, but I have to figure this out on my own, and like I told Dad and Lorenz, I need time to do that."

"Don't take too long. I can tell you from personal experience the longer the separation stretches the harder it is to mend the hurt. Often, time is the last thing you need. Seconds and minutes turn into hours, hours into days, and next thing you know days have become weeks. Time is a funny thing, Ethan. It passes you by whether you want it to or not. While you're thinking, time is wasting. Hours can be filled with the most precious and treasured memories, or the loneliest void. Please remember while you're thinking, so is she. And her thoughts will turn into insecurity and doubt. And you'll have done that to her."

My mom removed her hand from my cheek and stepped back. After a quick goodbye I put Carson in the truck and headed home. I couldn't stop thinking about what my mom had said about Chrissy. The petty, juvenile part of me was jealous she'd gone on with her life. She didn't have a care in the world. Chrissy hadn't put her life on hold for her child. She'd graduated high school with her friends and had gone to college—medical school even; she was a doctor now. She'd accomplished what she'd told me she wanted to. During one of the many post-sex talks we'd had as we'd lain on a blanket in the back of my truck, looking up at the stars, she'd told me all about her dreams. Neither one of us was under the illusion we'd be together for the long haul. Not like some high school kids who swore they were in love and would be together forever. She wanted to go off to college, and I was going to join the Army. We'd known our paths would be very different and would never cross again. Then the condom broke, and we were forever connected. How different my life would be if I'd never asked Chrissy out.

The normal guilt hit my chest anytime I thought about what my life would've been like if I didn't have Carson. I didn't regret a moment of having my daughter. I never felt like I'd given up my dreams for her, I didn't give up anything, my aspirations simply changed. Everything changed. The Army was no longer important—being a good dad was. Partying, hanging out with my friends, sports, and graduating on a stage . . . none of it could compare to Carson. Rounding the plate after hitting a home run used to be the best rush in the world. The excitement of the crowd. The cheers. My teammates' and coaches' praise. But none of that held a candle to what I felt when Carson smiled at me for the first time, or when she took her first steps, or hearing her jumbled da-da. I didn't give anything up, I'd gained the world.

Why didn't Chrissy feel the same way? For eight

years the question had plagued me. Was it me she hadn't wanted a child with? Did I do or say the wrong thing? Was I not good enough? Carson? What was it that made Chrissy leave us?

By the time I pulled into my garage and cut the engine, I was no closer to the answers I desperately needed.

The biggest one being—why in the fuck had I pulled away from Honor and why had I lied to everyone telling them I needed time?

I didn't need time, I knew what I wanted. I was just too scared to go after it.

18

I hadn't seen Carson or Ethan at all yesterday. Since Ethan was on nights, he slept all day while Carson was at school. What pissed me off the most was Ethan had devised a plan to avoid me. I'd left for my morning run and even though I was home ten minutes before Ethan needed to leave to take Carson to school, they were gone. Then he must've slipped back into the house while I was in the shower, slept all day, then waited for me to leave to go to the grocery store and bolted before I was back.

To say I was angry was an understatement.

This morning I'd skipped my run and had had my ass planted at the table with my laptop and coffee when he came down. He was fully dressed and looked like he'd planned on giving me the slip again. His mumbled good morning was awkward and forced. It was obvious he didn't even want to share the same space as me.

Some would say my reaction to Ethan's silent treatment was a little over the top, but I was mad and hurt and my least favorite feeling was that of being unwanted. So when he tried to beat a hasty retreat and take his coffee back to his room, I told him we needed to talk. I wasn't sure what I was going to say, but, in my mind, it'd played out much differently than it had.

Ethan had stood at the bottom of the stairs and made no attempt to come sit next to me. His gaze was faraway and uncomfortable. I hated he felt that way. With each passing second, I watched his look of unease grow. It was then I came to decision.

"Maybe it would be best if I looked for a new place to live."

"What?" He recoiled but still made no move to come closer.

"You said you wanted to slow things down. I don't think we can do that while I'm living here."

I waited for him to argue, say something, anything that would give me some sort of indication he wanted me to stay. But he didn't. He stood his ground, one hand white knuckling his coffee cup, the other in a tight fist by his side. He gave me nothing.

"I don't want you to have to tiptoe around your own house to avoid me."

"I'm not avoiding you," he denied.

"Sure you are. I won't pretend it doesn't hurt, because it does. I'll start looking for something this afternoon. I don't want to lose you, Ethan. Or Carson. But I can't live here in silence. I'll move out, you think, and when you're ready we'll see where we go from there."

"I don't want—"

Ethan was cut off when Carson came running down the stairs and beelined it straight to me. She jumped in my lap and told me all about the day I'd missed and what she'd done. I hadn't gotten up like I'd been doing and making her breakfast, instead Ethan set a bowl of cold cereal in front of her, and she talked around spoonfuls until it was time for her to go to school.

That's when Ethan had made his promise, one I bet he wished he hadn't. A promise he'd made to get Carson out the door to school. She hadn't wanted to go to his parents' house after school today, she'd wanted to come home and stay with me while Ethan was at work. The more he told her no, the more upset she got, until he gave in.

I STOOD off to the side watching Ethan and Carson argue. He was standing by the door in his uniform, trying to get Carson to go to his parents' house. Carson wasn't having it. Ethan had made a promise, and she wasn't letting him renege. We still hadn't finished our conversation from this morning. After he'd taken Carson to school, I took my laptop into my room to work. I waited, but he never knocked. He hadn't made the effort. As the day progressed it felt like the knife in my heart was twisting with each hour that passed.

"Daddy. You promised," Carson whined.

"Hey, maybe we can do a movie night some other night?" I tried to help Ethan, even though I was seriously angry he was trying to keep Carson from me after he'd promised her just this morning she could stay with me.

"But Daddy made a promise. Pop says, a man never breaks his promise."

Carson, wise beyond her years, had a very good point. However, Ethan seemed to be breaking a lot of promises lately. His attention turned to me, and he still didn't have the balls to open his mouth and ask me if I was okay with Carson staying with me. He let his expressive, green eyes ask for him.

I, however, wasn't acting like a prick, so I answered, using words, like a grown-up.

"It's fine, Ethan. Go to work. I'll help Carson with

homework then we'll watch a movie. Don't worry, she'll be in bed on time."

"Yippy. Can we make tacos again tonight?" Carson asked.

"Sure, darlin' we can make whatever you want."

Ethan said goodbye to Carson and offered nothing more than a lift of his chin to me before he walked out the door.

"Daddy's being grumpy," Carson complained.

"I think Daddy is grumpy because he doesn't like working nights. He likes being home, so he can eat dinner with you and tuck you in. So he gets grouchy when he can't do it."

"But if you're my mommy, he doesn't always have to do it. Mommy's tuck their kids into bed and read stories. McKenna's mommy tucked us in when she had a sleepover."

God, I hated Ethan. Not really, I was madly in love with the stupid jerk, that was why I hated him so much right then. Two days ago, I was thrilled Carson wanted me to be her mom. I thought that meant the relationship Ethan and I had been building was solid. I had Carson's seal of approval; we could continue. A day that was supposed to be happy and always remembered, I just wanted to forget. But I couldn't. Ethan's words played on repeat, overshadowing Carson's question.

Slow down.

Not ready for anyone to be her mom.

His words still hurt days later. I desperately wanted him to talk to me. Open up, trust me, something—anything. But he'd shut down. I wanted him to fight for us. Give me something so I could stay and fight, however, the statement about me moving out had been made and now it hung between us. He was probably relieved. I knew once I moved out, that would be it. He'd never try and work things out.

The worst part was, I had no idea what had happened. What had changed his mind? He offered me nothing by way of explanation. The only thing I was left with was assumption and everything pointed to Chrissy having said something to upset Ethan.

Thankfully, Carson was easily distracted, and I used it to my advantage, offering her a snack and told her we could eat at the coffee table and watch the movie if she finished her homework in time. I wasn't sure if Ethan had talked to Carson about her asking if I could be her mom or if he'd blown her off too. I knew nothing because he wasn't talking to me.

I got Carson a snack and we finished her homework. We were getting everything ready to start making tacos when I realized we didn't have any tortillas to make the shells.

"We gotta run to the grocery store, darlin'."

"Will we still have time to watch our movie?"

"We sure will. And we'll even grab a tub of ice cream and share it for dessert."

"Yippy. I'll get my shoes."

Carson took off then met me at the door. Her excitement was contagious, and I found myself smiling at her, despite my foul mood.

Damn Ethan!

I buckled Carson in and headed toward the grocery store. She was telling me a story from the backseat, one I'm ashamed to say I didn't hear. I was torn. On one hand I wanted to stay and demand Ethan open up to me. However, I couldn't deny I deserved better than a man who would close me out and break promises. I'd grown up with a father who'd promised year after year he'd be home more, be more involved, yet each year there was another excuse why that didn't happen. Promises made, promises broken. Each time my dad walked out the door, I watched my mom lose a part of herself. I would never lose myself like that, no matter how much I loved Ethan and Carson.

I was worth the fight, and if he wanted me, he'd have to chase me.

"I'll drive today." Lorenz swiped the keys to the squad car out of my hands. "I'm shocked I lived after last night's driving."

I rolled my eyes at his exaggeration. "Whatever."

"You get shit worked out with Honor today?" he asked once he had me trapped in a moving vehicle where I couldn't avoid his question like I'd done when he'd bombarded me earlier.

"Barely saw her today. By the time I dropped Carson off at school and came home she was working in her room."

"Did you knock?"

"What?" I shifted my gaze from the red light in front of the car to my partner.

"Jesus, Ethan. Did you knock on her door? Tell her you wanted to talk to her?"

"No . . . she . . . um . . ." Fuck, now I was stuttering. I couldn't even get myself to say the words out loud.

I knew I'd fucked up and hurt Honor, but I didn't think she'd want to move out. Once she'd suggested it, I was too angry to speak. Then when I'd found my voice, Carson came downstairs for breakfast. I couldn't believe she wanted to bail. And the worst part was I'd done it to myself. Both my mom and dad had tried to warn me not to wait, to talk to her immediately, but I didn't fucking listen.

After I'd lain awake tossing and turning after my last shift, I knew I needed to talk to her. I'd actually gone downstairs once to wake her up, but it was barely six a.m. and I figured I'd let her sleep an extra hour and catch her when she got home from her run. Only she surprised the hell out of me by changing up her morning routine and was sitting at the kitchen table when I'd gone downstairs for coffee. She looked so fucking beautiful, but the sadness in her eyes was like a shot in the chest.

I was going to go wake up Carson and come right back to talk to her when she dropped the bomb she wanted to move out. Then shit went downhill. Instead of telling her she wasn't going anywhere and explaining why I'd behaved like an ass, I stood there trying to get my anger in check. The longer I'd stood there, unbelieving what I was hearing, the more she mistook my silence for acceptance. I didn't fucking accept anything. Then Carson came downstairs and essentially ended any discussion we were going to have. After I got home from dropping my daughter off at school Honor had already locked herself in her room to work, or pack, or whatever the fuck she was doing. I was too pissed to knock and find out. I thought I'd done the right thing by calming down before I spoke to her. I'd already hurt her, I didn't want to say something else I'd regret. The day wore on and instead of getting my shit together I got more and more angry. How could she want to leave? *Because I was a dick, that's why.*

"She what?" Lorenz asked, pulling me from my memories.

"Said she wanted to move out," I told him.

"I thought things were going well."

"They were—until Chrissy showed up. Man, just seeing her sent me spiraling into my worst fear. I said some shit to Honor I regret."

"And you still haven't apologized or talked to her," he surmised and shook his head in disgust. At least that's what I assumed it was, considering I felt the same way about my behavior.

When the fuck did I turn into such a coward?

"I told you, I needed a minute to get my shit together before I talked to her."

"Right. And I told you, not to delay apologizing to

your woman. Now she thinks you don't want her there and is going to give you space to sort your shit. Am I right?" I grunted my confirmation, and he continued. "So, you gonna let her move out?"

"Fuck no. But I have to tell you, her wanting to run away at the first sign of trouble doesn't give me a warm and fuzzy feeling. We're gonna talk about that too."

"Yeah, I'd tread lightly about that, friend. You did this to her. You made her feel unwanted. I know you, when you freeze someone out, you freeze them the fuck out. I've never known anyone who can shut down like you. You don't burn when you're angry, you go arctic. A relationship can weather an argument, what it can't is silence."

"One-Palmer-One, what's your twenty?" The radio transmission cut off my retort.

"One-Palmer-One to dispatch, we're northbound on Everson, passing 3rd Street," I called back with our location.

"One-Palmer-One continue northbound to 7th. Single vehicle collision. Possible fatality. EMS and fire are en route."

"One-Palmer-One. Copy."

Lorenz hit the lights and sirens and increased his speed, veering around cars that had begun to slow.

"Move to the right, fuckers, don't stop in the middle of the damn road," he grouched.

"Shitty way to start a shift," I commented.

No one liked reporting to an accident scene where there were injuries or fatalities, but nothing set the tone of a tour when it was the first call of the night.

Ladder 61 was already on scene when Lorenz came to a stop behind the truck. The large rig was blocking the accident itself, and looky-loos had already gathered around.

"I'll take crowd control," Lorenz said when he put the squad car in park.

I rounded the fire truck and cringed. A white Honda Accord had jumped the curb and collided head-on with a traffic light pole. The front of the car was a mangled mess of crunched metal. The left bumper was smashed as well. I was looking for a possible second vehicle when I heard a woman screaming. That wasn't unusual for an accident scene, however, I thought I'd heard my name.

"Someone needs to call Officer Ethan Lenox, right goddamn now," she yelled again.

My attention went back to the white car and my heart dropped to my stomach, and I took off in a sprint. Honor drove a white Honda Accord. I tried to tell myself it was impossible, Honor was home, safe and sound, with Carson. They were going to watch a movie and make tacos. Carson! Fuck.

I skidded to a halt in front of the car, and my eyes

shifted from the driver to the small passenger in the backseat. I blinked and tried again, praying I was hallucinating.

Honor.

Carson.

I used to think my worst fear was Chrissy coming into Carson's life and turning everything upside down. I'd been very wrong. Seeing Honor's car smashed in front of me and not knowing if the two people I loved most in this world were hurt or worse was far scarier. The feeling was indescribable; it went beyond fear.

"I need that collar now. We have to move her."

What in the actual fuck? Why was Chrissy barking orders to the EMS squad? Why in the hell was she here to begin with?

"Ethan. Thank God. Carson is fine. Minor contusion on her forehead. She's alert and responsive. I've advised EMS to leave her buckled in until I can look her over better."

"Daddy!" Carson screamed, and my confusion immediately drained away. Thank God she was talking.

"Hi, baby, are you okay?" I asked, going for the buckle I desperately needed my daughter in my arms.

"Don't move her, Ethan," Chrissy barked. "Let me finish with Honor and then I'll check her again."

Who the fuck did this woman think she was, telling me what to do with my daughter?

"Please, Ethan," she begged. The desperation in her tone stopped me from scooping Carson up and holding her the way I wanted. Instead I grabbed both of her tiny hands in mine and squeezed.

"I'm scared, Daddy."

"I know you are, Squirt. Are you okay?" I asked again.

"I think so."

"How's Honor?" I asked Chrissy.

"She's in shock. Elevated heart rate. Decreased breath sounds on her right side." Two more paramedics ran over with a board and collar, stopping her from continuing.

"Miss, you need to move."

Chrissy ignored the EMT's order and continued.

"I'm Doctor Christina Krier, my ID is in my bag. Shallow, rapid breaths. Asymmetrical chest movement. Heart rate elevated. She needs to be transported now. Give me the collar."

"What does that mean?" I asked, not letting go of Carson's hand.

No one answered as they worked. What the hell was going on with Honor? Before I could ask again Chrissy moved from the front of the car and ripped off blood covered gloves tossing them on the pavement as she moved toward me. Fuck. The front of her shirt was covered in blood too.

"Let me check Carson over so you both can ride with Honor."

"I'll be right here, Squirt." I let go of Carson's hands and stepped back.

Chrissy took my place in front of Carson, and worry superseded any anger I felt because Chrissy was touching my daughter.

"How you feeling, sweetie? Does your head hurt or your tummy?" Chrissy asked and flashed a pen light in Carson's eyes before she used her fingers to press around Carson's neck and throat.

"Nothing hurts," Carson answered.

Chrissy's hand moved over every part of Carson before she stepped back and looked at me.

"You can take her out. She'll need to be checked over in the ER, but there are no signs of trauma. She's extremely lucky."

I wanted to yell at Chrissy for telling me Carson needed to be checked over by a doctor, as if I were some sort of idiot who wouldn't know a visit to the ER was necessary. Instead, relief mixed with fear about Honor, and I remained quiet while I removed Carson from the backseat.

"How's Honor?" I asked Chrissy again.

"She's critical."

"Critical? What's wrong?"

"Her right lung has collapsed and—"

"Will she be okay?" I cut her off.

Chrissy didn't answer, she didn't have to, the anguish that marred her face told me everything I needed to know.

"We need to move, Doctor," the EMT said and locked the stretcher in an upright position, giving me my first look at Honor.

"Jesus Christ." I turned and held Carson's face close to my chest uncaring my radio was probably digging into her cheek. It was better than her seeing Honor.

Blood covered her face and ran down, disappearing under the neck brace she was wearing. The stretcher was moving, but not before I noticed the huge gash on her forehead the EMT was dressing as they ran to the waiting ambulance.

"Head wounds bleed a lot, Ethan. The laceration looks worse than it is."

Laceration. Head wound. Collapsed lung. Please God don't take her for me.

"We're emoving," a man yelled as he loaded Honor in the back of the rig.

I took off in a jog, hoping I wasn't hurting Carson in the process, but there was no way I wasn't going with Honor.

"Officer," the paramedic stopped me.

"She's my fiancée. We're coming."

I didn't give the first fuck I'd lied, there was no way Honor was leaving my sight. I still didn't have answers, and, as badly as I wanted them, nothing mattered but Honor being okay. After the stretcher was locked in place, he helped me into the back and pointed to where I needed to sit.

"Carson, baby, keep your eyes closed."

"I'm scared. Is Honor okay?"

"She will be, Squirt."

"Promise?"

"Promise."

The doors slammed shut, causing me to jolt, and I hoped like hell I hadn't just made a promise to my daughter I couldn't keep.

Chrissy had a stethoscope pressed to Honor's side, below her armpit, her eyes were closed. I still had no idea how the fuck Chrissy happened to come upon the accident. Just when I was going to ask, all hell broke loose.

"Undo her collar," Chrissy demanded. The EMT finished taping the IV he'd inserted and opened the brace exposing Honor's throat and neck.

"The trachea is deviated to the left," Chrissy said as her fingers palpated Honor's throat.

"What's happening?" I asked.

"I need a decompression needle. Give me a ten-gauge cath." Chrissy cut open Honor's shirt and glanced around the surrounding supplies before she found the bottle she was looking for and squirted a brown liquid over the right side of her chest. The paramedic ripped open the packaging and handed Chrissy a long-ass needle.

What the fuck was that for?

"Call it in," Chrissy instructed.

"Calling County General. This is MediStar Bravo-Two-Zero-Seven."

"Country General, go ahead please."

"County, we have a priority trauma. Female patient, mid-twenties. Motor vehicle accident, air bags deployed. Absent breath sounds on the right. Tracheal deviation. Multiple injuries to head, face, left leg below the knee. Possible dislocation of the ankle. Heart rate is . . ."

I stopped paying attention to the paramedic and shifted all my attention to Chrissy.

"What are you doing?" I asked.

Chrissy didn't stop poking around Honor's collarbone and with the most compassion I'd ever heard from her she began to explain.

"Honor's right lung has collapsed. Air is collecting in the chest cavity causing pressure to build. Once that happens it causes the right lung to shift left, leaving no room for the lung to fully expand. Her heart is also being compressed and is under stress. I need to relieve the pressure and expand the lung before she dies."

Dies? Oh, Fuck. I squeezed Carson tighter, and tried to keep my panic at bay. This could not be happening.

"In," Chrissy called out. "I have air. Give me a chest tube."

"Heart rhythm lowering."

"ETA less than two minutes. Prepare to unload," the driver yelled.

"Ethan, when we stop. Stay where you are. Let the doctors take care of her."

"I'm going with her," I argued.

"The doctors need to concentrate on her. Let them work. We'll get Carson checked out, and when there's news someone will find you."

"There's no we," I seethed.

Chrissy held up her hands in a defensive manner, and I felt like a dick. She'd saved Honor's life, or at the very least bought her more time until she made it to the hospital. I shouldn't have barked at her, but my head was spinning, and my heart felt like it was no longer beating in my own chest, Honor held it in her hands. If she didn't make it, it would never beat again.

The back doors where flung open and Honor was pulled out. A flurry of medical professionals surrounded her stretcher and she disappeared through the doors.

Chrissy followed Honor into a cubicle, and I remembered I'd forgotten to tell Honor something. I quickly got out of the ambulance and chased after them with Carson still in my arms. I ignored the shouts of the nurses that tried to stop me until I made it to the space they'd taken Honor to.

"Sir, step back," a doctor said.

"I have to tell her something."

"It will have to wait," she replied.

"Let him through. This is his fiancée," Chrissy told them.

"You have one second," the older woman told me.

I didn't delay rushing to Honor's side.

"We love you so much. We'll be right here waiting for you to wake up, smalls. Fight, Honor. You hear me? Fight for us, baby. I'm so sorry. Please come back to us."

"You need to move, sir."

I moved out of the way and prayed.

Please, God, bring Honor back to us.

20

Carson had been checked out and had received a clean bill of health. She had a bump on her forehead that was most likely caused by her hitting herself when she'd tried to cover her face. No cuts, breaks, or any other injury. Chrissy had been right, it was a miracle Carson hadn't been hurt.

Honor hadn't been so lucky; she was in surgery to stop the internal bleeding.

"She's gonna be okay, son." My dad said, joining me at the window.

I'd been staring out into the parking lot, thinking over the last few days. All the words I hadn't said, the ones I had. The last time I'd kissed her, and all the missed opportunities since then.

Why the fuck had I been such an idiot? I should've talked to her. I never should've shut her out. Two days

I'll never get back. Two whole days I'd missed being with her, laughing with her, loving her. Two days since I'd seen her smile. Over what? Nothing, none of it was important.

Not only did I miss those days, but Carson had too. That made me an even bigger dick. *Please God do not let the last words I ever speak to Honor be in anger. Please don't let her die.*

"I can't lose her. We can't," I amended. "She has to be okay."

"She will be."

My parents, as well as my aunts and uncles, had been waiting with me in the sixth-floor surgical family room, hoping for good news soon. It had been hours since a doctor had been in to give us an update. I was getting ready to lose my fucking mind when the door finally opened, and Chrissy walked in. She'd changed out of her bloody clothes and now had on a pair of hospital scrubs, reminding me her life had indeed gone on. After she'd left Carson and me, she'd continued to chase her dreams. She was a doctor.

"Has the nurse been in?" she asked shyly from the doorway.

"No," I clipped not caring if I sounded like a dick.

"I'll take Carson out into the hall so you all can talk," my mom said, picking a sleeping Carson up.

It wasn't lost on me when my aunts stood and

flanked my mom, forcing Chrissy to move or be trampled.

Once my Aunt Emily closed the door, Chrissy began to speak. "She's out of surgery. It went well." Relief washed over me. And I had to close my eyes to keep the tears from falling. "Honor had a spleen laceration. The doctor preformed a splenectomy and was able to stop the internal bleeding. Luckily, the tension pneumothorax was caught and didn't cause any further issues. Her CT scan came back normal, the airbag did its job and prevented any serious head trauma. I'm sure the doctor will be in soon to go over all the details and what her recovery is going to look like."

Chrissy turned to leave, but I stopped her.

"What were you doing there?"

Over the last few hours reports had come in about the hit-and-run accident that'd caused Honor to hit the pole. But like any eyewitness accounts, they varied. It was rare any two observers reported the same details. Lorenz and my captain had been by to check on Honor and Carson and to tell me they were tracking every lead. Unfortunately, the intersection was not equipped with a traffic camera, so they had to rely on the bystanders' statements—and there were a lot of them. But the one person no one had interviewed yet was Christina Krier.

"I just wanted to see her," Chrissy said, lowering her head.

"What the fuck? Did you run her off the road?"

"No!" Chrissy shouted. "I would never hurt Carson."

"What about Honor? Would you hurt her?"

"I didn't run her off the road. I was following her."

My dad's hand landed on my shoulder, stopping my forward movement.

"Why the fuck were you following my woman and my daughter?"

"I was . . ."

"You were what, Chrissy? Doing exactly what I told you not to do?" It was becoming increasingly harder to exercise self-control.

"I wasn't going to talk to them. I promise."

"Son," my dad warned.

"What?" I snapped.

"Calm down."

"Calm down? My woman almost died with Carson in the car. I can't calm down." I really wanted to tell my daughter's human incubator to fuck off but there was one small detail I couldn't over look, she'd save Honor's life. "Did you see the accident happen?"

"Yes."

"Well . . ." I motioned for her to continue.

"Chrissy, why don't you sit down," my Uncle Jasper offered.

"Thank you, but I'd like to stand."

I bet she would. It'd be easier to run if she got uncomfortable. God knows she was good at that.

"We were coming up on the intersection and the car between Honor and me started to slow. Then, suddenly, when she was about halfway through, the person slammed on the gas and accelerated. They hit the back, left bumper. Her car went straight into the pole. There was no time for her to stop. The car that hit her swerved but regained control and sped off. They never slowed or stopped."

"Do you think it was on purpose?" My dad asked.

"Absolutely."

"Fuck," I roared.

"Anyone come to mind?" my Uncle Clark asked.

"Any threats lately?" Uncle Levi added.

"Yeah. Two, actually," I told them, then turned to Chrissy. "Did you get a make and model of the car?"

"Yes. And a partial plate. I'm sorry I didn't memorize it all, but I was more worried about Carson. And Honor," she quickly added.

What the hell was I supposed to do now? Someone tried to kill Honor and Carson. Chrissy was still breathing the same air as me. The person who'd hurt

Honor was at large. And I wanted to kill someone with my bare hands.

"Lock it down, Ethan." Jasper's gaze pinned me in place. "You have to keep your head straight. Honor will be in recovery soon and she'll need you. Carson is going to be looking to you about how to react. Give Lorenz the information and let him pass it along. You're needed here."

It amazed me my uncle could read me so well. He knew I was struggling about what to do with the information Chrissy had provided. I wanted to be the one to nail the son of a bitch that had run Honor off the road. But he was right, Honor and Carson needed me.

"I'm going to leave. Would it be okay if I came back to check on Honor before I fly back to California?" Chrissy asked. Now, what the fuck was I supposed to say to that? My first reaction was fuck no, I didn't want her anywhere near us. But I was torn. It all came back to Chrissy having saved Honor. "You don't have to answer now. I'll leave my number at the nurse's station. I'll come by when Carson's not here, if it's okay with you and Honor."

She started for the door and guilt slammed into my chest. As much as I wanted to let her walk out the door and never see her again, I couldn't. I wanted to, really, really wanted to but . . . there was always a but wasn't there?

"Let me talk to Honor and see what she says."

"Thanks."

"Thank you for . . ." I choked back the emotion, not wanting to lose it in front of her.

"No need. I'll write everything down for you and leave it with the nurse."

"You saved her life, Chrissy. There is a need. If you hadn't been there, I doubt she would've made it to the hospital alive. Listen," I paused and did something I never imagined myself doing, giving Chrissy what she wanted. "Before you leave would you like to sit and talk to Carson for a while?" Fuck, it pained me to offer, but I was stuck. If she hadn't been there, I would've lost Honor. I was trapped in a shit sandwich. I'd have a lot to explain to Carson, but I'd rather that than being plagued by guilt for the rest of my life.

"No." Chrissy didn't try to hide her tears, she let them flow freely down her cheeks. "I thought about what you said, and you were right. I was being selfish." She took a tentative step toward me but stopped before she was too close. "That's why I was following them. If I could see Carson from a distance, she'd never see me. She's so beautiful, she looks just like you when she smiles. Thank you for keeping her and giving her a good life when I couldn't. You're a great dad, Ethan. There was never a doubt in my mind you'd take good care of her.

"I'm sorry. I promised you I'd never disrupt your life but I did. Today when I saw her, really saw her, I knew I'd made the right choice. Something that was stirring around in my heart was laid to rest. I knew she belonged to you, she always has."

"Was there something I could've said or done back then to make you stay?" God, I hated asking her that question, but I had to know.

"Nothing would've made me stay. You know how some girls grow up and dream about their weddings and having babies? That was never me. I knew I'd never be mother material. Even now, Ethan, I don't want children. Damn, that makes me sound heartless, but I'm just not that person."

"Not heartless—honest," I corrected.

The door creaked open and a doctor walked in. "Honor Sullivan's family?"

"Here." I stepped forward.

"We've moved her to recovery. If you'd like to walk with me, I'll explain the procedure as I take you to her room."

"I'll tell your mom. We'll watch Carson," my dad told me.

"Thanks."

The doctor immediately started running through the list of injuries Honor had sustained. The only issue that Chrissy had not addressed was Honor's right ankle. The paramedic had thought it was a possible fracture, but it turned out to just be bruised. That was one less thing for her to recover from.

I stepped into Honor's room and ignored the beeping and whirring of all the machines and went to her side. All the fears I'd had about Chrissy had been wiped clean and the self-doubt I'd had was finally behind me. Nothing mattered in that moment but Honor. I need her to wake up so I could beg her to forgive me.

"Hey, smalls. You ready to wake up yet?" The doctor told me it could take a few hours before the anesthesia wore off and she was coherent enough to carry on a conversation or it could only take minutes. Every patient was different.

I pulled a chair close and picked up one of her small, cold hands in mine and brought it to my lips, kissing her fingers. Thank God she was alive. Seeing her broken and near dead was something I never wanted to experience again. It'd also made me contemplate the last few days, and how I'd behaved. Never again would I shut her out. I took in the bruises on her face and the stitches on her forehead near her hairline and was relieved. The angry purple marks would fade, her ankle would heal, so would the scrapes on her leg. I could only hope the hurt I'd caused would too.

"I'm so sorry Honor." I kissed her knuckles again

wishing I could climb into the bed next to her and hold her. "So damn sorry for being such an asshole. I didn't mean any of what I said. I promise. I was a coward and let fear take over. I don't ever want to slow down. I don't want you to move out. Baby, I need you to wake up. I miss you so much. Carson misses you, too. She needs you. We both do. I don't know what I would do if I lost you."

I rested my forehead on her hand and listened to the constant rhythm of her heart. Thank God it was beating.

Honor would be okay. She had to be. My life didn't work if she wasn't in it.

21

I slowly awoke and lay there a moment, disoriented and trying to figure out what had happened and where I was. The first thing I noticed was the unmistakable smell of a hospital. Antiseptic and bleach. The next were the sounds. Beeping, swooshing, and buzzing. Even as faint as it was, the hum hurt my head. I wanted to go back to sleep.

"Please, Honor, wake up. Let me see those pretty eyes."

"Ethan?" I croaked.

"I'm right here, smalls. Can you open your eyes?"

I tried, but they felt heavy and gritty, like someone had thrown sand in them. I finally got one cracked open a sliver and decided against it when the light felt like it was piercing my skull.

"Can't. What happened?"

"You were in a car accident."

A car accident? That wasn't right. I was at home making tacos with Carson.

Tortillas.

Carson.

No!

My eyes flew open, and I fought against the nausea that roiled in my stomach.

"Carson. Where is she? Is she okay?"

"Slow down. She's fine. Everyone's fine."

Slow down.

I hated those two words. My brain slowly engaged, and I remembered.

"Why are you here?"

His face was still a little fuzzy but not so much I couldn't make out the worry.

"Why wouldn't I be here. You're here. Where you are, I am."

What? Was he drunk? He hadn't wanted to be anywhere near me.

"You shouldn't be here. Where's Carson?" I asked him.

Ethan brought my hand to his lips and kissed it, then he peeled my fingers open and kissed my palm, placing my open hand on his cheek.

"I'm so sorry," he said, ignoring my question.

"My head hurts," I complained.

"Let me get the doctor. And I need to tell everyone you're awake. They're in the waiting room."

"Why is everyone here?"

"Smalls, we almost lost you. Where else would they be?"

Lost me?

"What happened?"

"I promise I'll tell you everything. But please let me have the doctor check you out first."

"Okay." With my head pounding, I easily gave in.

"I won't leave your side, promise."

Ethan pushed the call button next to the bed and moments later a woman in scrubs walked through the door.

"Don't make me promises you can't keep." I tried to pull my hand free, but he held it firm on his cheek.

"I deserve that. I'm so sorry."

"Oh, good, you're awake." The nurse interrupted. "Let me get the doctor."

"How long have I been out?"

"You've been out of surgery for two hours," he told me.

"Surgery?"

"Yes. Four of the longest hours of my life. I can't remember a time I've ever been so scared."

Before I could ask any more questions, an older man entered the room and smiled.

"Glad you finally decided to wake up. I thought I was going to have to sedate your fiancé here. He was worse than a two-year-old on a road trip asking, are we there yet," the doctor chuckled.

Fiancé? I looked at Ethan and he shrugged his shoulders.

"I'm Doctor Levine, I performed your surgery. How do you feel? On a scale of one to ten what's your pain level?"

I was trying to focus on Dr. Levine, however my head was still spinning at the revelation Ethan had told him we were engaged.

"Um, maybe a four, but I do have a headache and I feel like I might throw up."

"Both are normal. Your vitals all look great. Dr. Krier was able to treat the pneumothorax in the ambulance. I removed the cath she put in during transport and replaced it with a chest tube." The doctor pulled the unsnapped hospital gown down revealing a tube inserted just below my armpit. "You're connected to a wall suction, so you're leashed, so to speak, to the bed. Do not try and get up. Tomorrow you'll be able to use the restroom with assistance. For now, you need to be connected to the suction at all times. To stop internal bleeding I had to remove your damaged spleen. The incision will be sore for a few weeks. I'm more concerned with your lung at the moment. You were extremely lucky Dr. Krier was there; pneumothorax can be life-threatening."

"You removed my spleen? Don't I need that?"

"I've performed hundreds of splenectomies. You can live a normal, healthy life without your spleen. There's a chance you'll be more prone to infection; however, it's not significant."

"When I woke up, I didn't notice this." I pointed to the tube coming out of my chest.

"That's good. I don't want you in pain. You'll still feel a shortness of breath while your lung inflates. I won't sugarcoat it, young lady, pneumothorax is extremely painful. I was very impressed with Dr. Krier's original efforts."

"Who's Dr. Krier? Is she here? I'd like to thank her. It sounds like she saved my life."

Ethan's hand on my arm tightened, bringing my attention to him.

"What's wrong?" I asked. His brows were pulled together, and he was staring at me with wide eyes. He opened his mouth, and I narrowed my eyes. "Don't lie to me."

"Nothing's wrong. We'll talk after the doctor is done with his exam."

I continued to hold Ethan's gaze. I only broke contact when Dr. Levine asked me to look at him, so he could check my pupils and throat. Once he deemed I was fine, he left the room with a promise to return before he left for the evening.

"Tell me," I demanded.

"What do you remember about the accident?"

I tried to recall the moment of impact, but the details were fuzzy. "I was driving through an intersection and I was hit from behind. But it wasn't like I was rear-ended. I was being pushed. I tried to step on the brakes, but it was too late, I couldn't turn and there was a light post in front of me. Why? What does this have to do with why you look like you've swallowed a lemon?"

"What about after? Do you remember the EMTs working on you?"

God my head hurt, and the harder I tried to remember details the more it hurt.

"Not really. I remember opening my eyes and the airbag was in my face and it was hard to breathe. I could taste blood mixed with chalk. I called out to Carson, she was crying. Then the airbag was deflated. I remember a woman was trying to talk to me, but I couldn't understand her. I begged her to leave me and help Carson. I'm not sure if I was making sense, though, or if I was even talking. I hurt everywhere."

"Did you recognize the woman who helped you?"

"No, I don't remember. Why? Just tell me what's

wrong. My head hurts too fucking badly to play guessing games."

"The . . . um . . . woman who helped you was Dr. Krier. Dr. Chrissy Krier." Ethan looked like it physically pained him to say the words. What was the big deal about . . . oh, no . . . Chrissy.

Shit on a shingle!

"Chrissy? Carson's—"

"Yes," he said briskly. His jaw was set tight, and he looked like he had this morning when I'd told him I was moving out. *Shit, had that only been this morning?*

"Why was she there?"

"Do you need something for your headache?" he asked instead of answering me.

"Did she run me off the road?"

"No." Our eyes remained locked. I was unwilling to accept his one-word answer. "She was following you."

"Me? You mean Carson. Was she going to try and take her? Is that why you didn't want me alone with Carson? Did she threaten to kidnap her?"

"No, smalls, she didn't."

"What aren't you telling me?"

"A lot," he admitted. "I promise to tell you everything. But I refuse to pile more shit on your plate when you've just woken up from surgery."

"I don't believe you. I think you're putting me off.

You promised not to shut me out again, yet the first time something big came up you did just that. Only this time was worse than the first time. You didn't shut me out, you locked me out. And now you're doing it again. You should go home. Carson must be frightened. She needs you right now."

"I leave when you leave."

"What's the point? Nothing's changed."

"You're right, nothing has changed. I feel the same way about you right this very moment as I did the first time I kissed you. I know I fucked up. I'd planned on rectifying that this morning. Then you surprised me by telling me you were moving out, and I got pissed. But make no mistake, I was never going to let you walk out the door."

"You were pissed? That's rich coming from you. Don't forget, *you're* the one who's refused to speak to *me*."

"Yeah, Honor, pissed and hurt. I haven't forgotten I behaved like a jackass. I thought I was doing the right thing, trying to work through my issues on my own and not stress you out or burden you with them. I was wrong. But so were you. I may've been silent, but you were ready to give up."

"I wasn't giving up. I was giving you space. Space you admit to needing."

Damn my head hurt worse now than it did when I'd first opened my eyes.

"I'm not letting you walk away. I know I have a lot to make up for. A lot to prove to you. And I will while you are in our home. Where you belong."

"It's not my—"

"We're not arguing about this, Honor. Not while you're in pain. I'm going to go get the nurse and ask her to give you something for your headache. Then I'm going to go talk to my parents. When I come back, I'll watch you sleep, and we'll talk again when you wake up."

"I already told you, you should leave. Go home with Carson."

"That's not happening. She'll be fine with my parents. We walk out of here together."

Without another word, Ethan stood and made his way to the door, he hesitated a moment before he shook whatever thought he had out of his head and left the room.

I now had more questions, and Ethan still hadn't explained what had put him on edge in the first place. I should've been grateful Chrissy had been there to save my life, but now I was afraid Ethan felt indebted to her. And if she was there that meant she'd seen and spoken to Carson. What a fucking mess.

"She's fine, Squirt. The doctor even said so."

"I want to see Honor," she demanded.

I looked over Carson's head at my parents, hoping they held the answers I need to calm Carson down.

"I know you do. But you can see her tomorrow. You're gonna go home with Pop and Gran—"

Carson moved and grabbed my face in both her tiny hands and looked me dead in the eyes.

"I want Honor, now," she yelled.

"Okay, baby, I'll take you to see her."

I'd never seen fear like that in my daughter's eyes. Not even while she was strapped into the back seat after the car accident. Sure, she'd been frightened, but it didn't compare to the terror rolling off her now.

I scooped Carson up and held her close before I turned to my dad. "We'll be right back."

He gave me a chin lift, and my gaze slid to my mom, who was tucked against my dad's side with tears glistening in her eyes. She nodded her approval, and I left the waiting area.

"You have to be very careful and not touch anything," I told Carson. "There are a bunch of machines that may look scary—"

"Sir," a nurse cut me off midsentence as I was opening the door to Honor's room. "She can't be back here." The nurse motioned toward Carson.

"We'll only be a minute. She's scared and wants to check on her mom."

The nurse looked from side to side before turning back to us. "Please be quick. Children are not allowed in this unit. And if someone catches you, we never had this talk."

The woman turned on her heel and walked off down the corridor leaving us outside of Honor's door.

"Did you decide, Daddy? Can Honor be my mom?" Carson asked.

"We have to talk to Honor about it, Squirt. She's pretty mad at Daddy right now. I was a jerk this week and I hurt her feelings. I need to make things right with her. And you too. I'm sorry I was so grouchy."

"It's okay. Honor, I mean Mom, told me it was because you were sad you had to work at night and couldn't tuck me in like you like to. And Pop always says when Gran is mad at him, he kisses her until she forgives him. I don't understand how that works. I think it's silly."

I really didn't want to think about how my father got my mom to forgive him when he was acting like an asshole. I was sure it entailed more than kissing and the images made me want to gag.

I opened the door and found Honor sleeping peacefully. I was getting ready to tell Carson she'd have to come back later, when her eyes opened. The scowl she'd worn earlier while talking to me turned into a breathtakingly beautiful smile.

"Hey, darlin'. How ya feeling?"

Carson remained frozen for a moment before she wiggled in my arms, wanting to be set on her feet.

"Remember, no touching anything," I whispered.

Without looking at any of the machines, Carson marched to Honor's bed and started to climb up.

"Carson—"

"She's fine, Ethan. Help her up."

I didn't have to, Carson was already sitting on Honor's left side looking her over.

"Does it hurt?" Carson asked.

"A little. But I'll be okay. I even have a cool tube the doctor left in. I'm attached to a machine that's sucking out air from around my lung that shouldn't be there. Wanna see?"

I wasn't sure it was a good idea for Carson to see Honor's chest tube, but I remained quiet, trusting Honor knew what was best for her.

"Wow. Does *that* hurt?"

"Nope. I can't feel it at all. The doctor gave me special medicine to numb the area." Honor brushed Carson's hair from her forehead and turned to me. "You said she wasn't hurt."

The accusation in her tone was fierce. Just what you'd expect from a mother. How could I have been so fucking stupid? She loved Carson. She loved me. Why hadn't I trusted her with my thoughts about Chrissy?

"She's fine. The doctor said she hit herself in the head," I explained.

"I'm sorry you were hurt." Honor brought Carson close and kissed the bruise on her head. "I was really scared. Were you?"

"Yes," Carson told her. "I wanted to go up front with you, but I wasn't allowed out of my seatbelt. The doctor told me she needed me to help her and stay in the back, so she could get you out of the car."

"That was really brave of you. Thank you for helping her."

"Then Daddy came. You were scared, too, weren't you Daddy?"

"Yes, Squirt. I was very scared. My two best girls were in an accident and hurt."

When had Carson grown up? It felt like yesterday she was learning how to walk. Then suddenly she was running. The years seemed to have slid by in the blink of an eye.

"Then Daddy argued with the doctor but he let her shine a tiny flashlight in my eyes and she checked me all over before she let him take me out of the car."

Honor's face had turned to stone.

"She checked you?" Honor asked then pinned me with a pissed off look. "Did she get checked in the ER?"

I would've rolled my eyes at her if I hadn't been so taken by her concern.

"Yes. As soon as you were taken up to surgery, she had a full battery of tests. She's fine."

Not to be deterred, Carson continued with her story. "Then we got in the ambulance with you and the doctor. Daddy was holding me so tight all his stuff was poking me. But I didn't care because when all the beeping started I was scared."

Honor looked to me to fill in the holes. I wanted to wait to explain what had happened in the ambulance and the role Chrissy had played until after Honor had gotten some much-needed sleep. But by the look she was giving me, I no longer had that option.

"Your lung collapsed, and it was straining your heart. That's when the first chest tube was put in."

Honor nodded then returned her focus to Carson.

"That had to have been really scary. I'm sorry you had to see it."

"I didn't see it. Daddy told me to close my eyes. I only heard it," Carson informed her.

"Well, either way, I'm sorry."

"I didn't want you to die," Carson blurted out and started to cry.

"Come here." Honor opened her arm as wide as she could and waited until Carson's head rested on her chest. "I'm not going to die. The doctors and nurses did a great job patching me up, darlin'. I'm not going anywhere."

Relief washed over me hearing Honor's last statement. Even if it was only meant to reassure Carson, I'd take it. I'd do my damnedest to make sure I proved to Honor she could trust me. I let the two of them lay in silence for a few minutes before I told Carson it was time to go. Honor needed to rest, and I didn't want to push our luck with the nurse. Especially since I planned on breaking the rule again tomorrow. Carson needed to see Honor, just as much as she needed to see Carson. And I damn well needed all three of us together.

"Daddy said you were mad at him for being a jerk," Carson not-so-helpfully announced. I bit back a curse, and my daughter barreled on. "He said he has to make things right with us before you forgive him and can be my mom. He said he was sorry to me. So, I forgave him. I told him to kiss you like Pop kisses Gran, and you'll forgive him too."

Shit, motherfucker, damn. Honor was going to be so mad at me and think I was trying to use Carson to get to her.

"Carson, that's not exactly what I said."

"Yes, it is. You told the nurse I wanted to see my mom. Then you said, Honor was mad. Then you said, before we can talk to her about being my mom you had to make things right."

Jesus, the little parrot had me, but she was not helping my case.

"Okay. That is exactly what I said. How about you let me and Honor talk, yeah?"

"Okay," she easily agreed. "When do you get to come home?"

"I'm not sure, darlin'," Honor croaked then cleared her throat. "Maybe you can come see me tomorrow after school."

"Can I, Daddy?"

"Absolutely. Gran can bring you by when she picks you up. Now, let's get you back to Gran and Pop so you can go home and get some dinner, and Honor can rest."

"I love you, Honor."

"I love you, Carson."

I helped Carson off the bed and didn't miss Honor wiping a tear as it rolled down her cheek.

"I'll be right back," I told her.

She opened her mouth to argue but closed it and nodded.

It wouldn't have mattered if she'd argued or not. I was not leaving this hospital without her. It was one of the many ways I was going to prove to her how much she meant to me. Getting her to trust me again, was a whole 'nother battle, which would take longer than a few days.

I said goodbye to my aunts and uncles, promising frequent updates, then I was left with my parents.

"I can't thank you enough," I told my dad.

"No other place we'd be," he said. "Now, fix this, son."

"I'm going to."

His hand clapped on my shoulder and squeezed. "I know you will."

My mom gave me a hug and patted my check. "Love you, boy."

"Love you, Mama."

"I'll see you tomorrow, Daddy," Carson added.

I knelt in front of her and opened my arms. She stepped in and wrapped her arms around my neck. "I love you, Squirt. I'm sorry I'm staying here tonight."

"It's okay. Gran told me that Honor needs all your love right now, so she can get better and come home."

"Yeah, she does. She'll be home before we know it, and we can spoil her."

"Can I make her cookies?"

"You sure can."

"Night, Daddy. I'll miss you."

"Miss you, too. Be a good girl."

By the time I made my way back to Honor's room she was asleep. I sat back down in the chair next to her bed and did exactly what I told her I was going to do; I watched her sleep.

I'd like to think I was fairly self-aware and could recognize my shortcomings. I'd been wrong. I hadn't seen nor understood them until Lorenz, my parents, and Honor pointed them out to me. And even after they had, I still stubbornly thought I was doing the right thing.

Honor sighed in her sleep, and I vowed to make this right. Once again, I thought about what my father had told me. I hated to admit it, but he was right. The last eight years, I'd been content. Happy being a father, loving on Carson. However, I'd never known bone-deep, soul-consuming love. Now that I had, I wasn't going to let it go. I was going to hold on to it for dear life, fight for it until my dying breath, nurture it, and wrap myself in it until there is no beginning or end to it.

Honor would be my wife, Carson's mom, and the mother of our future children. That, I was sure of. It was time I opened up to her and let her see the real me —all the ugly secrets I kept hidden from the world. She deserved nothing less.

23

I woke up disoriented and uncomfortable. It took me a moment to get my bearings and remember I was in the hospital. Ethan was next to me, softly snoring. He was still sitting in the same chair from last night, and I winced at the angle of his head. He looked more uncomfortable than I felt, But, even in his slumber, he was handsome. Damn him for driving a wedge between us.

I thought back to what Carson had said yesterday, and my heart constricted. Ethan had told the nurse he was taking Carson to see her mom. A week ago I would've been thrilled. Now? I was angry he was trying to manipulate my feelings about Carson to his advantage. The realization only strengthened my resolve. I would not let him use Carson to get me to forgive him. Once bitten, twice shy.

The accident only proved to me that life was short, everything could be gone in the blink of an eye. The somber reality may've woken him up and made him think about the past week and how stupid he'd been pushing me away. But the near-death experience had sobered me, and now I knew, more than ever, I wanted more. As much as I'd loved my mom, I wouldn't allow my life to end like hers: one husband who repeatedly promised a better life, then another who promised the world only to put her through hell. Why had my mom resigned herself to an existence full of empty words? Whatever reasons she had, I wasn't going there.

"Morning, smalls. How are you feeling?" Ethan's sleep roughened voice pulled me from my thoughts.

As immature as it was, I wasn't ready to talk to him, so I shrugged my answer and turned my head away from him. Why was he doing this? Why now? After days of grunts and one-word answers. I'd given him the out he'd needed to sort his shit out. I was finally getting my life on course. I'd moved out of Frank's house with a determination to make it on my own and, stupidly, I'd fallen for my landlord, putting me back into a situation of having to rely on someone else. So fucking stupid.

"Why are you really here?" I asked, wanting to get the argument we were about to have over with. He needed to leave. I needed to use this time to think, which was hard to do with Ethan sitting vigil.

"I already told you why."

"No, you haven't. I want to know why, after days of not speaking to me, suddenly you love me and don't want to leave my side. You had no issues leaving me alone the last several days."

The sleep crept from his eyes, replaced with pure anger. His face turned to granite, and his eyes narrowed. "Suddenly? There is no suddenly about it. I have never stopped loving you. And I'm here because I'm going to prove to you I've learned from my mistakes. Remember when we started this, and I told you I was going to need patience? This is one of those times. I know I owe you more than an apology. I owe you honesty, something I'm prepared to give you. But, Honor, you need to understand this, I was never going to let you move out of the house without a fight. And I still won't. I will use everything within my power to make you stay."

"Like Carson? That wasn't cool the way you flipped everything around and made it seem like I didn't want to be her mom. Let's not forget it was you that said you weren't ready for anyone to be her mom."

"I did say that, and I regret it. I hope after I explain everything to you, you'll understand and forgive me. If you don't, I'll try harder. And for the record, I'm not using Carson. Last night I tried to tell Carson she had to wait to see you. She nearly screamed the waiting room down. She wasn't leaving until she could talk to you. When the nurse stopped us in the hall and told me children weren't allowed back, I said what was natural—she wanted to see her mom. Carson asked if that meant you were going to be her mom. I admitted I messed up, and you were mad at me. I also told her I had to make things right with you before we talked about her request again."

I was still pissed, however, there was a twinge of guilt for thinking the worst of him. I knew how protective he was of Carson and accusing him of using her was out of bounds. I knew better.

"Will you tell me more about Chrissy and why she was following me?"

There was no sense putting off this conversation nor trying to talk about how he'd behaved the last few days if we didn't address her presence. The truth was, I'd rather gouge my eyeballs out with a hot poker than talk about her, but it was time to rip the scab off, even if I'd be the one bleeding.

"Before we start, do you need anything? Pain medicine? Anything?"

"Are you stalling?"

"No, Honor. I'm trying to make sure my woman is comfortable and not in pain before we talk. And I'm going to get a cup of coffee and wake up a little. Then I'm going lay it all out for you."

That was nice. It'd been a long time since someone cared about my comfort.

"I'd like a cup of coffee, too, if I'm allowed."

"I'll ask on my way past the nurse's station. Be right back."

He stood and stretched, the hem of his T-shirt rode up, exposing a sliver of mouth-watering flesh. I may've been laid up in a hospital bed, pissed off at him, but I wasn't dead. There was no doubt Ethan Lenox was a fine example of male sexiness.

"I love you, Honor." He winked and leaned down to kiss my forehead.

He strode out the door, and I couldn't bring myself to care he'd caught me checking him out. Now that I was alone in my room, nerves set in and had me questioning my reasoning for bringing Chrissy up first thing in the morning. I'd always heard the saying, don't ask questions you don't want the answers to, and the more I thought about the possible answers, the less I wanted them. Then there was the added complication that the woman had saved my life. Of all the people in the world who could've been there to help me it had to be her.

"Good morning, Honor." A chipper nurse walked into my room. "I'm Betty. I'll be your nurse today."

"Hi, Betty." I smiled back, her friendly disposition infectious.

"Where's your pain level, sweetie?" she asked as she looked at one of the many monitors surrounding my bed.

"About a six."

"I'll get you something," she said and started to pump up the blood pressure cuff around my bicep.

"Please don't. Not yet. The pain medicine puts me to sleep, and I just woke up."

I didn't want to tell her it was because I wanted to hear what Ethan had to say and I'd need my wits about me.

She removed her stethoscope from my arm and tucked it into the pocket of her scrubs before she gave me an apprising once over. "Not that I blame you, wanting to be awake with a fiancé as handsome as yours, but you can't get behind the pain. Your body needs to recover and the best way for that to happen is if you are relaxed and not hurting." She walked around the foot of the bed. Coming to my right side, she pulled back my hospital gown and checked my chest tube. "Everything looks great. I told Ethan you could have one cup of coffee. I'll make you a deal. We'll wait on your pain meds until breakfast is served."

"Deal."

"Can I get you anything before I leave?" she asked.

I didn't know how to ask for what I wanted without sounding vain, but I wanted to see how bad I looked.

"Is there a mirror I can use? And maybe get my brush out of my purse." I looked around the room, not sure if my belongings had been retrieved from my car. "If it's here."

"Are you sure?"

Whoa. Her question gave me pause. What did she mean was I sure? Should I not have been? How bad did I look?

"Um, I thought I was."

"Oh, sweetie, I didn't mean the mirror. You're beautiful. I meant, the brush. You have stitches right on your hairline. You'll need to be careful not to tug them. Dr. Levine was very careful not to have to shave the area." Betty pulled a hand mirror out of a drawer and handed it to me. "I think he did a great job. You should only have minimal scaring."

I held the mirror with shaky hands. *Come on, Honor, just look.* I brought it up to face level and opened my eyes, the reflection staring back at me could've been worse—but it wasn't all that great. Tiny, black stitches ran nearly an inch across my forehead. Betty was right, the doctor had done a great job staying as close as he could to my hairline. If I wanted to, I could always wear bangs and the scar would be hidden. There was a yellowish bruise around the area and a faint greenish hue on my right cheek and lower eyelid. All in all, it was better than I thought it would be. I looked back at the stitches and changed my mind about brushing my hair.

"Maybe just a hair tie. I'll wait to brush it."

"Okay, sweetie." She opened up the same drawer she'd retrieved the mirror from and pulled a black, elastic hair band off the cardboard packaging. "We keep extras in all the rooms. You know how quickly these little buggers can break. Do you need me to help you? You can't lift your right arm over your head with the tube in."

Well, damn. I hadn't thought about that. Not wanting to put Betty out, I was ready to refuse when the grandmotherly woman stepped to my side and started to gather my hair.

"Thank you," I told her once she had my hair fastened in a low ponytail.

"Anything you need."

Ethan opened the door but stopped when he saw Betty.

"Do you need me to wait outside?" His gaze darted between Betty and me.

"No, sir, we're all done. Buzz me if you need anything." She patted my shoulder and started for the door. Before she could step back into the hallway Betty snapped her fingers and turned back to us. "Your mother already called the nurses station this morning to check on our beautiful patient. She didn't want to wake you but asked me to tell you, she'll be by around three with your daughter. As I know you are aware, no children are allowed on this floor. I will be on break from three to three fifteen." Then Betty lowered her voice. "Who am I to keep a cute little girl from her mama."

"Thank you," Ethan answered.

The door softly clicked behind Betty, and the room filled with trepidation. Mine—not Ethan's.

"Why didn't you correct Betty?"

"About what?"

"Come on, Ethan, you know about what."

"What do you want to start with first?" he asked, ignoring my question.

I knew what he was asking, I just wasn't sure how to answer. Chrissy following me or Chrissy showing up at the house and him shutting down, pushing me away, and acting like a sulking jerk?

With the ache on my left side intensifying I opted for the more to the point conversation about Chrissy behaving like a stalker and tailing me.

"The accident," I told him.

"Chrissy was following you, so she could see Carson. That was because when she came to the house on Sunday, I told her no. Her plan was to follow you into the store and watch from a distance so she could see Carson."

"See her? She didn't want to take her?"

"No. And she didn't even really want to talk to her. She just wanted to see her."

I didn't understand why Chrissy didn't want to take Carson. Not that I wasn't grateful she hadn't planned on kidnapping her, but that would make more sense to me. Why would a mother only want to see her child?

"That's crazy! What about Carson? Didn't she stop to think about what it would do to her? A strange woman shows up and says hey, I'm your mom. I just wanted to stop by and see how pretty you are, but I don't want anything to do with you. No fucking way!" Ethan's smile took me off guard. "What?"

"That's exactly what I said to her on Sunday before I told her to go home and never come back."

"But she didn't listen," I said unnecessarily.

"She didn't. And now I'm torn between being fucking furious and beyond grateful. Who knows what would've happened if Chrissy hadn't been there. She was the first on the scene and was able to give you the medical care you needed on site as well as in the ambulance."

Shit on a shingle. His feelings mirrored my own. I wished to God Chrissy would've never shown up at all, but if she hadn't been there, I could've died.

"What about Carson? What did she say to her? Did she tell her?"

Anxiety crept in and threatened to choke me. Carson would have so many questions.

"Chrissy didn't have any interaction with her other than treating her at the scene. When Chrissy came into the waiting area to tell everyone you were out of surgery, my mom took Carson out of the room." Ethan stopped and inhaled, holding his breath for a moment before he blew it out. So much pain passed over his features before he began again. "Though, you should know, after she told me she'd witnessed the accident and was able to give the make and model, as well as, a partial plate, I offered her the opportunity to talk to Carson."

"You what? Why, Ethan?"

"She saved your life," he mumbled. "I don't know what I would've done if I'd lost you. I felt obligated. If there's one feeling I hate, it's guilt. And I'd rather you and I have to answer questions from Carson, rather than feel guilty for the rest of my life. Chrissy gave life to the two most important people to me. One she saved, one she bore. I felt like I owed it to her."

I didn't know what to say to Ethan. I was in the same predicament as him. I didn't particularly like the woman and I really hated what this could mean for Carson, but the fact remained—Chrissy had been in the right place at the right time. And as much as I wanted to pretend she didn't exist, she did. And if I was going to be in Carson's and Ethan's lives, I'd have to accept that fact.

"What did she say? Did Carson talk to her?" I held my breath waiting for his answer. I was pretty sure the answer was, no. Carson would've told me.

"No. Chrissy changed her mind. Upon further reflection, she agreed it was selfish of her to speak to Carson when she had no intention of being a part of her life. But she did have a request."

"What kind of request?"

If Chrissy thought she was seeing Ethan again, she had another thing coming. As grateful as I was, I wasn't *that* grateful. There was no way I was allowing her to spend any more time with him just so she could fuck with his head.

"She wants to check on you before she goes home."

"Check on me?"

"That's what she said."

What the fuck? What was her game?

"What did you tell her?"

"That it was up to you and I'd talk to you about it."

"Huh?"

"If you don't want to, I'll tell her to fuck off. If you'd like to talk to her, I'll be here with you—or not. Whichever you prefer."

"You'd let me talk to her?"

"Why wouldn't I?"

I was about to remind him of all the reasons I'd think he wouldn't let me when a sharp, stabbing pain radiated from my left side.

"Time for your pain meds, smalls. We'll continue this later."

I didn't bother arguing with him, the pain was that bad. I knew I'd be out in a matter of minutes after the nurse gave me the medication, and I welcomed the dark abyss.

I was impressed Ethan had been so forthcoming. Not that he'd divulged any deep, dark secrets but at least he wasn't shutting me out. I'd give him points for that, though he was still a long way away from earning my trust back. I was relieved we had a start. I didn't want to lose Carson and Ethan, but I had to put myself first in this situation. Maybe I should've felt a little guilty, but I didn't. If I didn't value myself and my needs, how would he? And if he didn't, how would we ever truly be happy?

Relationships were about give and take, and right now it was my turn to take. If he could give me this one small thing, I could spend the rest of my life making sure he and Carson were happy.

24

I was happy Honor had spent most of the day resting. She woke up when my mom and Carson came for a visit and stayed awake for the fifteen minutes the nurse was away and Carson could be in her room. Within minutes of their departure she fell back to sleep.

Dr. Levine had come in and checked the incision from her splenectomy and assured us it looked great and was healing. He was also happy with the progress her lung had made. She'd have another x-ray tomorrow, and he'd make the decision then about when he'd release her. Honor drifted in and out of sleep the whole time the doctor was examining her and she hadn't woken up until dinner time. After complaining the food tasted like shit, I ignored her protests and called my dad. He dropped off a bowl of chicken soup and bread, along with some pre-approved snacks.

A knock on the door drew my attention from the conversation my dad and Honor were having, and I found Lorenz standing in the doorway with a huge bouquet of flowers.

"Hope this isn't a bad time" He entered the small room, walking towards me.

"Not at all." I stood and shook my partner's hand.

"I was gonna call but I wanted to bring these by." He set the vase down on a side table and turned to Honor. "How are you feeling?"

"Like I slammed into a pole." She smiled and laughed when Lorenz's scowl matched mine. I hadn't meant to allow the growl to slip past my lips, but I didn't see anything funny about her almost dying. "Jeez. Lighten up. I feel fine. A little tired and sore. But I think I'll live. Thank you for the flowers. They're beautiful."

"You're welcome. Mind if I steal Ethan away for a minute?"

"Wait. Is this about the accident?" Honor asked.

Lorenz shifted his gaze to me, confirming he indeed had news. I was stuck between a rock and a hard place, I didn't want to discuss the case in front of Honor. Yet, I knew I had to. I couldn't continue to keep things from her, even if I knew they were going to stress her out or scare her.

"It's okay. Whatever it is, Honor needs to know."

"All right, brother. But brace, this shit is whacked. We made an arrest this afternoon—Samuel Harris."

"What? Why did you arrest Sam?" Honor asked.

"I knew there was something off about that mother-fucker," I spit out. "Did you get a confession?"

"No and we won't need it. We ran the partial plate, and when Sam's name came up, we went to interview him at the Gold Suites, where he and his father are staying. We found his car in the parking lot. Left front bumper is torn to hell and white paint from Honor's Honda was clearly visible."

"What?" Honor repeated horrified. "Sam ran me off the road?"

"I'm afraid it looks that way," Lorenz told her.

Fuck. This was my fault, I should've done some-thing to keep Sam and Frank away from Honor. I didn't like the way Sam was eyeing her the night at the restaurant, and the congressman had out and out threatened her.

"What about Frank?"

"He has an alibi. His aide swears they were in his room all day going over budget cuts."

"Shit. You know he's involved."

"You'll never prove it," Honor spoke up. "Jessica, his aide, will lie through her teeth for him. She's one of his many mistresses. It's been going on for years. She'll swear to anything he tells her to. I can see Frank wanting me dead. But Sam? He's too weak. He's a puppet. But I guess if Frank ordered him to kill me, he obviously would. Or try at least."

"Frank is distancing himself from his son. He sent a lawyer but has yet to go to central booking and see him."

"Thank you for catching who did this to me." Her tone was hushed. "I'm sorry, Ethan. Carson could've been injured, and it would've been my fault. He was trying to hurt me."

"No, smalls. It would've been Sam's fault. I should've taken their threats seriously."

"HE THREATENED HONOR?" My dad had his hands tightly clinched, and the vein on the side of his neck pulsed. "Why didn't you come to me?"

"I asked him not to." Honor turned her head towards him, a pained look on her face. "I was embarrassed about my association with them. And then there was Frank's plan. I didn't want you and Lily to know."

"Don't make excuses for me, Honor. I should've known better. I told you, you don't have anything to be embarrassed about. This is on me. I didn't take him seriously."

I spent the next thirty minutes explaining Frank's desire to force Honor to marry Greg, the threats he'd made, however I did leave out the contract. That was something I'd tell my dad in private. Honor answered the questions my dad and Lorenz had, albeit with hesitation and rosy cheeks.

"I'll ask Levi and Blake to comb through Frank's life. Sam's, too," my dad announced when I was done filling them in.

"You don't have to," Honor told him.

"Yeah, I do. Neither of them will be a problem for you. From here on out, you're protected. If you see Frank, you call one of us."

Honor assessed the situation and came to the right decision. Arguing with my dad wasn't going to get her anywhere. Lorenz made his exit, and my dad stood to follow. Before he left the room, he gave Honor some truths about my family.

"I hope you don't think I'm stepping out of bounds here, but there are a few things you need to understand. We protect what's ours. And not just me and Ethan. Jasper, Clark, and Levi will protect you as well. It's what we do. You're family, Honor, one of us. That means you fall under the umbrella of protection. You never, and I mean never, feel ashamed or too embarrassed to come to us. Ethan loves you, and that's all we need to know about what kind of woman you are."

Honor didn't answer, instead her lips pinched together, tears filled her eyes, and she nodded her understanding.

"Thanks, Dad." I reached out my hand to shake his, and he pulled me in for a hug and whispered, "Do whatever you have to do to make sure she doesn't walk away. Now is the time to grovel. And son, it doesn't make you less of a man—it makes you a smart one."

"I plan to."

"Good." He stepped away from me and opened the door. "I'm out of here. My granddaughter has requested mint chocolate chip ice cream."

"Dad—"

"Son, there's nothing you can say that's going to stop me from spoiling her. Save your breath."

"Right."

"See you both tomorrow."

My dad left, leaving me with a crying Honor. I carefully sat on the bed and gathered both her hands in mine and waited for her to look at me.

"You okay?" I asked.

"I can't believe Sam tried to kill me."

"I can. I knew there was something wrong with the way he was staring at you at the restaurant. Combine that with all the stalkerish shit he did when you were teenagers—I should've been more careful.

"This isn't your fault."

"Sure it is."

"You mean like it would've been my fault if Carson got hurt?"

I clenched my jaw to prevent myself from sounding like a misogynist pig. I doubted she wanted to hear how it was my job, as the man, to protect her—and I'd failed. Not to mention, Carson had been in the car. It was absolutely my job to keep her safe.

"Point taken. How's your pain level? Tired?"

"I'm fine. Will you tell me about last Sunday?" she asked.

I wished we were at home, so I could lie next her and gather her in my arms. I didn't want to talk to her about Chrissy, but if I had to, I'd prefer it be done while I could hold her close.

"I was so scared to tell my parents. Did I tell you where we were when I told them?" She shook her head and I chuckled at the memory. "My cousin Nick's housewarming party. Everyone was there. I'd kept the secret for like a week, and it was eating away at me. I had to get it off my chest so I could breathe. I think I told them there so my dad couldn't kill me, too many witnesses. Which was stupid, my uncles would have helped him bury my body and never ask questions. I was most afraid to see the disappointment on their faces. But, as mad as they were, they supported me. My mom's only request was that I finish school. And my dad actually told me he was proud I'd decided to step up and be a father. But I was still scared and doubted I could do it."

"But you had your family, Ethan. You know they'd never let you fail."

"I knew that. But I was still secretly pissed I was willing to own my responsibilities, but Chrissy was going to walk away." I stopped to contemplate my next words. I had to tell Honor everything, even the ugly parts, if I wanted her to understand. I hoped like hell she wouldn't think less of me once she knew the type of person I was. "When I brought Carson home from the hospital my world changed. My friends disappeared, my opportunities, my goals, my dreams—all gone. I was no longer living for myself but for Carson. That's what a parent does. But a sixteen-year-old parent who never had a chance to grow up starts to become resentful. I resented Chrissy's ability to realize every dream she ever had. The military was no longer an option for me. Something I'd wanted since I was a little boy. I always knew I'd follow in my dad's footsteps. But I felt like Chrissy had stolen that from me. I hated her for it. Then there was no more going to regular school for me. I isolated myself because I was so different from all my old friends. I had a baby and all the responsibility that came with her. I refused to let her down. I threw myself into homeschool and then found a career where I could still protect and serve, even if it wasn't in the way I'd always dreamt of."

"Handsome, I think you're too hard on yourself. Of course you'd feel some sort of resentment. You were sixteen. Hell, I know plenty of people who have found themselves in your situation as adults and hate the other parent when they abandon their responsibility."

"I let the hate and resentment for her rule my life and every decision I made. I keep screwing things up with you because I'm so fucking afraid you'll leave me. In my mind, Chrissy was supposed to love Carson enough to want to stay. Even if she didn't love me, she should've loved her daughter. I've spent the last eight years wondering what it was I did or didn't do to make her leave her own child. It had to be me because Carson was perfect."

"Really? It had to be all about you. Are you so egotistical that you made a woman's decision about if she wanted to be a parent about you? What about her choice? Maybe it was about her and not you."

"Turns out it *was* about her. I asked her after she told me about your surgery, why she didn't stick around for Carson. She told me she never wanted to be a parent, still doesn't. She's happy living her life child-free."

"So why did you shut me out when she came by your house?"

"Our house," I corrected. "I've always been scared Chrissy would change her mind and come back and try and take Carson from me. That's why I overreacted when we first met at the park. I saw you taking Carson's picture and the first thing I thought was Chrissy had hired a PI to follow us and take pictures."

"Me? A PI?" Honor smiled at the absurdity. "Looking at it from your point of view I can understand why you'd be worried. Hell, I'm worried Chrissy is even in the same state as Carson. I love her so much, I don't know what I'd do if Chrissy tried to take her from you."

"From us."

God, I'd fucked up so badly. Why hadn't I listened to everyone and talked to Honor about Chrissy the day she came by the house? Instead, I'd let something so stupid draw out and had hurt the woman I loved due to my inability to man up and tell her the truth about my feelings.

"So, you thought she'd try and take her?"

"No. Chrissy told me she didn't want her. She wasn't there to take Carson, but her presence threw me back to a time where I'd begged her to stay and raise Carson with me. Every time I pleaded, she'd refused. It didn't matter what I said, she was leaving. Which brought me to you. If I couldn't compel the mother of my child to stay with me, what would happen when you tried to leave me, and I couldn't make you love me."

"You can't *make* me love you. Not in the way you're talking about. And why would you want to? You'd never be happy with me if you had to *make* me stay? I don't want to leave you, Ethan, but you have to trust me. You don't need to try and do anything. I love you because of who you are, both as a man and as a father. This is never going to work if we can't communicate."

"You're right. And I do trust you. I think I have to learn to trust myself and let go of the guilt I feel."

It felt good to get the weight of my issues off my shoulders and let Honor in. I've been so used to bottling up my feelings and keeping everything to myself that it was strange, in a good way, to have someone to share them with. I'd never trusted anyone enough to talk about how much I resented Chrissy for being able to go forward with her life. I knew it didn't mean I loved Carson any less, but I still worried how it would make me look.

"What do you have to feel guilty about?"

"That I'm not giving Carson—"

"Stop," Honor cut me off. "You're a damn good father. We've talked about this before. That little girl wants for nothing. She has so many people around her that love her and spoil her it's not even funny. Hell, your big, badass dad is making a special stop to pick up ice cream for her. I know all she had to do was ask nicely and he caved, uncaring it was a school night. He'd give her the world if she asked. And, handsome, Carson has everything she needs in you. The rest? The extras? They're just icing on an already delicious cake. You have a great job, a nice house, and you provide everything she needs. To hell with Chrissy. Her loss—not Carson's."

I loved how fierce Honor became when she spoke about Carson. Another regret, not falling to my knees and thanking my lucky stars this woman loved me and my daughter. Instead I'd behaved like a fucking coward and had run.

"I should also tell you, when Carson asked if you were going to be her mom, I was so fucking happy. I remembered what you'd said about me not having found the right woman before you. The woman I wanted as my wife and Carson's mom. I'd already recognized who you were to me and who I wanted you to be in the future. But hearing Carson tell me she felt it too was . . . well, it was beyond words. And I ruined it by allowing my insecurities about Chrissy to override what I knew to be true."

"Who am I to you, Ethan?"

"My everything. The woman I'm going to marry. The mother of my children. My teammate. My friend. You are my first thought each morning and last person I want to hold every night. I will prove to you I'm the man for you. I'll stop at nothing until you know, deep in your soul, how much I love you and how sorry I am. I didn't mean what I said to you in your room. I am ready. More than. I want us to be a family."

"You said you needed time and we were going too fast."

"Did you miss the part where I said I was an idiot, and a coward, and I was acting like a scared little boy, instead of a man who knew with great certainty he'd found his other half?"

Honor smiled, and, for the first time since Sunday, it was a real honest to God grin.

"I must've missed that part."

"I'll work on my communication skills. But next time I act like an asshole, please don't run. I'm begging you to stay and fight for us. I'm man enough to admit I will fuck up in the future. But we have to be in this together. I trust you won't abandon me and Carson if you can trust me when I tell you I am working on letting my past go."

"I can do that."

"Thank you."

There's a saying—once words are spoken they can

be forgiven but not forgotten. It would be a while before the careless words I'd said to Honor would be forgiven. But they would be. If I worked every day, giving her nothing but love and happiness, the sting of my stupidity would fade.

She was giving me a chance. That's all I needed.

"Are you sure about this?" Ethan asked, pacing the hospital room.

"Yes. We talked about it."

It was day four of my hospital stay, and I was going home. All we were waiting for was the final discharge papers from Dr. Levine. I was under strict orders to go home and rest. No running or exercise for three weeks, until my lung was fully healed. The stitches on my forehead and abdomen would have to stay in another week, but I didn't care. I was going home.

"We did. But it's not too late to change your mind."

"Ethan, she's on her way. I need to do this. I think you need it, too. What are you so worried about? And stop pacing, you're gonna wear a hole in the floor."

He finally stopped his patrol and sat down in the chair next to my bed; the one he'd been sleeping in every night. True to his word, he hadn't left the hospital. Lily had brought Carson in every day, however, the fifteen-minute visits weren't enough. I missed her, and I knew Carson was missing Ethan and her own bed. I'd pleaded with Ethan to go home and get Carson settled, but he'd refused. I leave when you leave is all he'd say. We'd talked well into the early morning hours last night and he'd opened up about his experience as a young dad. Once again, I was impressed by his love for Carson and his commitment to ensure she had a great childhood. Every story was about Carson, every move he'd made had been well thought out, keeping only Carson's happiness in mind. He told me how he'd struggled with the decision to become a police officer and how he still felt guilt over choosing such a dangerous profession. He was too hard on himself. And boy was he still pissed at Chrissy. He hid it well, I wouldn't have guessed he'd harbored so much anger, but he did. Most of it was on Carson's behalf. Ethan was worried Carson would grow up and feel cheated because she only had one parent. But the strange part was, Ethan never had made the effort to date. It was this weird cycle. Guilt, anger, resentment, fear. He had to break it.

I was hoping Chrissy's visit today would be a start.

"I'm not worried about anything," he answered.

"Fine. I'm worried. I don't know why, although, having her anywhere in Georgia worries me."

"Everything will be fine," I assured him. "There's nothing she can say that will change my mind or how much I love you. I want to thank her for her help and ask for myself what her intentions are with Carson." I held up my hand when he tried to interrupt. "I know what you've told me. But I need to hear it from her."

"I love you, Honor."

There was a knock on the door, halting my response. Ethan walked across the room and opened the door. When he turned toward me to allow Chrissy to enter, his brow pinched together, and his big, strong frame vibrated with uncertainly. I hated this for him. There was no reason for him to be nervous. There was nothing Chrissy could do to us.

"Thanks for seeing me." Chrissy's voice wobbled. She entered the room, and Ethan shut the door behind her.

I was thankful I'd been able to change out of the hospital gown and was in my regular clothes. Sure, I wasn't looking my best, but at least I wasn't still leashed to the bed by the chest tube. I needed to be on even ground with the woman who'd given birth to the little girl I'd come to love.

"Of course. Ethan said you wanted to talk to me before you left."

This meeting was her idea. She obviously had something she wanted to say. It was up to her to start the conversation.

"I . . . um . . . wanted to make sure you were okay. And apologize for following you and Carson."

I took her in, really studied her for the first time. She was an attractive woman, which wasn't surprising. Carson was beautiful. I noted the similarities between the two and was surprised when I didn't feel any jealousy—I felt sorry for Chrissy.

"About that. Why were you following me?"

"Do you mind?" Chrissy gestured to a chair near the window.

"Please, make yourself comfortable."

I watched as Chrissy crossed the room on shaky legs and sat, clasping her hands in front her. She briefly glanced at Ethan before her attention swung back to me.

"I'm sure Ethan told you I asked him if I could see Carson. For good reason, he told me no. I wasn't happy with his answer and, selfishly, still wanted to see her. As I told Ethan, I wasn't going to approach you or try to take her or even talk to either of you. I just wanted to see her."

"Why now?" I asked.

Chrissy flinched at my question and looked away.

"I wanted to see her just once before I go blind." She spoke so softly I thought I'd misunderstood.

"Blind?" I questioned.

"I have retinal denegation. I'm not telling you this to excuse my behavior or so either of you will pity me. But it's the reason why, after all these years, I came back. My doctor told me I needed to do and see everything I wanted while I still could. The only thing I wanted to see before I lose my sight was Carson."

"There's no treatment?" Ethan asked.

"No. I've already tried gene therapy, but there was no improvement. I've made peace with it. Carson was the only regret I had. Never seeing her has haunted me. I'm sorry, I went against your wishes. It was selfish and underhanded. You have my word, I won't bother your family again."

Shit on a shingle. What did I do with the news of Chrissy's illness? I couldn't blame her for wanting to see Carson before she lost her eyesight.

"She's beautiful, isn't she?" I asked Chrissy.

"She is. And smart. You've done a wonderful job with her, Ethan. I always knew you'd be a great dad. I can never thank you enough for keeping her and loving her. You've given her the family I never could have."

"She has a good life," I told her. "Ethan and his family love her very much. She has all of them wrapped around her finger. Lily has taught her how to bake. Lenox takes her fishing. Levi has taught her how to throw a football. Ethan has provided her with everything she needs. Carson wants for nothing."

I don't know why it felt necessary to reassure Chrissy that Carson was well cared for, but I knew she needed it. She may not have wanted to be a mother, but it was easy to see she did care for Carson. Perhaps it was because of her love for her daughter she was willing to give her up for adoption. If she knew she wasn't in the position to be a mom, and never would be, giving her child to a family that could provide all the things she couldn't would be the ultimate sacrifice. Chrissy was lucky Ethan had been ready and able to keep Carson.

"Thank you." Chrissy swiped at tears as they rolled down her cheeks. "I needed to hear that. Even though I know I made the right decision, it doesn't mean I don't think about her. That I don't love her."

"How long do you have? You know . . . before . . ." Ethan awkwardly asked.

"Maybe a year. Two at most. Retinitis Pigmentosa is aggressive and most patients are legally blind by forty. I'm one of the lucky ones that will be blind before thirty." Chrissy tried to laugh off her discomfort but failed miserably. "My night vision is all but gone. And within six to nine months my vision will no longer be correctable."

"Lucky for me, you didn't need your vision to save my life." My attempt to lighten the conversation fell short, just as hers had.

"That's true. I've put in hundreds of chest tubes. I don't need my sight, I can do it by touch alone." She smiled. "Though, I don't think I saved your life. I'm fairly confident the paramedic would've been able to insert the cath if I hadn't been there."

"I don't think that's the case. The EMT was more concerned with putting in Honor's IV, not her breathing and heart rate. You picked up on the signs, and, because of your quick assessment, she's leaving the hospital four days later with a promising recovery. You did that."

"How are you feeling?" Chrissy asked.

"Better. Still sore when I take a deep breath or laugh but I've been told it can take four to six weeks for the pain to subside."

There was a knock and then the door opened, and Dr. Levine walked in.

"Dr. Krier, nice to see you. Stopping by to double check my diagnosis?" Dr. Levine chuckled good naturedly.

"I wouldn't think of it. I was only stopping by to say hello."

Dr. Levine set the laptop he was carrying on the counter and pointed to the x-ray on the screen. He motioned for Chrissy to look at the black-and-white image, pointing out areas of interest. Their conversation faded into the background while I concentrated on Ethan. He looked conflicted. I could sympathize, I, too, felt the same way. I wanted him to find closure, however I was afraid the news of Chrissy's disease was going to leave him feeling more guilt.

"Everything looks great, Honor. You're healthy and active. I bet you'll be closer to the four-week spectrum as long as you take it easy," Chrissy said, not taking her eyes off the screen. I wondered how well she could see the image. How much longer did she have before she'd have to give up doing what she loved.

"She's going home and getting into bed. I'll make sure she doesn't overdo it," Ethan vowed.

I wanted to argue that I didn't need help, but the ache in my chest told me I did. And I didn't want any lasting damaged that would prevent me from living a full life.

"That's good," Dr. Levine said. "I left your discharge papers on the counter. The number to my call service is on there. Use it if you have any questions, and I'll see you in my office to remove your stitches."

"Thank you, Dr. Levine." I smiled at him. I was so happy to leave I could barely stand it.

"You're very welcome. Oh, and wait for the nurse to come and get you."

"Yes. VIP wheelchair service, she already told me."

He picked up his laptop and headed for the door, turning back to smile at Chrissy. "Nice to see you again, Dr. Krier."

"You too."

What? Did I sense some mild flirtation and interest between the two doctors? Ethan's smirk confirmed my suspicions. He sensed it too.

"What?" Chrissy asked when Dr. Levine closed the door.

"Nothing," Ethan laughed.

"Come on. What's funny?" she tried again.

"I think the good doctor was flirting with you," I offered.

"I think you bumped your head harder than we originally thought. He was being nice."

"Right," Ethan laughed harder. "He wasn't that nice to me, or Honor."

Chrissy blushed and lowered her head.

"You think?" She smiled.

"Oh, yeah," I answered.

"Huh. Too bad I live on the other side of the country. And besides, I've found that doctors are a pain in the ass. I don't date them."

Maybe it was weird the three of us were sitting in a hospital room discussing the type of man Ethan's ex now dated, but it was strangely nice.

"When are you leaving?" Ethan asked.

"In a few hours."

"Will you leave me your email address?" I blurted out.

Maybe I should've checked with Ethan before I'd asked, but there wasn't time. Chrissy was getting ready to leave.

She glanced at Ethan, and he nodded. "Sure." Her answer was unsure and hesitant.

"If you'd like, Honor can email you some pictures of Carson," Ethan told her, picking up on what I was offering.

"I'd like that."

"Chrissy, I can't say I'm happy with how you handled the situation, but I understand," Ethan told her.

"I know I screwed up. I promise you it will never happen again."

"But, I can't say I'm not pleased you were there to take care of Honor and Carson. Thank you for that."

"You're welcome." Then her gaze was on me, assessing me the same way I'd done to her. "Thank you for loving them. I'm glad you're all right."

"It's no hardship, and me too."

"Well, I'm sure you're eager to leave. I'm gonna go; I have a flight to catch."

"Be well, Chrissy."

"You, too, Ethan."

She waved and just like that she was gone.

Ethan didn't speak for a while and when he looked at me I wanted to flinch at the pain I saw. But I had to be strong for him. For us. So I waited until he was ready.

"Thank you for knowing what I needed even when I didn't."

His statement surprised me, and I was a little shocked he'd seen right through my intentions. I did want to thank, Chrissy, and I did want to hear for myself why she'd come back, but more than that I'd wanted Ethan to find the answers he needed.

"Did it help?"

"If by help you mean I feel like a jackass, then, yes. I've harbored some seriously fucked up thoughts about her over the years. Turns out my assumptions were wrong. I now believe she did have Carson's best interest in mind when she gave her up. I can't judge her for knowing what she could and couldn't offer Carson. And I also can't be upset that she gave me the greatest gift I've ever received." He stopped speaking and moved to my bedside, lifting my hand from my lap. He brought it to his lips and kissed each knuckle. "That is, until you agree to be my wife and give me more children. Then *that* will be one of my greatest gifts."

It was a start. Ethan could finally move on. And so could I.

"Take me home."

"With pleasure."

I really needed the nurse to hurry up. The no exertion rule was going to kill me. I wondered if kissing was considered a laborious action. Remembering the way Ethan's lips felt on mine, and the way his tongue drove me into a sex-crazed frenzy, I figured it did. But it wasn't going to stop me. It had been too long since I'd been in his arms.

"You're sure?"

"Ethan, go to work. It's been three days. I'm fine. And your mom is here to help me. You're driving me batty," Honor complained.

I didn't want to go to work. This was my first shift since I'd arrived at the accident scene. The vision still haunted me, not that I'd tell Honor that. She had enough on her plate, and I didn't feel one bit of remorse for not piling more on.

Sam was still in jail, having been denied bail, even after his over-priced lawyer had argued for his release. The judge had deemed him a flight risk and hadn't taken kindly to Sam's entitled attitude. It was worth noting the congressman had not shown up for his son's bail hearing. As a matter of fact, he hadn't been seen since Lorenz and Detective Wild had interviewed him.

He seemed to be lying low until the media shit storm passed. It had me worried that my dad and uncles hadn't been able to track him down. That meant he was purposefully hiding, and innocent men didn't hide, not even politicians.

"I won't be home until late. My dad said he and Carson would be done fishing in time to bring you and mom lunch when he drops her off."

"Okay. We'll be fine. Between you and your mom the house is fully stocked. I am capable of making dinner."

"No way. You need to rest."

"Handsome, you and Carson have waited on me hand and foot. I'm not saying I don't love the attention, but I'm fine. Please stop worrying and go catch some bad guys. The sooner you leave the sooner you'll be home."

She was right. The faster I got this shift over with, the faster I could crawl in bed next to her and hold her. Carson and I had taken up residence in her room. I didn't want her climbing the stairs to my room, and Carson didn't want to be left out. So the three of us had squished into her queen-sized bed. As soon as Honor was completely healed, we'd be having a discussion about her moving her belongings up to my room. She could use the downstairs bedroom as an office. But I wanted her in my bed every night.

Carson hadn't blinked at the change in our family dynamic. I no longer tried to hide my displays of affection and openly kissed Honor and held her hand. Child friendly of course, but I wasn't looking over my shoulder before I pecked Honor's cheek or forehead. Another thing that had changed, and had come quite naturally, was that Carson often told Honor she loved her, and Honor didn't hide the sentiment either. It wasn't discussed, and no one made a big deal out it. Things were simply moving in the right direction.

We'd quietly talked late into the night—about nothing and everything. Honor had been forthcoming telling me how much my silence had hurt her, and I vowed never to shut her out again. To say I'd learned my lesson was an understatement. I'd never do anything to jeopardize what we had. I'd fight to keep her. And as soon as she was up for it, I was going to ask her to marry me. I wanted my ring on her finger and a date set.

"All right, I can take a hint. I'm leaving."

"It wasn't as much of a hint as it was an 'in your face' request. You need to stop. You're stressing yourself out. I don't want you thinking about me when you need to be concentrating on staying safe."

"Sorry, but it's impossible for me to stop thinking about you. But, I will be safe. I love you."

"I love you, too, handsome. Now go."

"ANYTHING new on the Sam Harris case?" I asked Lorenz when he walked into the locker room at the station.

"The DA seems to think she has an open and shut case. But something's bothering me."

"What does Detective Wild think?"

I knew my partner, he always spoke his mind. If he thought there was an issue, he would've shared it with the detective investigating the case.

"He agrees with me. The DA is jumping the gun. She thinks she has a straightforward case because the car is registered to Sam, the paint transfer matches Honor's Honda, and he has personal ties to her. With your statement corroborating hers about the altercation at the restaurant. She thinks she has it in the bag. But we both know a good defense attorney is going to poke so many holes in her case it's going to leak like a sieve. However, she won't listen. But we need more."

"Can I look over the evidence?"

"No go. You need to keep your nose out of it."

He was right, but I still wanted to see the case file. Conflict of interest was a bitch. If Sam's attorney caught wind I'd even glanced at the evidence he'd scream foul. I wouldn't jeopardize the prosecution's case, but I would offer Lorenz my opinion.

"How's Honor?" He changed the subject.

"Apparently, I hover. Other than me annoying her, she's fine. The bruising has faded, and her stitches come out in a few days."

"That's good. When she's ready, Maria would like to have you guys over for dinner." I tried to stifle a groan, but Lorenz caught the most inaudible grumble. "You're not going to get away with hiding her for much longer. Maria's already pissed as hell I'd kept Honor a secret from her this long. She wants to see for herself that you and Carson are happy."

"I know. I'll talk to Honor."

Maria had been trying to get me to date for several years. She'd even tried to set me up with several of her friends, telling me I needed a Latina woman. She was of the opinion that Latina women knew how to take care of their men, and if the way she pampered Lorenz was anything to go by, she was right. Though, Lorenz spoiled the hell out of her and their kids as well. It was the perfect balance of give and take.

"LENOX, A WORD?" My captain stopped me after the afternoon briefing.

"I'll wait for you outside," Lorenz told me and walked toward the exit.

"How's Honor recovering?" he asked.

"Very well. Thank you for asking. I appreciate you approving my leave."

"And Carson?" he asked, not bothering to acknowledge my gratitude.

"Five by five."

"And you?"

"Not sure I'm tracking, Captain."

"I need to know if your head's in the game. I can't have you out on the streets when you're thinking about home."

"Copy that."

"And stay the fuck away from Detective Wild and the Harris case. I don't want IA down here breathing down my neck."

"Understood."

"Good. Have a safe tour."

"Thanks, Captain."

When I made my way to the patrol car, Lorenz was already in the driver's seat. I rounded the vehicle and got in.

"What was that about?" he asked.

"Head check," I answered.

"Figured."

I waited until Lorenz pulled out of the station parking lot before asking, "Did Sam give a statement?"

"You just can't help yourself, can you?" He shook

his head but answered, "He's maintained that he's innocent and someone must've stolen his car. He swears he's being set up."

"What do you think? About the being set up part. We both know the car being stolen is bullshit."

"He doesn't have an alibi. He says he wasn't feeling well after lunch, went to his hotel room and fell asleep—alone. But the fact remains there are no traffic cameras that captured an image of him driving the car. Even though it's registered to him, I think the DA is going to have a hard time placing him as the driver."

"I agree. The congressman could've hired someone to run Honor off the road. Why would he set up his son?"

"That's the question. He has the means, motive, and opportunity, but setting up his own son is a stretch."

"One-Palmer-One. This is Dispatch."

"One-Palmer-One. Go," I responded to the radio call.

"Active shooter at Autumn Lake Nursing Home. Three twenty-five Gilmore. Repeat 3-2-5 Gilmore. Male is wearing jeans, a white T-shirt, and a black baseball cap. Caller advised shooter has one hostage— female doctor."

"Copy that. En route."

"Nothing like starting our shift with a bang," Lorenz deadpanned.

"One-Palmer-One. Go in soft. South side of the building."

"Copy, dispatch."

Lorenz turned off the sirens but left on the flashing lights and slowed his speed just enough to allow the traffic to move right.

It didn't take long for Lorenz to pull into the south driveway of the nursing home. He'd just put the vehicle in park when the back door of the building flew open. A man fitting the suspect's description fled the building with a female dressed in a white lab coat in front of him.

"Fuck," I muttered and drew my weapon from my holster, using the open door of the cruiser as cover.

"Let her go and drop your weapon," the officer closest to the suspect yelled and started to retreat to find cover.

The man brought the gun he'd had pointed at the doctor's side up to her head and stopped.

"Move back or I'll shoot her," the man yelled.

I shifted my attention from the suspect to the hostage. She looked oddly calm, her arms limp at her sides, hands unclenched, and staring straight ahead. Before I had time to further analyze her behavior, she nodded slightly and dropped her weight in the suspect's grasp. He tried to catch her as she fell to her knees in front of him. The distraction was all the officers needed.

A series of shots rang out, and I took off running toward the woman as the injured suspect crumpled on top of her. Lorenz got to them the same time I did and kicked the suspect's gun out of arms reach and pulled his bleeding body off the woman.

"I got you," I told her and pulled her to her feet. Holding her tightly I moved us away from the man's dead body. "I'm not sure if that was the bravest or stupidest thing I've ever seen."

"My . . . my . . . dad and brothers are cops at the 727," she stuttered. "It was my best chance. He was going to kill me."

"Sounds like they taught you well."

Her legs buckled, and I picked her up before she could fall.

"You're safe now," I reminded her.

She buried her face in my chest and started to sob. "Shit. I'm sorry."

"Don't be." I found a bench and sat with her, still crying, in my arms.

"Will you radio my dad?"

I took in the scene around us, the SWAT was pulling in, even though they were late to the fire fight, and an ambulance was coming in behind them. The sea of red and blue flashing lights was overwhelming. It went against regulations, but the woman in my arms needed her dad.

"One-Palmer-One to dispatch," I called into the radio on my shoulder. "What's your dad's name?"

"Sergeant Hudson. Steve Hudson," she answered.

"Go. One-Palmer-One."

"Call the 7-2-7. Sergeant Hudson's attendance is requested at this location, forthwith. Be advised, his daughter was the hostage. Unharmed. I repeat, she is unharmed but requesting his presence."

"Copy. One-Palmer-One."

"He'll be here soon," I told her.

"Thank you, Officer . . ."

"Lenox," I offered.

"I'm Lauren Hudson."

"Nice to meet you, Dr. Hudson."

I continued to hold Lauren on my lap as the other officers secured the building. Lorenz caught my attention from across the parking lot and started toward us.

"Miss," he greeted and stopped in front of us. "The EMTs would like to check you over."

"Not yet. I'm fine." Her death grip around my neck tightened.

"You don't have to do anything you don't want to do. They can wait."

"He . . . he . . . killed his mother. She was my

patient. He just shot her right in her bed. In front of me," she cried. "Why would he do that?"

Jesus.

Lorenz lowered himself to a kneeling position in front of us.

"I'm sorry you had to see that."

Tires screeching into the lot had Lorenz standing and stepping in front of me, offering us protection if need be. The car had barely stopped when the door flew open and a man held up a shield and ran toward the crime scene tape.

"Sergeant Hudson. 7-2-7," he announced and ducked under the tape. "Where's my daughter?"

Lauren's body started to shake in relief as her father neared.

"Here," Lorenz hollered and waved the man to our location.

"Christ almighty." Sergeant Hudson stopped in front of me. I stood and offered the man his crying daughter. He happily transferred Lauren into his embrace and took my place on the bench.

Lorenz and I started to walk away to give the two of them privacy when his booming voice stopped me.

"Is the fucker dead?"

"Yes," Lorenz answered.

"Thank you," Hudson gruff voice cracked as he spoke.

"Just doing our job," I told him.

I took a moment to soak in the view of father and daughter. It didn't matter how old your children were, you always wanted to protect them. And when you couldn't, it must be something akin to torture. I would do anything to keep Carson safe. I couldn't begin to imagine what Steve Hudson had felt when he'd learned his daughter had been held at gun point. Nor the relief he'd experienced when he found out she was safe.

"Thank you all the same."

We left them, and, as we were walking away, Lorenz clapped me on the shoulder.

"You're such a softie." He chuckled, poking me in the ribs.

"Fuck you," I replied with no heat.

"Let's wrap this shit up, I'm starving."

"You're the only person I know that can eat five minutes after seeing a dead body."

LORENZ WAS DRIVING and telling me a story about his sons taking apart their brand-new, two-hundred-dollar Xbox because he'd been bitching to them that kids these days didn't know how stuff worked. He'd also told them that back in the day, boys played outside and got dirty. They also took shit apart and knew how to fix something when it broke. That conversation had led to the boys dismantling a perfectly good video game console to make their father happy.

"Two hundred fucking dollars down the drain. Maria thought that shit was funny because she doesn't want them playing on it anyway. I told them I wasn't buying a new one. If they wanted to use it, they'd better fix it."

My phone vibrated in my pocket. I pulled it out, and seeing my father's name on the screen I answered.

"Hey, Dad," I said, still laughing at Lorenz's story.

"Get home. Now," my father thundered.

"What's wrong?" I sobered.

"Honor's gone. Your mother was tied up and gagged. The team is on their way."

Holy fucking Christ.

"My house. Now." I told Lorenz. "Fuck. ETA five minutes. Where's Carson? How's Mom?"

"Pissed as fuck. Details when you get here. Out."

My father had gone into combat mode and, strangely, it was comforting. I'd need all the help my family could give me to find Honor. I relayed the information I had to Lorenz and dialed my Captain.

"Rolland," he answered on the first ring.

"Someone broke into my house and tied up my mother before they abducted Honor."

"You en route?"

"Yes."

"I'll call you out of service and have Detective Wild meet you there."

"Warn Wild, my father will be armed, as will all of my uncles."

"Jesus H. Christ. I wouldn't expect anything less. I'll meet you there."

He hung up as Lorenz was pulling into my neighborhood. I spotted my Uncle Jasper's big ass pickup in front of us, speeding toward my house. When we pulled up, my father, Uncle Clark, and Uncle Levi were all standing on my lawn.

Lorenz stopped the patrol car in the middle of the street, uncaring he was blocking traffic.

"What happened?" I ran toward the group of men.

"Congressman Harris pushed his way in when your mom was leaving to go to the store. It was dumb fucking luck he got the drop on her. He tied her up and held a gun to her head and Honor left with him."

"Motherfucker!" I roared. "Did Mom see a car?"

"Negative. He was at the door fixin' to knock when she opened it to leave. He bum-rushed her."

"Where's Carson?"

"Fuck, son. We walked in and saw your mom tied

up, I untied her, cleared Honor's room, and locked them in so I could check the rest of the house. Blake's in there with them now."

I was happy my Aunt Blake was with my mom and Carson.

"How is she?"

"I told you, pissed as fuck."

"Physically?"

"Fine."

"I need to talk to Ethan," my mom yelled from inside the house.

I jogged to my front door, and my anger spiked. A kitchen chair was in the middle of the living room, plastic zip ties, which had obviously been cut off my mom, lay on the floor, and a blue bandana I'd never seen was on the coffee table.

"I asked you to stay in the bedroom," my dad scolded.

"Not now, Lenox."

Yeah, my mom was furious. If looks could kill, my father would be dead on the floor.

"You okay, Mom?"

"No! I'm so sorry, Ethan. I tried to stop her. I knew your dad was on his way. But when he put the gun to my head, she told him she'd go with him."

"It's okay, Mama. We'll find her."

"She wanted me to tell you something."

"What did she say?"

I stared at my mom as she told me Honor's last words about how much she loved me and had known from the first day she saw me in the park. Her message sounded a lot like a goodbye and my gut knotted at the idea.

"I'm so sorry, son." Seeing the look of fury and devastation in her eyes, I knew Mama Bear was in full force. "That son of a bitch caught me by surprise."

"I know, Mama. There's nothing to be sorry for. We're gonna find her."

I was one lucky son of a bitch having Lily Lenox as my mom.

27

Frank had officially lost his marbles. He was screaming at me about videos I'd stolen from his house. I had no idea what he was talking about and now I was up shit creek without a paddle. When he'd put his gun to Lily's head and demanded I tell him where they were, I'd lied to him and told him they weren't at the house, and I'd hidden them. I'd already given him my camera, memory cards, and laptop. He thought he'd successfully confiscated the images I'd taken of him sneaking in his whores. Idiot. He'd forgotten about cloud storage.

"You better not be lying, or you'll end up like your mother. You've always been a pain in the ass and you never could follow directions."

My mom? What did he mean by that? My mom had died in a car accident.

"Don't talk about my mother," I bravely demanded. He could say whatever he wanted about me, but I never wanted to hear my mom's name come from his lying, cheating lips.

"Your mom was a blackmailing bitch. Bet you didn't know that, did you?" He laughed. "She thought she could play me. In the end, I taught her the same lesson you're about to learn. I always win. Now, where the fuck is this park?"

"What did you do?" I yelled, not bothering to answer him. "Did you have Sam run her off the road too?"

"Samuel? I wouldn't trust that nincompoop with anything of importance. He's lazy and doesn't have what it takes to get the job done."

And I wonder who made him that way? Frank had given Sam anything he'd wanted when we were teenagers. He'd made him into the spoiled, entitled prick he was today.

"Then who, Frank?"

"You know the saying: if you want something done right, do it yourself."

"You wouldn't dare get your hands dirty."

Frank slammed on the brakes and pulled into a fast food parking lot and turned to me.

"Wouldn't I? You have no idea what I'm capable

of. Now tell me which goddamn park you buried the videos in."

"Not until you tell me what happened to my mom."

Fuck him. If I was going to die, I wanted to know the truth about my mother's car accident.

"The bitch had gone too far. She wanted me to kick Sam out. She'd caught him in your room being a normal teenage boy, and, as always, she over reacted and demanded I tell my own fucking son he had to move out of my house. The nerve of that bitch. It was easier to let her believe she'd been blackmailing me into not divorcing her. I knew she didn't want to go back to being a waitress and living in a shitty apartment with her brat, and I needed her on my arm for state dinners. It was a win-win. She was useful until she wasn't. Then it was time for me to dispose of her."

"Fuck you! Fuck you! Fuck you!" I screamed and did my best to swing my zip tied hands in his direction. I only made contact once before he grabbed my hands and yanked them to a stop.

"You're gonna pay for that, too, bitch." Spittle landed on my forehead and cheeks as he yelled in my face.

I couldn't believe my mom had actually said something to Frank about Sam. All the times I'd talked to her about what he'd been doing, she'd blown me off and told me I was wrong. I wanted to ask what she had on him, but it didn't seem all that important at the moment. Instead I thought back to the accident. Frank was home with me when my mother lost control of her car and slammed into a semi.

"What did you do?" I demanded.

"Made sure when she left the hotel where she'd met with her lover her brakes wouldn't work. It really was simple."

He did it. He really killed my mother.

"Fuck you. You're a lying murderer. My mom would never cheat. You're the one who was fucking every prostitute in Atlanta."

"Your mother had been fucking Barry Wells for years. Why do you think he agreed to my proposal when I offered for you to marry his son? He didn't want his wife to find out."

My head was spinning with all this new information. Everything had been a lie. I was so furious and hurt I was numb. I didn't know if I wanted to scream at Frank or crawl into a corner and cry.

"Why did you want me to marry, Greg? What was in it for you?"

"To keep a leash on you. I knew you were planning on moving out and I couldn't risk you opening your mouth. You'd seen too much."

"And when that didn't work you decided to try and

kill me, too."

"I warned you. It didn't have to be this way. But again, you never fucking listen. You're just as stubborn as your mother was. Confession time is over. Either tell me where the park is, or I'll kill you now and after I dump your body, that little girl will be next. What will that trash cop think of you then—the woman who got his daughter killed?" He pulled his gun out of his coat pocket and pointed it at me.

I hated Frank with every fiber of my being. First, he'd hurt Lily and threatened to kill her, now he was threatening Carson. What had I gotten them into? I should've left after our run-in at the restaurant, but I'd been selfish and hadn't wanted to give them up. Now, because of me, they were all in danger. And there was no denying it was my fault. I hoped Ethan and Lenox would find him and make him pay.

"Head to the West End Motel. Make a left at the intersection. There's a park a few blocks down."

I prayed I'd stalled Frank long enough for Ethan to figure out where I was. If not, at least I'd make Frank kill me in a public place. He hadn't thought out his plan very well. I guess desperate people really did do desperate things. Couple that with Frank's ego and belief he was above the law, he thought he'd literally get away with murder—and why shouldn't he, he'd gotten away with my mother's.

28

"Repeat it again?" I asked my mom.

I was only just keeping my temper in check. If I'd thought waiting for Honor to pull through surgery was torture, I was wrong. This was worse. Way fucking worse.

"She said for me to tell you she loved you. She knew the first day she saw you. Then she said, tell Ethan everything always comes full circle. The beginning is often the end."

Honor's words cut me to the quick.

My Uncle Levi came out of Honor's room holding a box that had *Katie—misc.* written in black marker. "Who's Katie?" he asked.

"Honor's mother."

"Okay, so, Honor's online activity is boring," my Aunt Blake said from the dining room table. Her fingers were flying across the keyboard as she spoke. "No social media. She spends most of her time online reading blogs related to photography. Professional print labs and gallery websites. Most recently she'd been searching parenting websites. One in particular called Baby Center. She's joined two groups—Stepparent Adoption and Mothers and Daughters."

My heart did a somersault, Honor had been looking up parenting and adoption sites. I should've felt guilty about invading her privacy but if any of the information could lead us to her, I couldn't summon the feeling.

"Mom. You said Frank wanted to know where the videos were?"

"Yes. He wanted some pictures she had, and she gave him her camera stuff and her computer."

"When we saw him at the restaurant, she told him she had pictures of him with women. But she never said anything about videos."

"She has cloud storage, but it's password protected," Blake announced. "It'll take me a while to figure it out."

"Try Buck Sully," my dad offered.

"She told Frank she'd take him to where she hid the videos?" I asked my mom for clarification.

"Yes. She told him if he didn't hurt me, she'd show him. He told her if she was lying he'd kill her and be back for me. I tried to tell her not to go. I knew your dad was on his way. But Frank had already gagged me, and she refused to make eye contact with me. She was more concerned about me than herself."

I glanced at the box now in front of me on the coffee table and started to peel back the packing tape. Most of the adhesive had worn off, a testament to how long it had been since the box had been opened.

"I'm in," Blake told us. "You were right, Lenox. Buck Sully for the win."

I moved the items in the box around and wondered why Honor had never opened it. There were pictures of her with both her mom and dad. A scrap of fabric, baby shoes, a lock of hair taped to a piece of paper. It was a box of keepsakes from Honor's youth. The only thing out of place were two flash drives. I fished them out of the bottom and turned to Blake, just as she was turning the screen of her laptop in our direction.

"Back up of the pictures of the congressman with the women."

"Here, check these." I handed her the drives.

Nothing we'd found was going to lead us to where Honor was. However we did have enough to nail the son of a bitch. But none of that mattered if we didn't find her before Frank hurt her.

Fuck.

Where are you Honor? Where would you hide the videos?

"There's not enough eye bleach to erase what I just saw," my Aunt Blake complained. "Guess we now know what videos he's after."

I turned toward the screen and watched in horror as Harris's pasty white ass drilled into a redheaded woman.

"That's not Katie." Jasper said holding up a picture of Honor and her mother. "She had light brown hair."

"I don't think she knew about the videos," I said.

"If she did know, she was leading him away from the house to protect Lily, because there are a bunch more videos on these memory sticks," Blake told me.

I looked at my dad, his arms were crossed across his chest, and when I looked at my uncles, they were mirroring his stance, they all had matching scowls. What the hell were we missing?

"Everything comes full circle. The beginning is often the end." I contemplated Honor's words again.

"Does that mean something to you?" Levi asked.

"No. But I feel like it should."

"She said she knew the first day she saw you," my dad reminded me.

"First day, the beginning, full circle. Where did you meet her?" Clark asked.

"The park off Gambler by the West End Motel," I answered.

"Would she take him to a park or the motel she was staying in?" my dad asked.

Neither made sense if you were hiding videos. A room would be cleaned, there would be no good hiding places. And a park? That made even less sense, but if Honor was trying to send me a message—the park was the answer.

"Detective Wild and Lorenz will come with me to the West End Motel. What room was she staying in?" Captain Rolland asked.

"Three hundred," I answered.

"We'll head there now. You head to the park. I don't think I have to remind you there are—"

"You don't," I cut Captain Rolland off. "I promise to use my best judgment, but I can't promise I won't protect my woman at all cost."

Captain Rolland sighed long and hard before turning to Lorenz. "Change of plans. You go with Ethan. I'll take Wild with me. Don't let him get his ass in a sling. Necessary force only."

"Copy that," Lorenz replied.

"Let's head out," my dad said, and my uncles followed.

"I love you, Mama. I'm sorry you were caught up in all this."

"Don't start. I'm fine. Go get Honor and bring her home to us."

"Carson—"

"Is fine. Your aunts are upstairs with her now. Go."

Lorenz was waiting for me next to the police cruiser by the time I made my way outside.

We were half-way to the park, my dad and uncles following behind, when Lorenz spoke. "We'll find her."

I gritted my teeth to prevent myself from lashing out. He couldn't know that for sure. We had nothing. A hunch based on a cryptic message from Honor. I still didn't understand why she would have pointed us to the park, if she had at all. And was the congressman so stupid he'd believe she hid the flash drives at the park like some kind of buried treasure?

Not a goddamn thing made sense.

"The swings where I first saw her are on the north side of the park. Pull into the south entrance."

I checked the mirror and saw my dad was still following us. Lorenz pulled into a parking spot concealed by a row of thick evergreens.

My dad and my uncles had exited my dad's SUV and were already on high alert, scanning the area around us.

"Jasper, Clark, and Levi you take the west side of the park. It will be harder to conceal your movements because there aren't a lot of trees. We'll take the east side," I told the group. I watched as each man lifted their T-shirt, exposing the guns sheathed at their hips. They each tucked the material behind their Kydex holsters, giving them easy access to their weapons.

Fuck. This was not the middle east nor was it a war zone. None of my uncles would give zero fucks about shooting Frank dead in a park full of people. Not that there looked to be many people there in the middle of the day if the empty parking lot was anything to go by.

"If deadly force—"

"This is your op, son. You make the calls but don't think I won't place a bullet between his eyes if the opportunity presents itself. The motherfucker put his hands on my wife, your woman, and scared my grand-daughter. And they. . ." he stabbed his finger in my uncles' direction. "Feel the exact same way. He fucked with our family, and no one fucks with our women."

"I know, Dad. I don't need the reminder, He took *my* woman out of her home and he had the balls to touch *my* mother." I ground my teeth. "But I don't need you in lockup until we sort out whether it was justifiable homicide, while mom is freaking the fuck out. I have the badge here, not you. Your carry permit won't do shit to protect you. So, I'm telling you, if it comes to it, I have the fucking honor of putting him down. The four of you are backup only."

"Chip off the old block," my Uncle Clark chuckled. "Copy that, Officer Lenox."

"Just like the good old days. Glad to see the Lenox retribution gene was passed down," Jasper added.

Not wanting to waste any more time on mindless banter, I flipped the two of them the middle finger and broke from the huddle, heading for the thick tree line on the east side of the park. The extra foliage was necessary for me and Lorenz. We were both in uniform, Frank would spot us from a mile away. Branches snapped under my feet as I made my way through the thick brush at a fast clip. With more than two hundred yards until the woods opened at the play area, I wasn't worried about Frank hearing us. If they were even here.

The sweltering humidity had my T-shirt under my uniform top and vest soaked and my hands clammy. Or was it my anger bubbling over? I slowed my pace and balled my right hand into a fist, lifting it to stop my dad and Lorenz from progressing.

"Did you hear that?" I whispered.

All three of us stood in silence, straining to hear.

"There it is again," I told them.

"Copy," my dad mouthed.

A few moments later the voice was louder and easier to understand.

"You better not be lying to me, bitch."

It was Frank. Holy fuck, she had brought him to the park. My dad pointed to the right and broke off, silently disappearing behind the shrubbery. Lorenz nodded to the left and he, too, disappeared. I continued as silently as I could, hoping we could surround Frank before he spotted one of us.

"I'm not. It's under a magnolia," Honor yelled. Good, she sounded more pissed than scared.

"That's what you said about the last two fucking trees. This is your last chance. If it's not here we're going back to the house and I'll shoot that asshole cop's mother in his living room. Then we'll come back here and see if it helped jog your memory."

The anger I'd felt had transformed into something indescribable. As I slowed my breathing the fear and rage mingled together into clarity. Frank Harris was a dead man walking. I took one more cleansing breath and fortified my decision. There would be no demands for him to surrender. I would not give him the option to drop his weapon. All I needed was the gun to still be in his cold, dead hand when the CSI officers arrived. I didn't need him to point it in my direction. There would be no fear of imminent danger. He was simply going to die by my hand, and there would be no remorse.

"You'll never get away with this. Ethan and his dad

won't stop until they hunt you down," Honor said, her voice getting closer.

"I'm not worried about some baby killer, ex-military low life and his trashy son. It will be their word against mine. And, let's face it, it's all about who you know. I have more capital than either of those two."

"I wasn't talking about in a court of law, you asswipe. They'll hunt you like the animal you are and kill you. The only thing I'm sorry about is I won't be alive to see it."

I came to the last of the tall cherry laurel bushes that would conceal my position and peered around the waxy leaves. My Glock 22 felt abnormally heavy in my hand, I clutched the grip tighter, until the hard, plastic ribbing bit into my palm.

Frank's hand pulled back and he pistol whipped Honor across her face. She fell to her knees and covered her face with her hands. Her sob nearly broke my concentration.

I'm sorry, smalls. Just a minute longer.

"Fuck you, bitch. I'll kill them all, starting with that little brat you love so much, then the—"

The recoil of my weapon barely registered as I watched Frank's body fall. I'd never been more thankful for all the hours my dad and uncles had spent with me at the range. Years of practice had earned me the nickname Deadeye Dick, something I'd hated until today.

Lorenz was the first to dart out of the shrubs and run toward Honor. I holstered my weapon and did the same. Coming to a sliding halt in front of Honor I dropped to my knees and scooped her up into my lap.

"Thank God. I knew you'd find me," she cried.

"Always, smalls. I'll always find you."

"How's your mom?"

"She's fine, baby. Let me see your face."

"No. It doesn't matter. Where's Carson?"

How had I been so lucky to find this perfect, self-less woman? I knew her face had to hurt like a bitch, but she was more concerned with Carson and my mom.

"She's safe. I need to look at your cheek."

Honor slowly lifted her head off my chest, and blood trickled down her face and dripped from her chin.

"Fuck."

"Here." My dad handed me his shirt. It wasn't ideal but it was something to stop the bleeding. He knelt in front of us and flicked his knife open. "Let me see your hands."

She held them out to him, and they were filthy. I also noted several broken nails. The fucker had made her dig with her bare hands. With a single pass of my dad's blade he sliced through the zip tie.

"Thank you," she whispered. "I'm—"

"No, Honor. Thank you," my dad said.

A look passed between me and my dad. A silent communication. There were no words necessary. She was my bone-deep, the woman I would breathe and die for. I would fight for the rest of my life to be worthy of her love. She was my Lily Lenox, my one and only. My dad stood and walked to join my uncles. Even though the threat was no longer present, the four most important men in my life still stood guard, reminding me I was never alone. They always had my back, my front, and my sides. They had Honor's too.

"I called it in. The captain's on his way," Lorenz said. "It's a shame he wouldn't drop his weapon."

Not that I wasn't prepared for any consequences resulting from the shooting and death of the jacknut who'd kidnapped my woman, but it seemed my partner wasn't going to allow it to come to that.

"Appreciate it."

"I want to go home," Honor said.

"We have to wait for the ambulance to get here. You need to be checked out. I think you may need stitches."

"I'm not staying in the hospital, Ethan. I want to go home. I need to see Carson and Lily. They can look at my face, but that's it. I'm going to be in our bed tonight. Do you understand me?" She was almost hysterical. "I want to be in our bed, with you and Carson."

"Okay, smalls."

"He hurt her," she yelled. "He pushed his way into our home and tied her up."

Four menacing growls came from beside us.

"I couldn't stop him. I was too afraid your dad would show up with Carson and she'd get hurt. I didn't know what fucking video the dumb bastard wanted. But I had to get him out of the house." She continued to yell, her sobs turned into venom, and she angrily swiped a tear from the eye that wasn't covered by my dad's shirt. "He kept threatening to hurt them. He killed my mom. The asshole killed her. Oh my God. All those years I lived under the same roof as the man who killed my mother. And he did it, not Sam. I told you that bitch was covering for him. He tried to kill me and Carson. Fucking prick."

I rocked her back and forth and let her get it all out. I was thankful she wasn't bottling up her anger. I knew we'd have other things about Frank kidnapping her to deal with down the line, but for now, this was good.

"I'm so sorry, Honor."

"I fucking hate him. I hate him so much. I wish he could die all over again. He killed her and hurt Lily." Her shouting turned back into tears and she pinned me in place with the saddest look I'd ever seen. "I just want you to take me home. I want my family. Please, don't leave me at the hospital."

"Honor, I'll never leave you anywhere. You're coming home with me. Carson will be there. My mom will be there. You will be surrounded by your entire family. I promise you. None of us will ever leave you."

"That's the goddamn truth," my dad choked out. He, too, was overcome with emotion.

"Blake and I will be there," Uncle Levi added.

"Regan and I are staying," Clark put in.

"Nowhere else Em and I would be," Jasper told Honor.

"You're one of us, Honor. And family always sticks together. You'll never be alone again. And that's a promise you can take to the bank," my dad finished.

"I love you, Honor."

"God, I love you. Thank you for saving me."

"You saved yourself with the secret message you left me. Smart and beautiful. You're a special kind of dangerous, Honor Sullivan."

She smiled, just as I'd hoped.

The wooded area we were in was suddenly swarming with men and women in uniform. I didn't move a muscle. I had Honor in my arms, safe and sound, and there wasn't a damn thing I was going to do but hold my woman.

29

"You really do love this statue, don't you?" I laughed at Carson posing.

"She's waving hello to all the ships coming home. And goodbye to the ones leaving on their long voyages out to sea."

Carson was something else. She certainly had a flare for the dramatic.

"I love it down here." I sighed and cuddled closer to Ethan.

It had been three months since that horrible day in the woods with Frank. Three wonderful months. My breakdown, as I called it, Ethan called it a moment of cleansing and closure, whatever you wanted to call it, it seemed to bring us closer. All of us. Not only me, Ethan, and Carson. But it seemed to reinforce the family bond of the uncles too. Lily had commented last week how much she loved that the family was all getting together more. The four families all had individual families of their own and schedules didn't always coincide, but these days more of an effort had been made. Even Jason and Kayla had come to as many get togethers as Kayla felt up for. Her cancer was progressing quickly. It was heart breaking to watch. She was shy and reserved, but once you got her talking, she was the sweetest, kindest person I'd ever met. She didn't have a mean bone in her fragile body. I was going to miss her.

Carson had opted to pass on cheer camp but still wanted to go to her dance classes. As it turned out, the girl was talented. And that wasn't me being biased, even the teacher was impressed. After a few weeks, she was switched to a competition squad, which meant more classes and practices for me to take her to. I loved every second. I loved cheering her on and watching her grow.

"Honor?"

"Yes, darlin'?" I chuckled at her antics. She was on one knee in front of me smiling like a loon. I loved how silly and playful she was when she wasn't acting like she was a mini version of the adults around her.

"Will you please do me the honor," she giggled but quickly recovered, "of being my mother?"

She opened her little palm and nestled there were two bands. One adult size and one much smaller.

Tears filled my eyes and the rings disappeared behind the watery haze.

"What?" I whispered, praying I hadn't heard her wrong.

"It's a fancy way of asking you if you'll be my mommy from now on. I want you to be my mommy, and Daddy said yes and told me all I had to do was ask you. Daddy said you can make it official and adopt me if you want to. I don't know what that means. As long as it's all right with you that's all that matters to me."

"Yes, Carson. Yes, I want to be your mommy. Forever and ever."

"Did you hear that, Daddy? Honor is now my new mommy," Carson announced.

"I did, Squirt."

"Oh, wait, I forgot. Your hand please," Carson asked. I wasn't sure which hand she wanted but I presented her with my left.

"With this ring, you're my mommy." She slipped the ring on my finger. "Here's mine." She handed me the smaller ring and gave me her hand.

I slowly slipped the tiny gold band onto my daughter's finger and closed my eyes, savoring the moment. "With this ring, you are my daughter." I opened my eyes and Ethan was holding Carson's other hand.

"My girls," he said quietly.

"There's only one thing left to do." He let go of Carson's hand and lowered himself to a knee. "Honor Sullivan would you make me the happiest man on earth and marry me?"

"Yes! A thousand times, yes."

He pulled a ring from his pocket and slipped it next to the one Carson had placed there and brought my hand to his lips, kissing both rings.

***

IT WOULDN'T BE until much later when I finally inspected both rings Carson and Ethan had given me. I was tucked close to Ethan's side after he'd made love to me. My left hand was resting on his chest and I'd caught sight of the proof I was going to be his wife. I remembered back to all those months ago when Ethan had vowed to prove to me he was the man he said he was. It turns out, I am worth it. He's proven it to me every day by how fiercely he loves me. And he's worth it too. I now understand what bone-deep means. The Lenox family loves with an intensity you feel down in your bones, in your soul.

My family.

30

One year later

Jason Walker

"It's time, Jay."

Panic rose at Kayla's words and the lump in my throat threatened to choke me. I couldn't swallow past the fear. Selfishly I wasn't ready. The finality of the situation was more than I could comprehend.

"Just . . ." I didn't know what I was trying to say.

Just hold on.

Just let go.

"You've given up enough for me. It's time to let me go."

"Don't say that, Kayla. You know I'd give up everything if I could save you."

"And you have. You've given up the last seven years

of your life taking care of me. It's time for you to move on. Live. Be happy. Find someone to love."

Love? What the hell did I know about love? I didn't know the first thing about loving someone. I had failed in every way possible. My wife's frail body in my arms was proof. She's wasted away in front of me. I helplessly watched as cancer had ravished her body. Stolen years from her. Love? Yeah, fuck love.

"Kayla."

"Promise me, Jason. You'll never know how grateful I am that you've stuck by me. Because of you, I had seven extra years. I'm just sorry it was at your expense."

"I love you, Kayla. I don't regret anything."

What I felt for Kayla was as close to love as I'd ever feel.

"I love you, too, Jason." Her voice was starting to fade.

"I'm right here, Kay Kay. I won't leave your side." I couldn't stop the tears as they streamed down my cheeks. "It's okay to let go. I promise everything will be okay."

"Thank you, Jay." She sounded sleepy, her voice raspy. "Love . . ."

"I love you, too."

Sweat beaded on my forehead as I jolted awake in a cold and empty bed.

I'd lied to Kayla in her final moments of her life. I

promised her everything would be okay. It wasn't. Every night I dreamt of that promise. I relive the worst day of my life over and over again. It's what I deserve. I've lived a nightmare for the last year.

A husband fresh out of high school and a widower by twenty-eight—ain't life grand.

Not bothering to straighten the crumbled comforter I header to the shower to scrub away the lingering effects of my dream. The sweat and tears were easy to wash down the drain. The guilt and regret were etched so deep nothing would ever clean the stains away.

With my skin damn near raw from my shower I went through the motions of starting my day. I was like a fucking robot. I was numb. So many times, I'd considered selling the house but I couldn't. I was trapped behind the wood and bricks. Locked inside with the ghost of Kayla.

Remembering I had to grab files from my home office, I darted into the room to grab them before I headed to work. I picked up the envelope with the documents I needed, and my heart constricted.

A separation agreement sat on the desktop taunting me, reminding me, mocking the memory of my wife. Kayla's pretty handwriting flowing across the page. She'd signed it. This stupid fucking piece of paper was supposed to be her way out. She was supposed to finally find happiness. Get her happily ever after. The one she could never find with me.

I was a shit husband. A shit human being.

No. Nothing was ever going to be okay again.

Are you ready for Jason Walker and Mercy James in Finding Mercy?

"So much emotion it flew off the page and knocked the wind out of me. Finding Mercy was another great story by the absolutely brilliant Riley Edwards." Jennifer Pierson: The Power of Three Readers

DEA AGENT JASON WALKER became a widower at twenty-eight. Two years later he's still torturing himself with guilt. They'd married young, and she'd been his first love, but her illness changed everything. They'd fought a losing battle and he'd held her to the very end. Now he just wants to be left alone with his misery and memories.

MERCY JAMES IS no stranger to grief and loneliness. Her brother's death of a drug overdose, and her police officer father's death in the line of duty were the driving forces behind her pursuit of a career in the

DEA. In spite of—or maybe because of—her past, Mercy doesn't believe in feeling sorry for others, or for herself.

WHEN A CASE BRINGS Jason and Mercy together, and their attraction heats up, can her tough, straightforwardness help Jason learn to live in the light again? He'd lost his first love, but is he ready for a forever love?

Finding Mercy is up next

Riley Edwards

www.RileyEdwardsRomance.com

Takeback

Dangerous Love

Dangerous Rescue

Dangerous Games

Dangerous Encounter

Dangerous Mind

Gemini Group

Nixon's Promise

Jameson's Salvation

Weston's Treasure

Alec's Dream

Chasin's Surrender

Holden's Resurrection

Jonny's Redemption

Red Team - Susan Stoker Universe

Nightstalker

Protecting Olivia

Redeeming Violet

Recovering Ivy

Rescuing Erin

The Gold Team - Susan Stoker Universe

Brooks

Thaddeus

Kyle

Maximus

Declan

Blue Team - Susan Stoker Universe

Owen

Gabe

Myles

Kevin

Cooper

Garrett

The 707 Freedom Series

Free

Freeing Jasper

Finally Free

Freedom

The Next Generation (707 spinoff)

Saving Meadow

Chasing Honor

Finding Mercy

Claiming Tuesday

Adoring Delaney

Keeping Quinn

Taking Liberty

Triple Canopy

Damaged

Flawed

Imperfect

Tarnished

Tainted

Conquered

Shattered

Fractured

The Collective

Unbroken

Trust

Standalones

Romancing Rayne

Falling for the Delta Co-written with Susan Stoker

Riley Edwards is a USA Today and WSJ bestselling author, wife, and military mom. Riley was born and raised in Los Angeles but now resides on the east coast with her fantastic husband and children.

Riley writes heart-stopping romance with sexy alpha heroes and even stronger heroines. Riley's favorite genres to write are romantic suspense and military romance.

Don't forget to sign up for Riley's newsletter and never miss another release, sale, or exclusive bonus material.

Rebels Newsletter

Facebook Fan Group

www.rileyedwardsromance.com

facebook.com/Novelist.Riley.Edwards

instagram.com/rileyedwardsromance

bookbub.com/authors/riley-edwards

amazon.com/author/rileyedwards